THE BEGINNING
OF REVIVAL

The THIRD book of a multi-part series.
Book 1: *The Beginning of the End*
Book 2: *The End of the Beginning*

By John Jacobsen

Acknowledgements

M any thanks to my readers for their encouragement, feedback and editing, especially to my brother Bill (Jake), Sue and Tracy Villone, Barb Trost and my wonderful wife Kristin.

Foreword

This story is fictional, but based on many truths. The characters are strictly fictional and do not represent any actual persons, myself included.

Many direct and indirect Scriptures are employed. Where not specifically noted, the Scriptural references are included in the Appendix.

Statements about Freemasonry, the Illuminati and the New World Order are based on extensive research which can be accessed on my Lion of Judah website at www.lofj. com under the End-Times tab. Some readers will question the truth of demonology as portrayed in this book. However, I have directly experienced quite similar situations in my pastoral counseling career.

Warning: Some readers have experienced physical and emotional reactions when reading details about demons, Freemasonry and the Illuminati. If this should happen to you, seek out pastors or ministries who know how to handle these situations. You can search for them on the Internet.

As for my personal background, which many readers like to know, I was a Director of Management Science at two Fortune 100 corporations, an executive in the software industry and then President of Meals-on-Wheels in Prescott, Arizona. I have a BS in Engineering and an MS in Management Science. I became a pastor in 2001, and was the founder of the Gospel of Grace Food & Clothing Bank and the Lion of Judah ministries in Prescott Valley, Arizona. I also served as the Prayer Coordinator for Yavapai County in Arizona for several years. I was reared a Lutheran, became a pastor in a Pentecostal church, and now consider myself to be non-denominational.

Prologue

The first book, *The Beginning of the End,* concluded the end-time period Jesus called "the beginning of sorrows" (Matthew 24:8) leading up to the seven-year Tribulation. The "covenant with many" (Daniel 9:27) was signed, presumably bringing peace to the entire world. The anti-Christ (Alexis D'Antoni) and the False Prophet (Pope Radinsky) were also revealed.

The second book, *The End of the Beginning,* covered the start of the seven-year Tribulation period through the identification of the two witnesses of Revelation 11, namely Pastor Gabriel and Rabbi Abraham. This story picked up with our characters where the first book left them and introduced several new characters.

The final book in this series, *The End,* will go through the end of the world as we know it into the New Heaven, the New Earth and the New Jerusalem at the start of the Millennium following the Second Coming of Jesus Christ.

At the end of the second book, the two witnesses were identified and were now ready to fulfill their prophetic roles for the ordained 1,260 days through the first three-and-a-half years of the seven-year Tribulation.

Meanwhile, Jerome and Sue managed to hook up with Brandon and the Harrison family after they'd escaped from the detention center.. They were able to escape detection and began to descend the far side of the mountains to their rendezvous with Jesse and Francine in Silver City, New Mexico.

The militia group, under General Wycliffe, that had freed Brandon, Sue and the Harrisons from the detention center, was forced to abandon their once secret headquarters in the New Mexico mountains. However, they were intent on reforming elsewhere, trying to establish working relationships with other militia groups across the southwest.

Jim connected by phone with Jesse and Francine, and these ex-CIA and FBI agents began to hatch counterintelligence plans against the forming New World Order and the soon-to-be enacted Universal ID System, the dreaded "mark of the beast."

With Big Dog eliminated, life back in the Havenwood1 hideaway (the first of twelve nationwide, with two having been destroyed) returned to a semi-normal routine. Residents still had to deal with the two captured gang members as well as integrating the other gangbangers who had chosen to join with them. There was much counseling and pastoring for Wally to do.

Juanita devoted her energies to keeping prayer going 24/7 and was able to train and recruit new members for the prayer team. While Abby managed the Havenwood1 hideaway and their ongoing evangelism efforts, Jermaine coordinated the other hideaways and seven remote campgrounds around the country.

Alexis and Pope Radinsky were able to quell the Islamic uprising and return a state of peace over the earth for all except Christians and Jews. With generous funds, they also assisted the United States in rebuilding the White House, making it more grandiose, fully and openly reflecting Masonic and Illuminati symbolism.

Montrose and Sir William continued their hostile working relationship as further detention centers were constructed and filled with "traitors" and "violators" of the various Universal Directives.

Chapter One

The television networks ran and reran videos of Pastor Gabriel Ramirez calling down fire from out of the sky and destroying incoming missiles aimed at the Vatican, immediately followed by Rabbi Abraham Cohen similarly obliterating heavily armed terrorists who were charging the Papal Palace.

The talking heads of the media didn't quite know what to make of it all. Some were calling Gabriel and Abraham the new "superheroes" of the day, as if comic-book characters had stepped out of the pages into reality. Others sought to discredit the amateur videos as fraudulent and called the onlookers victims of "mass hysteria." Those "Bible thumpers" who said the pastor and rabbi were the "two witnesses" of the Book of Revelation[1] were mostly ridiculed.

The media was clamoring for statements from Pope Radinsky and Alexis D'Antoni, the "Global Czar." It was rumored that the Pope had directly witnessed the events in question. Behind the scenes, Alexis and the Pope were mobilizing their own network of global influencers to sow confusion and generate controversy before they would step in to "clear things up."

Technical experts were called upon to analyze the videos shot by tourists on their camcorders and cell phones. Leaks from anonymous sources were preparing the foundation for an exposé of an elaborately staged plot using holographic images and "magical tricks" to create sophisticated illusions. Christian spokespersons were marginalized as "crackpots" who were the primary targets of the scam.

Back in the Havenwood1 hideaway, the entire crew gathered around the various plasma TVs and computer screens to watch the unfolding drama in absolute astonishment. There, before their very eyes, was their leader, Pastor Gabriel calling fire down from heaven. They had no doubt that it was real, but it still boggled the mind to think that he might indeed be one of the two end-time witnesses.

Carmelita, Gabriel's wife, danced a jig in the middle of the central chamber of their underground hideaway. She was simply grateful that he was alive, having not heard from him in weeks since he had turned himself over to Sir William to try to infiltrate the New World Order. Abby and Juanita jumped in and joined Carmelita as the others surrounded them clapping and singing praises to the Lord.

Pastor Wally declared a holiday in honor of Gabriel. The evangelism teams would take a day off, facility maintenance was postponed, and all meetings, classes and counseling were canceled. "It's party time!" Michelle exclaimed, winking at her pastor husband to show her approval. The cooks broke out cakes and pies while the Worship Warrior band set up their sound system.

As excitement rippled throughout the hideaway, Jermaine, Abby, Jim, Wally and Juanita slipped away into the small conference room to discuss the ramifications of what they had just viewed on television.

"Is Gabriel really one of the two Biblical witnesses?" Abby asked, recalling Pastor Gabriel's own teaching on the subject. "Isn't it supposed to be Elijah and Moses, or Joshua and Zerubbabel?"[2]

"I guess not," Wally answered slowly, not quite believing what he'd just seen.

"What is it with you people," Juanita scolded. "Pastor Gabriel is the most Spirit-filled, wise, powerful Christian I've ever met or seen. Why couldn't he be God's holy witness?"

"I agree," Jermaine added forcefully. "Just because he isn't famous and doesn't hold some high-level position in the world, does that mean he can't be used by God in a mighty way?"

"You're right," Wally admitted. "Look at Jesus' twelve disciples. They didn't hold any positions of authority at all. They were mostly uneducated men and look what they were able to accomplish!"[3]

"That's what we keep coming back to, over and over again," Juanita explained. "God uses the foolish things of the world to confound the wise, just as the Bible tells us."[4]

"Yes, that way it's God who gets all the credit and glory," Jim added. Everyone smiled at the newbie Christian and former CIA Director. Abby leaned over to give her new husband an appreciative kiss, causing Jim to blush bright red.

The group, still astounded at this new development, sat in quiet contemplation for awhile. Abby waited a polite few moments before she would begin nudging the group along in their thought process. Everyone had come to appreciate her leadership skills and counted on her now to call the meetings and set the agenda.

Jermaine, Gabriel's second in command, was still the overseer of the ten remaining hideaways and the seven remote campgrounds. When Gabriel surrendered himself to Sir William for his "divine appointment" with Alexis D'Antoni, the Global Czar, Abby was appointed Havenwood1's leader according to Juanita's vision, and Jermaine replaced Gabriel as the overall General.

After Jermaine's hideaway in upstate New York was discovered and overrun, he relocated to Havenwood1 in Virginia, where he willingly and graciously ceded local authority to Abby, despite some initial misgivings. Now, he admired and respected her, as did all the others.

Jim too might have taken umbrage at Abby's leadership. After all, he had been her superior back at the CIA. But now, he'd begun a new life and was quite content to sit back and let her take the lead. He'd decided he would make amends to Jesus for his lifetime of work in the Illuminati opposing Christianity by following His admonition, "If anyone desires to be first, he shall be last of all and servant of all."[5]

Abby, though, encouraged Jim to become the "spiritual head" of their marriage as the Bible directed.[6] This was daunting to Jim, still a "baby" Christian. Together they sought Pastor Wally's counseling in this regard. He pointed out that being a spiritual leader didn't require knowledge as much as it did devotion and obedience to Jesus Christ.

Pastor Wally also explained that this didn't mean a husband should be the boss over all aspects of married life, just over spiritual matters. The Bible clearly showed the woman as the one who ran the household.[7] He also showed Jim and Abby that this elevation of men to a superior spiritual position was actually the result of curses God placed over men and women as a result of Adam and Eve's disobedience in the Garden of Eden.[8]

While men now had to labor hard by the sweat of their brow to earn a living, women were cursed to have their husbands rule over them. "This wasn't the initial pattern that God intended," Pastor Wally clarified. "When God made woman, He intended her to be 'comparable' to man. Counterparts, equal partners," he said."[9]

Abby gently interrupted the group reverie, "So, with Pastor Gabriel and Rabbi Abraham being the two witnesses, what does that mean to us? To the world? Does this change what we do and how we do things?"

"You sure do ask difficult questions." Juanita feigned exasperation, and then chuckled at her spiritual protégé. Jim winked his appreciation.

No one seemed to have any immediate answers to her questions, so she noted, "Well, it certainly means some changes in Carmelita's life. Do you think Pastor Gabriel will come back for her?"

"The Bible doesn't give us much to go on," Pastor Wally said as he turned to the relevant verses in Revelation.[1] Just like we saw on TV, the Bible says that no one can harm them, that they can call fire down on their enemies. They can also call for drought and strike the earth with plagues. So I don't think we have to worry about Gabriel's safety."

"Right, but that only lasts for forty-two months," Jermaine recalled. "Then the beast will overcome them and kill them, right?"

"Yes, that's what the Scriptures say," Wally confirmed. "Sad to say, but the Word also indicates that the world will rejoice over their deaths because the two witnesses tormented them."

"Surely they wouldn't be tormenting people just for the fun of it," Abby reasoned.

"No, certainly not," Pastor Wally agreed. "But, as God's two primary witnesses during the end-times, they would be the most persecuted and hated of all Christians. However, they would also be triggering droughts and plagues as God's judgment upon sinful people and nations. That would undoubtedly incur the wrath of a hedonistic world. That's why they've been given great powers to defend themselves."

"Remember, though, that after three-and-a-half days, the two witnesses are raised from the dead by God," Juanita noted. "Then they rise up into heaven in a cloud for all the world to see."

"Wow, what a great honor!" Abby exclaimed. "How could the world not believe in God and Jesus then?"

"I don't know," Wally said, shaking his head sadly. "But we do know from other sections in Revelation that many won't. [10] Perhaps it's because their hearts are hardened and their consciences seared, just as the Bible tells us."[11]

"So we need to pray all the more!" Juanita declared emphatically. "The more we pray, the more we save."

"Amen to that," Jermaine agreed. "But back to Abby's questions. Since we don't know much about what the two witnesses actually do for three-and-a-half years, I suggest we simply wait to see what happens. However, we need to be prepared to follow Pastor Gabriel wherever he and Rabbi Abraham lead us."

"Yes, I suppose you're right," Abby reluctantly agreed. She'd been hoping for something more definitive, something they could do other than just wait and pray. She was a doer, not a very good waiter.

"Well, I suppose that Pastor Gabriel must be feeling elated and jubilant over his selection as one of the two witnesses," Jim suggested, just before Juanita led them in a closing prayer.

Chapter Two

E lated and jubilant were not the words Pastor Gabriel and Rabbi Abraham would have chosen to describe their current feelings. After the awesome display of God's power in St. Peter's Square, they both felt quite overwhelmed. As sirens approached Vatican City, they felt a strong unction to leave the premises, continuing their flight from Pope Radinsky.

The onlookers were in a state of shock, alternating their wide eyes back and forth between the decimated terrorists and the two men who had called down tongues of fire from the heavens. No one said a word or even moved as Gabriel and Abraham ran out of the square and headed north on Via di Porta Angelica. As the sirens grew closer, they made a quick right on Borga Vittorio and slowed to a fast walk to avoid calling attention to themselves.

"Where should we go?" Pastor Gabriel asked Rabbi Abraham.

"I don't have a clue," Abraham replied. "Let's allow the hand of the Lord to guide us. He's obviously with us in a mighty way."

"That's for sure," Gabriel agreed, shaking his head in wonderment at what just happened.

Neither of them had been to Rome before, so they were blindly going where they felt the Lord was leading them.

They soon came to a major intersection with Via di Porta Castello. All the sirens seemed to have passed by and were behind them now, so they cautiously crossed the main thoroughfare. After walking one more block, they came to another major intersection.

Gabriel's head was spinning. He placed his hand against the wall of the building to his right to keep from falling over.

"Are you all right, my brother?" Abraham asked, leaning his back against the building as well. He was still panting from all the exertion and excitement.

Gabriel nodded. "Yes, I just need a moment to clear my head."

Abraham glanced ahead to see if he could figure out where they should go, what they should do. He could see a walled compound with a lot of trees. Perhaps they should take shelter there for awhile?

A passerby looked over at them and Abraham caught his eye. "Excuse, me sir, do you speak English?"

"Yes, a little," the young man replied cautiously.

"Can you tell me what that is across the street?" Abraham asked, smiling and pointing like a foolishly lost tourist.

"Yes, of course, it is the Castel Sant' Angelo," the studious, bespectacled man answered.

"Ahh, and what might that be?" Abraham inquired, shrugging his shoulders to indicate his complete helplessness.

The young man allowed a faint look of contempt to cross his face as he looked over these two typical tourists who come to a foreign country without any knowledge or preparation, expecting everyone to cater to their every whim.

"It is the Mausoleum of Hadrian," he answered officiously. "It was originally built by the Roman Emperor Hadrian for himself and his family. It is now a museum. The entrance is two blocks down to your right and one block to the left."

With that, the young man turned and strode away, his offended nose lifted slightly into the gentle autumn breeze. Abraham and Gabriel had to hold back their amusement lest they offend him any more.

"I feel that the Lord is saying we should take refuge in the Mausoleum," Abraham said, watching Gabriel for signs of disagreement or ongoing dizziness. Gabriel shrugged. "Okay, let's go."

There was a lot of foot traffic on the main street, so they blended in and followed the flow down Piazza Pia to Via della Conciliazione. After traversing the prescribed two blocks, they turned left onto a large plaza which led up to a small entrance through the massive walled structure into the towering cylindrical castle.

Gabriel paid the entrance fees in his American dollars, earning some more contempt and probably getting cheated in the currency exchange, but that was the least of his concerns. They made their way inside the compound and Gabriel quickly led them out of the Mausoleum/Museum toward the adjacent grounds, finding the Italian signs easy to read, very close to the Mexicali *Español* he'd grown up with.

They followed the footpaths northward again out into a broad park resplendent with a forest of trees. They quickly found a secluded bench and sat down to rest and consider what they should do. The afternoon sun bathed them in deep shadows, giving them a sense of privacy and peace that was quite welcome.

"Perhaps we should wait until dark before we venture outside again," Gabriel suggested.

Abraham nodded, giving in finally to the weariness and shock. They sat awhile in silence, lost in their own thoughts, trying to sort out what had just happened.

"So, do you think it's true then?" Gabriel eventually asked, not quite able to say the words.

Abraham's bushy eyebrows lifted and his mouth pursed in deep reflection, his ample gray beard quivering. "I must reluctantly admit that the evidence is hard to refute," he finally concluded.

"I hate to think that Pope Radinsky was right after all," Gabriel conceded, also hesitant to pick up the heavy mantle.

"Well, he's obviously wrong about cheating death and hell," Abraham snorted. "Imagine thinking Satan can alter time!"

"Yes, Lucifer is quite deluded," Gabriel agreed. "I always wondered how he could rationalize his certain fate and keep on going as though the end would never come."

Abraham sensed they were dancing around the core issue like a couple of moths around a flame, afraid to land but compelled to stay near. "The two witnesses. You and I. How can that be?"

Gabriel sighed. "I suppose your namesake must have had a similar feeling when God first called out to him and told him to leave his family and country and go to a land he'd never seen." [12]

Abraham chuckled. "Yes, and think what he must have felt when God gave him such grandiose promises. The 'father' of nations.[13] It must have seemed quite absurd at the time."

"Or Gideon," Gabriel mused, "when the angel of the Lord singled him out to lead the army against the Philistines," [14]

"Yes, Adonai seems to pick commoners to do His great works," Abraham agreed. "So I guess we're amply qualified."

They both laughed nervously, giving vent to the tension that gripped them like a vise. The burden weighed heavily upon them.

"If it *is* true," Abraham said between guffaws, "then Adonai must make it happen. This isn't something we can just go off and do on our own."

Gabriel breathed deeply, as the laughter calmed his frayed nerves. "It is an awesome responsibility. But just as God empowered others, we must believe and expect that He will do so for us as well."

"Yes, my brother, we must always keep that in mind and remind one another," Abraham asserted. "And we must seek Him constantly to know what it is He would have us to do."

"Like maybe right now. Where do we go? What should we do?" Gabriel pondered.

"Let's pray," Abraham suggested. They joined hands across the picnic table. Abraham began praying aloud in Hebrew and Gabriel prayed in tongues. [15]

It was a good thing that they were fairly isolated from the throng of tourists, because their voices rose in unison to resounding levels. The ground shook under their feet even as the picnic table vibrated beneath their hands. A pair of young lovers fled from behind a nearby stand of trees.

At the very peak of their vociferous prayers, each stopped suddenly at the very same moment. Their eyes opened and they stared at one another. Their bodies shook and their souls trembled. They had seen the future in a joint vision. It was both awe-inspiring and overwhelming.

They gripped each other's hands tighter, knowing for certain now that it was true and that the two of them were to be joined together at the hip for the next forty-two months. They rose as one without a word to follow the path that the Lord Almighty had laid out before them.

Chapter Three

J esse and Francine pulled into Silver City, New Mexico a couple of days after they'd spoken with Jerome and Sue. They had agreed to meet at the southern end of a vast range of mountains surrounding Baldy Peak in the Gila Wilderness, referring to the map Jesse had purchased when they made their first pit stop off I-10 in New Mexico.

Francine drove her jeep off Route 180 in Silver City and headed north on Pinos Altos (Route 15) to a small enclave of the same name. They had seen in their travel guide a listing for the Bear Mountain Motel and Cabins that lay in the foothills below Black Peak. This would be the closest they could get to where Jerome and Sue were last known to be, deep in the mountains.

After they got settled into the large comfortable cabin, Jesse called Jerome and Sue to give them the GPS coordinates so that they could work their way down out of the mountains to Route 15 and then on down to Pinos Altos. However, the call didn't get through, so Jesse left a message. He assumed that cell phone coverage was hit or miss in the mountains and hoped they would get the coordinates before wandering too far off course. He had no idea how long it would take for them to make the difficult journey.

"No wonder no one knew about the detention center there," Francine observed as she flopped down on the sofa. "It's really in the middle of nowhere."

Jesse nodded in agreement but seemed preoccupied. "What's the matter?" Francine asked.

"Well," Jesse began slowly and uncomfortably, "I think we'll have to reserve another cabin for Jerome and Sue. There are only two bedrooms here."

Francine smiled knowingly. She'd wondered when the circumstances of their burgeoning relationship would strike the committed Christian man who tried to live out his faith in all its aspects. She decided to let Jesse dangle in the wind a while longer before releasing him from his conundrum.

Jesse waited for the normally expressive young woman to say something. It was rather odd for her to be so quiet. He didn't want to offend or disappoint her, but he wasn't prepared to share a bed with her unless they were married. It was that thought that rendered him incapacitated.

It had been several years since his wife left and divorced him. He hadn't entered into any relationships since. It was clear that he and Francine had established a connection, but how deep did it run? What was she expecting of him?

"Okay Mr. Mum," Francine laughed as she jumped up off the couch. "I'm a dedicated Christian too, so I already knew we weren't going to share a bed. Pressure's off."

Jesse breathed a sigh of relief and then braced himself as the tiny effervescent woman leaped into his arms. "But that doesn't mean you can't come near me!" As Jesse held her close, he was beginning to think that marriage just might lay in the immediate future.

Meanwhile, Jerome and Sue were getting on each other's nerves. Against her advice, Jerome had driven his Land Rover down a narrow gorge that he guaranteed would bring them to the other side of some imposing mountains, thus saving them a lot of time and effort.

However, the gorge had led them into a dead-end canyon. There wasn't even room to turn the Land Rover around. Backing up over the rocky trail would be difficult at best. The supposed time-saver would cost them at least half a day before they could get back to where they had broken camp that morning.

Sue wanted to be forgiving, but the stress of imprisonment and escape from the detention center into the wilds of mountainous wilderness was more than she could handle. "You stupid, ignorant, stubborn oaf!" she shouted and began walking back up the gorge.

Jerome was exhausted and deflated. He was well aware of the ongoing consequences of his impulsive behavior, but he couldn't seem to stop himself from repeating the pattern over and over again. It was like something just took him over. Oh well, nothing to do but to begin the arduous process of backing up the narrow canyon.

First, though, he climbed up on the roof of the Land Rover and waved wildly at Brandon who had been making slower progress in the jeep he'd taken from the detention center. "Go back, go back!" he shouted and waved.

Brandon pulled out his binoculars and realized what Jerome was signaling. He sighed. It was difficult enough driving the jeep through the rough terrain, but much more so loaded down with the Harrison family. James was still recuperating from his bout with food poisoning. While getting better, he was still dead weight as far as the difficult journey was concerned.

Trudy Harrison and her four young children were real troopers, helping out with everything. However, when they all squeezed into the jeep, the children in the open caboose, the overall weight severely compromised ground clearance. So the two older kids traveled in the back seat of Jerome's Land Rover. Brandon still couldn't drive the Jeep everywhere Jerome could go in his Land Rover, or, if he could, it took a lot longer. *Now that clown has driven us into a dead-end*, Brandon grumped to himself.

It had seemed like such a blessing when Jerome approached them that first night away from the detention center. To have traveling companions as they retreated from government forces deep into the mountains was a welcome relief. That Jerome was big and strong and had a good four-wheel drive vehicle was a definite plus. Now, on their second day of travel together, Brandon was seriously thinking of cutting loose from this circus.

It took a couple of hours to get back to their morning campsite, just in time for lunch. Jerome wept and apologized – over and over again. "Enough already!" Brandon finally shouted to shut him up. "We get it. You're sorry. We forgive you. So now let's just get on with things, okay?"

Jerome nodded weakly and retreated meekly into the hills. After Trudy and Sue made the sandwiches, Sue brought lunch up to her chastened fiancé. This kind of behavior was why she had postponed their wedding plans. Then, as now, when he came down from his manic state, her heart went out to him. Afterward, it was all she could do to keep him from sinking into a deep depression.

She assumed Jerome was what they now call bipolar, what she still thought of as manic-depressive, which seemed to describe it a lot better. Jerome was loathe to go to some "shrink," so Sue had coped as well as she could. When Jerome was "himself," he was just what Sue wanted and needed. Someone big and strong to hold and protect her. A good man who cared about her and didn't take advantage of her.

That he'd charged clear across the country to rescue her from that despicable prison just reinforced her image of him as her "knight in shining armor." Then he'd pull a stunt like this. Did she really want to go through such extreme highs and lows? She decided to leave all that for another day. Take one day at a time. Get out of these mountains and back to civilization, or at least what was left of it.

Chapter Four

CNN's own Blaine Whitney was overseeing the final preparations for the special news conference with Alexis D'Antoni and Pope Radinsky in the Sistine Chapel. Although the producer was there, everyone got out of the way when Blaine was in one of her moods. That charming sweet woman whose warm smiles melted the hearts of her viewers was an angry tigress off screen. She would allow nothing to get in the way of her continued meteoric rise.

There were only a few minutes to go until the unprecedented news conference began. Because of the venue, the Vatican restricted the news media to one pool reporter. After much debate, Blaine and CNN were chosen. This ultimate coup weighed heavily on the already stressed-out blonde bombshell. She was determined to demonstrate that she deserved her exalted position because of her talent, not just her looks.

Sure, she'd purposely used her stunning beauty to open doors. She'd be foolish not to take advantage of all her assets. But once inside, she'd quieted her many critics through outstanding performance. Over and over again. But still, some critics ranted and raved, making disgusting suggestions that she'd slept her way to the top of the ladder. Nothing could be further from the truth. In fact, she was somewhat of a prude when it came to sexual matters. No one believed that, though.

No one except her one steady beau who remained a carefully guarded secret, because he was the respected anchor on a major TV network. They'd met and began dating back when they were both cutting their teeth in the news business at a local L.A. station. Both had been monogamous, or at least she was, but didn't marry because both of their careers were on the fast track. They didn't see one another all that often, but when they did she was sure that Patrick was the love of her life.

Just as Blaine was shouting one last set of instructions at the third cameraman located high on the gangway, the organ resounded within the vaulted chamber, announcing that the news conference would begin shortly. As the choir sang, Blaine glanced around the grandiose chapel, putting visual images to the research she'd completed on the hurried trip over the Atlantic. She possessed a prodigious memory.

The chapel was built between 1475 and 1483 in the time of Pope Sixtus IV, she reminded herself in preparation for her live report. It is one of the most famous churches of the Western World. The name *Sistine* was derived from the Italian *sistino* meaning of or pertaining to Sixtus IV. Overall, the chapel is rectangular and measures 134 feet long by 44 feet wide, the exact dimensions of Solomon's Temple as given in the Old Testament. It is 68 feet high and roofed by a flattened barrel vault, with small side vaults over the 6 centered windows.

Its exterior is unadorned by any architectural or decorative details, as is common in many Medieval and Renaissance churches in Italy. It has no exterior façade or doorways, with ingress always from internal rooms within the Papal Palace. It can only be seen from nearby windows in the Palace. The internal space is divided into three stories of which the lowest is a huge basement. Above that is the Chapel itself. Above the vaulted chapel rose a third story with wardrooms for guards and an open gangway projecting outward, encircling the interior of the entire building. It was on this gangway that her cameraman was precariously balanced.

The chapel was famous for its many frescoes, the murals adorning the ceiling, walls and wall hangings. Of course, the most famous were those painted by Michelangelo. Under the patronage of Pope Julius II, Michelangelo painted 12,000 square feet of the chapel ceiling between 1508 and 1512. That ceiling, Blaine saw, was magnificent, giving credence to the claim that it represented Michelangelo's crowning achievement.

Frescoes from other famous painters also graced the chapel, including Raphael, Bernini and Botticelli. During ceremonies of particular importance, as this one today, the side walls were covered with a series of tapestries designed by Raphael but looted a few years later in the 1527 "Sack of Rome." The tapestries were redone in 1983 and depict events from the lives of St. Peter and St. Paul.

As a procession of Cardinals streamed into the chapel, Blaine took note of the floor, or "pavement" as the literature called it. It was done in an "Opus Alexandrinum" style using marble and colored stones which also marked the processional way from the main door. Altogether, it was most impressive, and Blaine felt an unaccustomed chill up her spine. She was not a religious person at all, so she thought her reaction must have stemmed from the ancient beauty and majesty of the chapel itself.

At the end of the procession came a regal Alexis D'Antoni followed lastly by Pope Radinsky in all his regalia. One of the Cardinals said an opening benediction followed by a formal choir presentation. At that point, Pope Radinsky strode to the podium. Blaine had been studying videos of the new Pope as part of her always meticulous preparation, but she was unprepared for the aura that emanated outward from

'His Eminence.' Waves of power flowed from him which she felt pushing her backward. Most remarkable.

After obligatory remarks of introduction, Pope Radinsky wasted no time getting down to the matter at hand. Again Blaine was surprised, being used to the bloated hot air of politicians seeking to impress or obfuscate. She turned and gestured to the forward cameraman to move in for a close up. Then she began taking notes.

"Many questions have originated from the events earlier today in St. Peter's Square," the Pope commenced to address the issue that the entire world was debating. She wondered whether this might wind up being the most watched television event ever. That sure sent her nerves atwitter.

"I wish today to dispel many of the myths and conjectures that have arisen from the rather shocking assault on the Vatican. It is clear that these were not the same terrorists from the group that briefly occupied the new Jewish temple and who later bombed the American White House. It is also clear that the two people who appeared to thwart the attack are not, and I repeat *not,* the so-called 'two witnesses' described in the Bible."

That sent a ripple of hushed whispers among the audience of high and mighty officials from governments around the world. Pope Radinsky flashed one of his ultra-charismatic smiles and in a sarcastic tone continued, "Were that to be true, then Alexis D'Antoni would have to be the anti-Christ and I would have to be the False Prophet, and that, of course, is patently ridiculous."

As if on cue, the Cardinals and guests burst into raucous laughter. Now the Pope's countenance turned dark with outrage. "These two imposters are nothing but charlatans, magicians who put on an amazing display of illusion worthy of an Oscar but totally unreal."

Again the Pope waited while the august audience chattered in increasingly angry voices. It seemed to Blaine that she and the others could feel the Pope's own outrage welling up inside them. She allowed herself to wonder if he was a master manipulator or truly God's spokesman on earth. She quickly rejected the latter idea, as her admiration of this extraordinary man rose dramatically.

When the irate noises subsided, Pope Radinsky peered directly into the closest camera with a look of sincerity that was felt as much as seen. "I have it on the highest authority that these two men are representatives of the Christian right wing who staged this phony attack to lend credence to their twisted theology. In their rejection of the Universal Religion which unites all the people of the world under one umbrella of tolerance and peace, they seek only to insist that their way is the only way to connect with the Architect of the Universe. How utterly self-serving and pathetic."

This time, as the angry voices in the gallery rose again, the Pope spoke over the background noise in rising indignation. "These false Christians debase the name and message of Christ. These right-wing extremists are an affront to God and society. They are the most dangerous people on the face of the earth today and must be stopped!"

The audience rose as one screaming their outrage in accord with the now red-faced Pope. Fire seemed to flood outward from his eyes, enflaming the congregation into a tidal wave of fury. Blaine couldn't seem to help herself as she rose to her feet shouting agreement and shaking her fist at these Christian terrorists. She hadn't felt such powerful emotion in all her life.

As the Pope made his way majestically back to his throne-like seat, the Global Czar, Alexis D'Antoni stepped forward to the podium. In contrast, he appeared to be the antithesis of the Pope's charismatic personality. As he stood imperiously waiting for the hubbub to subside, not a flicker of emotion showed on his countenance. And yet, he was able to grab the attention of the audience as surely as Pope Radinsky had.

Everyone waited breathlessly to hear from the one many called "savior." His was now the voice of reason in a world gone mad. Alexis allowed quiet to linger before he began his remarks. "My friends, my colleagues, my compatriots, it is so good to be with you today. I would only wish that it wasn't under such unpleasant circumstances. However, this latest threat to our universal peace must be addressed. Ordinary terrorists with their bombs pale in comparison to the danger these Christian terrorists represent."

Heads nodded silent assent. "Nothing is more dangerous than misguided ideology. Nothing is more of a threat to the peace we've established than dissenters who use fakery and illusion to project themselves as the only voices of the Almighty on earth today. They subjugate Biblical symbolism to create nonexistent truth. They take God's holy Word and twist it to their own purposes. They seek to divide not join. They seek to disrupt, not pacify. They seek to destroy harmony in order to elevate themselves and their absurd beliefs above everyone else."

Even though Alexis spoke quietly and evenly, the response of the gathered elite was just as strong, albeit unspoken. The silence of total agreement was palpable, impossible to resist. "These two imposters and those they represent must be stopped immediately. We have identified the two men as a Pastor Gabriel Ramirez from the United States and Rabbi Abraham Cohen from Israel. It is important that we do not ascribe blame or guilt to these two countries because of the isolated actions of these two lunatics. However, it is of utmost importance that these two be captured and exposed for the charlatans they are.

"I urge every citizen of the earth to join with law enforce-ment agencies to hunt down and capture them. I am offering a one-million dollar reward to anyone who provides the information that leads to their apprehension or their death. We will distribute flyers and information about these two terrorists and those who stand with them to all media outlets in the world. They must be found and stopped and held up as a symbol that says to every religious nut that we will not allow anyone or anything to disrupt the unprecedented peace and harmony that we have established across the face of the entire globe."

As Alexis stepped back from the podium, everyone stood and gave him a standing ovation that lasted for six minutes and thirty-two seconds, according to Blaine's Rolex. The Global Czar blushed with embarrassment at the spontaneous burst of adoration. He humbly made his way back to his seat next to the Pope who shook his hand and then embraced him, causing another roar of approval from the spectators.

While the choir began the closing ceremonies, Blaine worked her way down the side and back out into the Papal Palace. She had to get set for her live interview with the two leaders of the world, the first they had ever granted to anyone. Blaine tingled with anticipation of the greatest coup in the history of news media coverage.

Chapter Five

Unbeknownst to Pastor Gabriel and Rabbi Abraham, the entire world was being galvanized to hunt them down as they made their way out of the Castel Sant' Angelo. The tourists who jostled them as they made their way back out the entrance onto the plaza had no idea that they had rubbed shoulders with the two most hated men on earth.

Following the vision they'd both experienced simultaneously, they turned east and continued along the Piazza dei Tribunali and then wordlessly turned north on Via Ulpiano. In the twilight of evening, they made their way anonymously up three blocks to the corner of Via Marianna Dionigi, where the Chiesa Di Altri Culti Valdese stood in grandiose splendor.

The church stood imposingly in its elegance and eclectic combination of German Romanesque and Byzantine styles. The towering structure had two cylindrical side-towers, which were built to join the church to the buildings on either side. Both Gabriel and Abraham hesitated as they stared at the monolithic building which was as imposing as it was impressive.

But this was what they each had seen in their mutual visions, so they slowly made their way to the entrance and knocked gently on the large, solid door. When there was no answer they knocked louder. Still no one came to the door, so Abraham grabbed the handle and pulled it open. Inside, they looked around to see if anyone was visible, but they saw no one. So they explored the church with their eyes, wondering at the lack of holy images. There were, however, Christian and floral motifs in the windows.

Just as they were about to start wandering around, a voice called out to them in Italian from a doorway off to the right. Abraham looked at Gabriel to see if he'd understood. Gabriel spoke back in Spanish, asking if the gentleman spoke English, which the two guests both understood.

"Ahh, yes, English. A little. I get the Majoralis. He speak English good," the young man answered and disappeared back through the open doorway.

Shortly afterward, an older priest in robes came out to greet them. He shook their hands heartily and asked in heavily accented English, "What can I do for you two fine gentlemen?"

Abraham and Gabriel had not spoken about what they should do or say when they followed God's lead to this nearby church. Gabriel looked at Abraham, who shrugged his shoulders and admitted, "I'm not quite sure, Father. We both saw in a vision that we should come here."

"A vision, how remarkable. But please don't call me Father," the wizened priest asked with an ironic smile on his face. "We Waldensians are not overly fond of Catholic terminology."

"Oh, excuse me then, I meant no disrespect," the rabbi apologized sincerely. "What shall we call you then?"

"My official title is 'Majoralis' or Major, but it really means bishop. However, I don't like to stand on formality, so you may please call me Alessandro."

"The protector and helper of mankind," Gabriel translated.

"Yes, that's right. I try to live up to that name in whatever small ways I can," the Major said humbly and sincerely. "So, who are you two that have seen this church in a vision?"

"I am Messianic Rabbi Abraham Cohen and this is my new partner, Pastor Gabriel Ramirez."

"Ahh, two ministers of the faith. It is a pleasure to welcome you to our church. So how may we be of service?" Bishop Alessandro inquired again.

"Well, I guess we need shelter for the moment," Pastor Gabriel admitted. "Beyond that, we'll have to wait and see what else God shows us."

The Majoralis studied them for a moment. Before he could respond, the young man they had first seen came running out of the doorway and hurried up to whisper in Alessandro's ear. The Bishop's eyebrows rose and his eyes narrowed.

Gabriel and Abraham supposed that news reports on TV might have reached their tentacles into this sanctuary, but they waited to see what would happen.

Alessandro nodded to the young man in dismissal and waved to Gabriel and Abraham to follow him. They went through the church, past the altar to a back door that led down a hallway to the office area. He opened a door into a combination storage room and lounge.

"You may stay here for the night," Alessandro advised them. "Before our evening service starts, I will bring two cots for you to sleep on. There is food in the refrigerator, so please help yourselves."

With that, the Majoralis bowed and left the room, closing the door behind him.

"Well, here we are," Abraham laughed. "Do you think he's aware of the events in St. Peter's Square today?"

"I suppose that's what the young man told him about. I'm sure someone got some videos of us, so I guess we're famous now," Gabriel observed as he scrounged through the fridge.

"Famous, hmm. I'm not so sure I'll like being famous," Abraham observed.

Chapter Six

The celebration in the Havenwood1 hideaway came to a screeching halt as TV images from the Sistine Chapel shocked the partiers into complete silence. Chills of terror replaced euphoria as the words of Pope Radinsky and Alexis D'Antoni echoed off the stone walls of the underground chamber.

"How can anyone believe that nonsense?" Abby asked disgustedly.

"It sure looks like all the Cardinals and dignitaries do," Jim observed sadly.

Carmelita's sobs grabbed their attention. Juanita ran up to her and held her tightly. She couldn't imagine what it would be like to hear her husband so vilified on worldwide television. Thoughts of her own missing husband, Brandon, forced their way out of suppression and brought tears of their own.

"It looks like your questions, Abby, were just a bit premature," Jermaine noted wryly. "Or perhaps you were being prescient."

"Prescient?" Abby asked.

"Knowing things beforehand," Pastor Wally explained. "Maybe the Holy Spirit was leading you to ask those questions, because now we really do need to figure out what this means for us."

"Yeah, it sounds pretty ominous when the Global Czar said they would hunt down all Gabriel's and Abraham's associates," Jermaine said as he waved for them to follow him back into the meeting room. The sounds of fear and agitation among the residents followed them until they closed the door.

"We need to bring every one of our relatives and other strong Christians we know into our remote camps right away," Jermaine stated before they even had a chance to sit down.

The urgency in his voice stunned Abby, Jim and Wally.

"You think it's going to become a witch hunt?" Wally asked.

Jermaine nodded emphatically. "Yes I do, and not just for the people who are directly associated with Gabriel or Abraham. All strong Christians are now labeled terrorists and must fear for their lives."

Jim cleared his throat. Whereas he normally felt like a newly commissioned private in the Lord's army, he now realized this situation was more up the old CIA/Illuminati dark alleys he used to roam.

"This was all a well-planned and well-executed end-run around the truth of what really happened," Jim began to explain. "The best way to undermine the truth is with well-crafted, highly believable lies. Trust me, I used to be an expert in lies, distortion, misinformation, etc."

The group's ears perked up. Here was the voice of experience. "If I didn't know any better, I'd think that Alexis and the Pope knew beforehand that this was going to happen. Either that, or they are extremely gifted. In either case, they've quickly turned around what could have been a devastating blow to their credibility and have gone on the offensive."

"So what can we do?" Abby asked plaintively.

Jim debated within himself, not wanting to sound contentious or disrespectful. However, it was high time for these believers to act on what they believed. He took a deep breath and looked each one in the eye.

"Looking at things from a military point of view," he began, "you have been operating as urban guerillas, sneaking out to bring supplies and truth to the people and then scurrying back into your holes like scared rabbits."

The shocked looks from his wife and friends almost stopped him, but the urgency of the situation propelled him forward. "I keep hearing about how God is so much stronger than the devil, and yet you act as though the opposite was true. Look at what Gabriel and Abraham just did! Juanita keeps saying that the anointing will increase exponentially in the end-times making miracles more common.[16] Isn't this the time that we need God's power to manifest through us instead of slinking around scared and weak?"

"Out of the mouths of babes," Juanita observed from the doorway. "Listen up, folks, 'cause he's preaching the truth!"

Jim watched their facial expressions go through a major paradigm shift right before his eyes.

"So what are you suggesting, exactly?" Wally finally inquired.

"I don't have specifics for you. That we'll have to strategize with the guidance of the Holy Spirit. But I think we need to start thinking like Joshua and David instead of like Gideon hiding in the winepress,"[14] Jim stated emphatically.

"Glory be, aren't you something else," Juanita exclaimed. "You must have been studying behind our backs!"

Abby looked at her husband through new eyes that began to mist over.

"We need to start going on the attack," Jim continued. "We need to start setting the agenda, the terms of engagement. We need to become offensive minded, not always on the defensive."

"Yes, indeed," Juanita said as she clapped her hands in joyful anticipation. "I think we're finally ready for the Lord of Hosts to come lead his army to victory. We're going to see the walls of Jericho fall again,[17] and the enemy's troops frightened into disarray by the sound of troops marching in the mulberry trees."[18]

Now it was Jim's turn to be perplexed. "Mulberry trees?"

"Pastor Wally, could you lead us in a Bible study of how the Lord led his troops to victory in so many different ways?" Juanita asked. "I think we first need to better understand how God works before we try and determine what we should do."

Everyone agreed and Wally headed off to prepare for the all-day class they scheduled for later that week.

Chapter Seven

Night was falling rapidly as it does in the cloudless southwest. The weary travelers felt much better than during
the morning's dead-end episode. Following lunch, they had
made excellent progress once they found an old mining road
that wound down into a valley awash with vegetation. It was
like finding an unexpected oasis in the midst of the desert.

Although Jerome's GPS unit didn't show that road or
any others in the surrounding area, it appeared that they were
closing in on Gila Hot Springs, a sparsely populated farming
community along local Route 15, which was a paved country
highway that would take them south down to Pinos Altos
where Jesse and Francine awaited them.

Before descending completely into the valley, they
stopped on a southern facing slope to see if they could get
a cell phone connection. With clear sight lines all the way
down to Silver City, Jerome cheered loudly when two bars
appeared on his cell phone. He was able to call Jesse and
bring him up to date on their journey, saying that he thought
they could make it in one more day. Knowing Jerome's
consistent optimism, Jesse told Francine it would probably
be two days before they arrived.

The biggest cheer came when Brandon was able to reach
Juanita over the still functioning fax line at the hideaway.
Abby ran down the hall to the prayer room, grabbed Juanita

without any explanation and dragged her back to the communications hub and handed her the phone.

Juanita's hands trembled as she slowly raised the receiver to her ear. She vainly attempted to keep her escalating hopefulness in check. She hadn't seen, talked to or heard anything at all about her beloved husband since he and the Harrison family were whisked away from her house in what seemed like ages ago.

"Hello?" she said tentatively into the phone.

"Juanita, it's me, Brandon, I'm alive and all is well," Brandon shouted into the cell phone.

For a moment, Juanita didn't recognize his voice because Brandon very seldom got excited and shouted.

"Blossom, are you there?" he asked more quietly, using the term of endearment that always caused her heart to flutter.

Tears began cascading down her cheeks. "Honeybunch, it's really you! Oh how I've missed you. When can I see you?"

Brandon excitedly explained what had happened to him and the Harrisons, how he'd escaped and hooked up with the militia, and where he, the Harrisons, Jerome and Sue were headed to meet up with Jesse and Francine.

"I don't know what we'll do when we get to Pinos Altos but I'll let you know as soon as we figure it all out," Brandon concluded his long monologue in the same quiet, dignified voice she'd grown to love so much.

Abby had brought Juanita a box of tissues and then left her alone, shepherding the communications team away from the area. Juanita dabbed away the last tear just as Brandon completed his story.

"Honey, I can't wait to see you and hold you again, but there's something you all need to know," Juanita began in a more serious tone that put Brandon on edge. She then explained to him the events on St. Peter's Square and the subsequent condemnation of Pastor Gabriel and all his associates, perhaps any strong Christians.

"You all need to be real careful," she warned. "We don't know what's going to happen, I've been praying and seeing visions of lynchings like in the old South, only this time it's Christians instead of black folks."

When they'd finished the call, Juanita collapsed into the swivel desk chair near the fax machine. She was overwhelmed with both relief and concern. For some reason, she felt quite uneasy. Well, she sure knew what to do about that. She quickly assembled the hideaway leaders and the prayer team and explained what was going on out west.

Jim was relieved and delighted to hear that Jerome had actually rescued Sue, and that Jesse and Francine were alive and well. For the first time, he stayed with the prayer team and even surprised himself when he chimed in a few times. They all felt a tremendous burden to cover the fugitives with a constant blanket of prayer and protection.

Chapter Eight

When Jesse and Francine realized it would be another day or two of waiting at the cabin, they decided to take a drive down to Silver City and find a nice restaurant to celebrate. Their journey out west had been a hurried, anxiety-ridden trip. Now that they had been able to relax at the cabin for awhile, knowing their friends were safe, they looked forward to their first real date.

After asking around, they wound up at the Jalisco Café, an enchanting brick building in the historic district. It advertised itself as serving "authentic" Mexican food, and Francine claimed it was the best she'd ever had. Jesse only knew that it was a lot hotter than anything he'd had before, but he believed Francine because he knew she was a real connoisseur of fine food.

The restaurant wasn't very crowded for a weekend evening. Perhaps it wasn't tourist season. Those who were there seemed to know one another and were engaged in animated conversations, some verging on hostility. Jesse and Francine were able to pick up some words and phrases that severely dampened their enjoyment of the meal and each other's company.

It appeared that those who were known as Christians were being cornered and forced to either defend or deny their faith. What had stirred up this peaceful little town?

Apparently some event had occurred at the Vatican. Were their ears playing tricks on them? Was that the same Pastor Gabriel they'd heard about from Jim?

Two of the more vociferous men who appeared to be drunk began to drag an older gentlemen away from his table and out the back door while his wife screamed hysterically. Jesse jumped to his feet to intervene.

A large red-faced lout rushed over to block Jesse's path. Francine ran over and grabbed Jesse's arm. "I think we should leave," she said urgently.

Jesse hesitated and reluctantly turned to leave. But then he heard the older man scream in pain. That wasn't a fair fight. They were apparently beating the man just because he was a Christian. That got Jesse's blood boiling.

He turned back and quickly delivered a knock-out blow to the chin of the large man blocking his path. Stepping over the fallen body, he ran out the back door and saw one young man holding the older gentleman while the other beat on him repeatedly with his fists.

While not a field agent, Jesse was well-trained by the FBI. Before the two young men even saw he was there, he delivered a swift, hard kick against the outside knee of the man holding the older gentleman. That attacker collapsed in pain, holding onto a now useless knee.

The older man fell over backward, his face mashed and bloody. The other attacker began to charge at Jesse who ducked under the wild haymaker and delivered a stiff-fingered karate chop to his mid-section. This one also collapsed, unable to take a breath.

The large man inside the restaurant charged outside toward Jesse. As he ran past Francine, she kicked at his ankle and he fell head over heels. She quickly opened her purse and pulled out the small revolver she'd purchased when she first went into hiding back east, and pointed it at him.

The older man's wife also came running out, stopped and looked around, and then ran over to her husband who was just getting up.

The large man scrambled back to his feet and hesitated when he saw Francine's gun. Then his lips curled into an angry grimace and he charged at her before Jesse could grab him. The man clearly thought Francine wouldn't have the nerve or the quickness to shoot. He was wrong.

The small gun popped and the large man fell past Francine grabbing at his thigh. She turned to face the two young men who were attempting to get up. "Stay where you are," she commanded.

Jesse took hold of the older man and guided him out to the parking lot while Francine kept the pistol trained at the three thugs. The wife pointed out their vehicle, opened it and Jesse helped the bloodied man inside. "I think you'd better follow us and get out of town for awhile."

The woman was quivering in fear and simply nodded. Jesse ran to the Jeep, drove over to pick up Francine. She fired a warning shot into the ground near the second young man who'd regained his breath and appeared ready to spring into action.

The Jeep roared off followed by the four-door sedan. Jesse led them out of town and back up to Pinos Altos. In the dark of night, Jesse parked the Jeep on the far side of the cabin, out of sight from the main road. Then he helped the older man out of the car. While Francine and the man's wife helped him inside the cabin, Jesse parked the sedan behind the cabin as well.

Inside, Fran was already ministering to the older man's wounds. "You might have a broken nose," she said gently. The man appeared to be in shock and didn't respond.

Jesse took the man's wife aside. "I think you should stay here for the night."

She, also in shock, simply nodded again.

"Do you live in Silver City?" Jesse asked.

The woman nodded again and then looked plaintively into Jesse's eyes. "My husband is pastor of the Baptist Church."

Chapter Nine

B laine Whitney glanced one more time around the Sistine Hall in the Vatican Library. In yet another coup, this would be the first time the public had seen anything of the Papal Library since July, 2007 when it was closed for restoration. One of the oldest libraries in the world, it contains one of the most significant collections of historical texts. Pope Nicholas V established the library in 1448, combining books from many sources, including the imperial Library of Constantinople.

She didn't know why the Pope had decided to use the library for the interview, but she was quite pleased about it. She and her producer had set up the three cameras in such a way as to capture not only the interview, but the exquisite frescoes on the walls, columns and ceilings. These magnificent murals sparkled in the brilliant sunlight streaming through the bank of windows running along the side wall.

Blaine wished she had known in advance about the location of the interview so she could have done some more research about the library, but she'd have to make the best of it. Just as she was repositioning the wide-angle camera for the fourth time, the entourage entered. Pope Radinsky and Alexis strode majestically to the elaborate throne chairs and turned around to face the cameras.

Although Blaine had researched the appropriate protocols for greeting the Pope, she had been undecided about
whether or not to kiss his ring. Born into a Catholic family
and surrounded by the church in all aspects of her forma-
tive years, she had nonetheless renounced her faith, if she
ever had any. Not officially though. Catholics were supposed
to bow and kiss his ring; all others should bow and shake
hands.

As an ardent atheist, it rankled her to pay obeisance to
anything religious. She'd already compromised her values
by setting aside her usual clinging, revealing wardrobe
for the frumpish dress that covered her shoulders and ran
down past knees that weren't used to being in the shade.
She'd chewed out her personal assistant who'd hurried out
to purchase the ungainly garment in the few minutes they'd
had before boarding the private jet.

But now, stirred by the earlier pageantry and speeches,
standing before the radiant, charismatic Pope, her hidden
knees trembled and her heart fluttered like a smitten school-
girl. She curtsied and placed her lips on the Pope's ring that
he'd extended in her direction. In an unaccustomed stupor,
she lamely prayed that the blush she felt burning brightly on
her cheeks wouldn't show through the heavy makeup.

Alexis likewise held out his hand with a gleaming, ostentatious ring. Thoroughly undone, Blaine curtsied yet again
and kissed the Global Czar's ring as well. The producer,
cameramen and various assistants were stunned. The worldwide viewing audience gasped in unison, then cheered wildly,
though not quite understanding why. It was as if the apparent
homage bestowed by the world's objective, secular heroine
broke down any remaining walls of resistance to recognizing
the two leaders as more than just authority symbols, but as
gods.

It was a good thing Blaine had rehearsed her opening
questions. They went by in a blur and she barely heard the

responses. She and most of the viewers were captivated and mesmerized by the charm, wit, intelligence and charisma of the Global Czar and Pope. Afterward, no one seemed to remember much of what they actually said, but it felt good. Wonderful, actually. Hearts were raised in limitless hope for a world of peace, love and reason.

When the interview was over, Alexis put his arm around Blaine and led her to follow the Pope back to his private quarters. René was steaming. *Who does this tramp think she is? Just wait till I get hold of you, Alexis you two-timer!*

But Alexis had other things in mind. When they were seated and a tea service proffered, Alexis looked deep into Blaine's bright blue eyes. "Thank you, my dear, that was most impressive. You have a knack for bringing out the best in your subjects."

Blaine still had not recovered her wits. She smiled bashfully and basked in the glow of unabashed love and admiration emanating from the two most powerful men in the world. As with any narcissist, she fed on such responses in others, but gave nothing back in return. But here her heart and soul opened wide to pour out her unquestioned faith and respect.

Faith? *Perhaps this is what those religious nuts feel when they worship their various gods?* Blaine pondered. But that was blind faith in unseen forces. Here before her were flesh and blood, and yet the epitome of all that humanity could be, the essence of perfection, the fulfillment of everyone's hopes and dreams. Finally, something, someone to believe in.

"Thank you, but it was you and Pope Radinsky who carried the day. I was merely the conduit that enabled you to reach out and touch the audience. I'm sure that everyone felt quite reassured that our world is in the best possible hands," Blaine replied with uncharacteristic praise.

Alexis leaned forward toward Blaine. "I'd like you to become the spokesperson for the Global Governance

Committee. You're the Walter Cronkite of our day. People believe in you, in your honesty, objectivity, intelligence. It would enable me to step back some from the public spotlight so I can concentrate on the great responsibility that has been bestowed upon me."

Blaine was so taken aback, she began to stammer. Alexis smiled charmingly. "I'll take that as a yes."

Blaine nodded weakly, all her ambitions fulfilled.

René wanted to puke, but now she understood what Alexis had in mind. *Nevertheless, he'd better keep his hands off her or there would be hell to pay.*

*****

The Havenwood1 gang also felt like puking as Abby switched off the large plasma screen on the wall of the hideaway.

"Who could believe such garbage?" Tara wondered aloud, reflecting everyone's thoughts.

"Surely people can see right through all that malarkey," Ryan O'Donnell agreed, and smiled shyly at Tara who was shaking her head in disgust.

"Yeah, what happened to the hard-hitting Blaine Whitney?" Dmitri wondered. "She just rolled over like a puppy dog. No hard-ball questions at all."

"I think they must have been in cahoots," Stella Rose snorted. "It was all planned out from the get-go"

"Maybe not," DeShawn interjected. "After all, the Bible says the whole world will eventually worship the beasts."
[19]

"It's as if some spirit blinded her eyes and clouded her mind," José observed.

"That's exactly the case," Juanita called out from the back of the gathered group of well over a hundred. "There have always been unclean spirits around to attack our minds and hearts. Now they're more empowered than ever."

With a collective sigh of resignation, the group slowly disbanded. They had each gotten a glimpse of the future. It was far more deceptive and subtle than they'd expected.

Pastor Wally hurried through the crowd and waved to get Juanita's attention.

She smiled knowingly and waited to hear what was troubling their resident pastor.

When Wally drew up alongside her, he looked around to see if anyone was close by. Then he spoke softly, not wanting others to hear his confession.

"Uhm, this spiritual warfare class I'm working on isn't going so well. I've gathered all the relevant Scriptures, and I know what it all means, but I can't seem to put it together in a way that makes it practical."

"It's always a good idea to build a teaching around real life examples," Juanita offered.

"Yeah, that's just what I was thinking," Wally nodded his head vigorously. "So I was wondering if you'd work with me on that aspect of the course. After all, you're the one with all the experience."

Juanita laughed. "Yeah, the school of hard knocks. I learned the hard way, made all the mistakes. I can certainly tell people what *not* to do."

"Sometimes that's just as important, maybe even more so," Pastor Wally agreed.

"Well, I'd be happy to share my experiences, both good and bad. I don't have the gift of teaching like you do. I could never put a course together, but I sure can share my hard-earned lessons," Juanita said. "That's why the Holy Spirit gives each of us different gifts.[20] Then we can work together to make a whole that is greater than the sum of its parts."

"You know," Wally observed with a sly smile, "you're very wise, more so than many people realize."

"Well, let's keep it that way. I prefer to stay under the radar, if you know what I mean," Juanita said carefully. "Pride has been the downfall of most people and it opens the door wide for all kinds of demonic influence." [21]

Chapter Ten

Rabbi Abraham and Pastor Gabriel were famished, so they helped themselves to some left over Chicken Parmigiana, spaghetti with meatballs and some kind of bean soup. They could hear the stirrings of people arriving for the evening service, but sleep quickly overtook them.

They awoke with a start, though, when the massive organ and choir announced the start of the service. The building vibrated in harmony with the organ, stirring their souls. They simply lay on the two cots and soaked in the wonderful spirit inside this blessed sanctuary.

Too tired to talk, they drifted off each time the organ ceased and awoke when it started up again. It was a pleasant interlude during which each chose not to give much thought to their circumstances or to what would come next. Gradually the sounds dissipated until Majoralis Alessandro opened the door and turned on the light.

As Gabriel and Abraham sat up on the cots and rubbed their eyes, Alessandro pulled up a chair. "So how are my two fugitives doing?" he asked with a twinkle in his eye.

"So you know about us now?" Rabbi Abraham inquired gingerly.

"Yes, indeed, and I feel quite privileged that you, or God, chose this place as your sanctuary," Alessandro stated emphatically.

Seemingly in good hands, Gabriel asked, "So what is the media saying about us?"

"Well now, not just the media. You have been condemned by the Pope and the Global Czar, no less, as the most dangerous men on the face of the planet. They have offered a million dollar reward for your capture."

Abraham's bushy eyebrows shot straight up. "And neither you nor your assistant are interested in such a substantial sum?"

Alessandro chuckled. "No, in keeping with our Waldensian roots, we have both taken vows of poverty."

"Waldensian? I've never heard that term before, what does it mean?" Gabriel asked.

"Ahh, that's a very long story. Allow me to summarize," Alessandro said as he settled deeper into the ragged but well-cushioned arm chair.

Abraham and Gabriel shifted into more comfortable positions as well. They had nowhere to go at the moment and it was a relief to be talking about something else.

"Waldensians derive their name from Peter Waldo, a wealthy merchant of Lyon who decided to give up all his worldly possessions in 1177. He went through the streets giving all his money away and became a wandering preacher who relied on donations for a living," Alessandro began what sounded like an oft-repeated explanation of this obscure Christian sect.

"A real ascetic, a man after my own heart," Rabbi Abraham noted with approval.

"Yes, and he gathered quite a following which grew all around Europe. So much so, that the Waldensians came to the attention of Pope Alexander III in 1179. Preaching required official permission in those days, which Peter couldn't secure from the Bishop of Lyon, so he appealed to the Pope who also ordered him not to preach. When he and other Waldensians continued to do so, they were declared heretics and had to meet secretly."

"Were his teachings really heretical?" Pastor Gabriel asked.

"Not at all, but he did specifically renounce such Catholic doctrine such as purgatory, indulgences and prayers for the dead."

"Oh, that would get him in trouble in those days of Papal authority," Gabriel nodded knowingly.

"Yes indeed, and widespread persecution followed the Waldensians through the centuries, culminating in a general massacre by the army of the Duke of Savoy in 1655. The massacre was so brutal it aroused indignation throughout Europe, which eventually led to our legal existence and protection from further persecution. We became part of the reformed movement. In 1975, the Waldensian Church joined the Italian Methodist Church."

"Well, that's quite a history," Rabbi Abraham exclaimed. "You've experienced much of what we Jews have dealt with."

"Oh, not nearly as bad, but we do have a heart for the persecuted and downtrodden. We specialize now in building schools for the poor."

"And so that brings us back to the present," Pastor Gabriel prompted. "What do you intend to do about us?"

Alessandro laughed heartily. "I am absolutely delighted that God chose to bring you here. How utterly fitting! For we have no love for the Pope, nor do I ascribe to the Universal Religion Directives. We are too small to be noticed for now, but are a perfect haven for God's two witnesses."

Abraham and Gabriel breathed a sign of relief. They really had been led by God to this church. But what did God have in store for them next?

Chapter Eleven

Jerome, Sue, Brandon and the Harrisons were reluctant to leave their little oasis in the Gila Wilderness, so they stayed and rested up through late morning and then continued their journey down the old mining road. Just before the end of daylight, the rugged, rocky, narrow trail intersected with a wider dirt road headed west. It was a much better road in spite of the sign that declared it to be a "primitive, unmaintained" road.

When Jerome checked his GPS unit it identified the artery as Little Cherry Creek Road which would take them to Cherry Creek Lane and then on down to Route 15. "We did it!" Jerome exclaimed excitedly.

Everyone was greatly cheered and relieved. As they set up camp in a swale just off the road, Jerome called Jesse to give him an update on their progress.

"Jerome, that's great," Jesse replied. "But listen, man, we've had a change in plans." He then related to Jerome what had occurred in the restaurant with the Baptist pastor.

"There are gangs of vigilantes out looking for us," Jesse explained. "Fortunately, the owner of these cabins is a strong Christian, so he allowed us to hide our vehicles in a nearby barn and told the mob that he hadn't seen anyone answering our description."

Sue was watching Jerome whose face had turned pale. "What is it, Jerome? What's the matter?" That brought everyone over to hover around Jerome.

"So what do you think we should do?" Jerome asked Jesse plaintively.

"We need to get out of this area, so instead of you coming down here to meet us, we'll drive up tonight to meet you. Then we'll only travel at night and take back roads through Little Walnut Village around Pinos Altos and on down to Silver City."

"Okay, I guess, but we were sure looking forward to getting off these dirt roads," Jerome lamented. He gave Jesse their GPS coordinates and then turned to tell the worried group about the change in plans.

Jesse then called Jim back at the Havenwood1 hideaway to alert him as to their predicament and plans.

"I'm sorry to hear about all that. We've been hearing about other Christians getting beaten by mobs. We'll have to be extra careful now. But I've got some good news that's going to make your day," Jim said mysteriously.

"Let's hear it, we could use something uplifting," Francine ran over and Jesse put the cell phone speaker on.

"I've been contacted by Alan Morrison. He's one of the billionaires who funded all the hideaways and remote camps. His internet companies have been put under intense pressure by the FCC who claim they're violating recently enacted laws about adhering to the Universal ID Banking System."

"Yeah, so why is that good news?" Jesse asked.

"He wants to use his tremendous infrastructure and assets to undermine the Universal ID system. I told him about you and Francine, and he wants to meet with you as soon as possible."

"Woo hoo," Fran hooted loudly. "I've been having Internet withdrawal pains. I can't wait to get started!"

"Well, first of all we need to get out of this area alive," Jesse reminded Fran.

"Party pooper. We'll be fine, just you wait and see. The Lord is on our side and I feel in my heart that this is what he wants us to do.'

Jesse had to grin and shake his head in wonder at this little dynamo. His first wife was so pessimistic and gloomy. What a welcome change Francine was.

"Where do we meet up with this guy?" Jesse finally asked between chuckles as Fran kept pinching his side and stomach.

"He's holed up near Colorado Springs where he has a large ranch under an assumed name, so you're not too far away," Jim explained.

"Stop that," Jesse chortled, and tried to grab Francine's arms, but she was too quick for him. As they tussled, the cell phone dropped to the floor with the speaker still on.

Finally Jesse wrapped her up in his strong arms and looked down at her, a serious glint in his eye.

"What? Why are you looking at me like that?" Fran asked, still wriggling to get free.

"Will you marry me, Francine? We've got a preacher man right here, and I love you so much."

That brought an immediate halt to Francine's attempts to escape his arms. Instead she melted into them and began to cry.

"Say yes, Francine!" Jim called out through the speaker phone.

"Yes, yes, yes, yes!" she finally exclaimed.

Jesse lifted her off her feet and swung her around and around until they collapsed in a heap on the floor, laughing and crying hysterically. Truly a match made in heaven.

Chapter Twelve

Pastor Wally had been waiting in the small conference room for a few minutes before Juanita came charging through the door.

"Sorry I'm late, but it's hard to just shut down in the middle of a prayer session," she apologized and began pacing around the room.

"That's okay," Wally replied, watching and wondering what was going on.

Juanita saw the questioning look on the pastor's face and laughed ruefully. "I get charged up when we engage in warfare and it takes awhile before my insides begin to calm down.

"Anything specific I should know about?" Wally asked, dreading the response. Good news was becoming a rare commodity in these days of 'peace.'

Juanita stopped for a moment and pondered her response. "Well, Jesse and Francine became engaged."

"Wow, that's great! First Abby and Jim, and now those two. I guess we really are getting to be a close-knit family," Wally chuckled

"Yes, I guess we are. But now for the bad news," Juanita continued, her voice edged with concern. She related how Jesse and Fran had rescued the elderly Baptist pastor and were now being hunted by vigilantes. Then she resumed her pacing.

"On my," Wally mumbled. "So while I've been studying up on spiritual warfare, you've been out in the trenches actually doing it." He always felt insecure and inadequate around the legendary prayer warrior.

"Yes, that's right. But that's what I do, that's what I'm called to do. That's my gift. Yours is teaching, counseling and pastoring. If we all were gifted in the same way, we wouldn't make a very good army, would we?" she pointed out, somewhat out of breath.

Wally had to concede the truth in that, but still felt uneasy about having the responsibility to develop a workshop in her bailiwick.

Juanita began to slow down her pace. "So what did you find out from your study of how the Lord's warriors won their battles?"

Wally appreciated the opening to plunge into all his notes. She was right. This was an area in which he excelled. He loved to search the Scriptures and find all the golden nuggets of truth.

"Well, let's just go through a list of them first and then I have some conclusions I'd like to discuss with you to see if I'm on the right track," Wally began, his nose buried deep in his notebook.

"I've divided my findings into two areas; the victories and the defeats. It's just as instructive to determine what not to do as it is to see how to do things right."

Juanita finally sat down on the edge of the chair, looking like she was ready to pounce at a moment's notice. "I couldn't agree more," she stated emphatically.

Wally looked up and smiled at her. She was an imposing person, physically and spiritually. Just short of six feet tall, a former college basketball player, she still kept herself quite fit. When not pacing during prayer, she regularly jogged around the wooded trails outside the hideaway. Ran actually, as Wally had observed a couple of times. She'd also brought her weight bench and treadmill over to the hideaway and set up a small fitness room for herself and the others. Truly an impressive woman.

"So, first the victories. I'll just summarize now. If you'd like to see my detailed notes you can take them with you after our meeting," Wally proposed.

"A summary would be good. I don't need to see the details. I trust your analytical skills. I'm not much of a detail person myself," Juanita said and chuckled at the understatement.

"Okay. Of course the first battle recorded in the Bible was between Moses and the Pharaoh," Wally began.

"That's very interesting," Juanita replied, beginning to settle back into her chair. "I hadn't really thought of that as warfare."

"No, neither did I until the Lord impressed it upon me as I began to search through the Bible for wars and battles," Wally admitted. "But when I re-read it all from within that framework, it made perfect sense. While Moses went head to head against Pharaoh and his magicians, it was really a war between the one true God and all the false gods of the Egyptians."

"Yes, I guess it was," Juanita agreed, finally settled and relaxed. She already was appreciating the fruits of Wally's gift.

"Every one of the ten plagues that God brought down on Egypt were in direct opposition to the false gods and beliefs that consumed the people," Wally continued. "In reality, those gods were actually demonic entities that Satan used to construct strongholds, mindsets, that deceived the people. The power of the magicians to replicate the first two plagues was demonic.[22] We tend to forget that the devil and his minions do have supernatural power, but they pale in comparison to the Creator of the universe.

"The only reason that Moses was able to bring those plagues down on Egypt was because God had already told him what to do and say. It wasn't that Moses had any power himself, but rather the Lord who worked through him."

"Yes, that's always the case, isn't it," Juanita observed thoughtfully. "Sometimes we lose sight of that fact and think it's us. That's when we get into trouble."

"Right. Later, when Moses used his staff to part the Red Sea[23] and bring water out of the rock[24], it wasn't him or the staff. If he tried that again at a later time, it wouldn't have worked. It only works if we do precisely what God tells us to do at the moment he says to do it."

"Like when Moses used the staff a second time[25] after God had told him to *speak* to the rock," Juanita recalled. "While God allowed it to work, he made an example of Moses. It cost him his life and he didn't get to enter the Promised Land."

Juanita was really getting into it now. She too had been somewhat wary of this meeting. Despite being quite bright, she'd never been that good a student due to mild learning disabilities. She always felt uneasy in a classroom environment.

"Yes, exactly," Wally exclaimed enthusiastically, delighted that he and Juanita seemed to be working well together. "What works one time will not necessarily work the next time. We have to seek God's will and ways each and every time."

"God never seems to do things the same way twice," Juanita nodded in agreement. "That's so we know it's Him and not us. Witchcraft spells and curses, however, have to be performed exactly in order to work, because they're not of God. Satan's counterfeits of God's ways are always upside down and inside out."

"Yeah, I guess you're right. I hadn't thought of it that way before," Wally responded enthusiastically. This was going a whole lot better than he'd thought it would.

"Like that whole Jericho thing[17] where they had to march around the walled city seven times, then blow the trumpets and shout. When the walls fell down, it was God's power doing it through the obedience of His people," Juanita suggested. "If we did that without God telling us to do so, it would be like spitting into the wind."

Wally laughed. "Well, I hadn't thought of it quite like that, but it would be somewhat similar. Ineffective, and it might have deleterious effects."

"Whatever that means," Juanita chuckled, comfortable enough to admit she didn't always know the meaning of the big words Wally sometimes used.

"Oh, sorry. It means that harmful things might happen as a result. By the way, do you know what Ph.D. actually stands for?" Wally asked with a twinkle in his eye.

Juanita's nerves jumped up a notch. She'd always hated to be put on the spot and not know the answer. "Uhm, no I guess I don't."

"It means, Piled Higher and Deeper," Wally explained.

Laughter exploded out of Juanita, partly in relief and partly from the humor.

"Sometimes too much education gets in the way of communication," Wally added on a more serious note. "So please stop me, any time, just like that."

"Will do," Juanita agreed as she sighed to release more of the tension. *This is actually fun!*

"Now it's really interesting what happened right after the big Jericho triumph," Wally continued, turning back to his notes.

"You mean about Ai?" Juanita asked.

"Yes, because two things happened that caused them to lose the initial battle there," Wally stated.[26]

"Two? I know about Achan having stolen booty hidden away in the camp. What's the other one?"

"Yes, the first and most significant was sin in the camp. The second, however, is quite important too. Unlike at Jericho, Joshua hadn't received a word from the Lord to go ahead and attack Ai, nor did he seek the Lord for a green light," Wally pointed out.

"Oh, yes, I hadn't thought about it that way."

"So we learn two lessons from the Ai experience," Wally summarized. "First, don't go to war if you have sin in your life or in your prayer group. Get clean first. Pray for forgiveness. If you don't know whether you've got any hidden sin, the Bible says to ask God to point it out."[27]

"Good point. I do that sometimes, but not all the time," Juanita admitted.

"The second lesson is always to seek the Lord first and don't go into battle until He tells you to."

"You know," Juanita said thoughtfully, her gaze turning inward. "I'm guilty of that sometimes too. Oh, I'd never go out into a major battle without seeking the Lord first. But in some of our prayer meetings, I'll start doing spiritual warfare over a situation just because it's important to me. But I guess we should check it out first."

"Yes, we always should but often don't. That goes for all of us, not just you. Have you ever experienced any backlash as a result?" Wally asked.

"Oh, yes indeed. I've realized sometimes that some of my stomach ailments have occurred because I acted... presumptively? Is that the right use of the word?"

"Yes, it is. Presumption opens the door to the devil, just as any form of sin does.[28] It's not God punishing us, but rather the law of sowing and reaping that comes back to hurt us. Like spitting into the wind."

As they both laughed together, they each realized that they were also forging a closer bond. While both had the utmost respect for the other, they had never established a true relationship. Each was grateful that the divide of preacher and practitioner, educated and uneducated, had been broken down.

Just then a rapid knock on the door startled them. "Yes, come in," Wally called out.

It was Tara. She was trembling. Tears tracked down her cheeks. "Reaper attacked Ryan and they had a big fight. They both got hurt before we could get them separated. Doc's fixing them up now."

"What were they fighting over?" Wally asked as he got up to go with her.

"Me," Tara said meekly as she stared at the floor.

Chapter Thirteen

B laine was so excited she couldn't stand it. She looked again at her smart phone where she had both the local time in Rome as well as the time in New York prominently displayed. Patrick wouldn't be back from lunch until 1 p.m. He was such a creature of habit. Same schedule, same restaurant, every weekday. So that would make it 7 p.m. local time, still an hour away.

She called the hotel's room service. Blaine didn't want to be in the restaurant when she shared the news about Alexis' job offer. Too many ears around. She usually loved the spotlight, a true narcissist and proud of it. She'd actually been disappointed when she first arrived in Rome earlier that day and walked through the airport without anyone rushing over or calling out her name.

But after the worldwide broadcast of her interview with the Global Czar and Pope Radinsky, she'd been mobbed wherever she went. Not that she was objecting, but it wasn't conducive to a serious, private conversation with her fiancé. And so she paced about, ate her dinner, showered and finally called Patrick on his cell phone.

"Well, that was really something," Patrick said as he answered the call. "What that something was, however, I haven't a clue."

Blaine was completely thrown off by this cryptic remark. "What do you mean?"

Patrick recognized that hurt, little girl voice and regretted his opening salvo. "Sorry. I didn't mean to rain on your parade."

"It was an absolute triumph!" Blaine declared defensively.

"Yes, so all the media are saying, ours included." Patrick agreed, but there was still something in his tone that Blaine didn't like.

"But you think I botched it?"

Patrick hesitated. If they were together, he would hold her and tell her gently what he thought about it all. Perhaps he should have waited to say anything. But what now? Lying or covering up wasn't part of his nature. "No, it's not that I think you botched it. But the woman I saw on my screen didn't look like you, nor did she act like you, so I'm quite perplexed about the whole thing."

"Oh, you mean that silly dress that my stupid assistant got for me." Blaine sat down on the edge of the bed, relieved. "Papal protocols and all that."

"Yes, but kissing his ring? You're not Catholic anymore, not that you ever really were," Patrick pointed out.

"Oh, well I just thought it would add a touch of magic to the whole scene," Blaine explained, beginning to get defensive again. Actually, she wasn't quite sure why she did it.

"And all those softball questions? The preening and fawning? That was all premeditated and calculated?"

Blaine was getting angry. Here she had such fantastic news to share and Patrick was quibbling over the details of what everyone said was the absolute pinnacle of her storied career.

"Yes, of course it was. What else would it be?"

Patrick paused. This could get quite messy. However, the upside of Blaine's volatile personality was that every day was a new day. Sometimes every hour. They might argue one minute, make love the next.

"I don't really know, but you didn't seem to be yourself. It was like watching someone else up there. I thought you seemed mesmerized, hypnotized even," Patrick said carefully and then braced himself for the explosion.

Blaine's mouth opened to shout out a curse, but her throat froze. The truth of it was that she didn't really remember much of the interview. Her subconscious had brought that one up before, but she'd quickly repressed it. Why couldn't she remember? Why did she feel so unsettled about it?

"Blaine? Are you still there?"

"What? Oh, yes, sorry. I don't feel quite right," Blaine said softly.

Now Patrick was really confused. The little girl was back instead of the fire-breathing dragon. Something had happened, but what? "I'm sorry if I've sounded harsh. I was just puzzled about it, that's all."

Blaine tried to recharge the rush she'd felt about Alexis' job offer, but it fell far short. Where had it gone? "Alexis has offered me a job," she finally said in a flat monotone.

"A job? Doing what?"

"Being the spokesperson for the Global Governance Committee." Where did the excitement go? Maybe it was jet lag.

Patrick was stunned. "You mean becoming the Global Czar's public relations flack?" He regretted his comment even as it left his larynx. But investigative objectivity was what he and Blaine had always thrived on. How could so much have changed in such a short time?

"I'm very tired, Patrick. It's been a long day. I'll call you tomorrow." Blaine hung up before Patrick could respond.

Yes, it must be jet lag. Surely she'd feel better tomorrow. The thrill and excitement she craved would come back. It always did.

Chapter Fourteen

General Charles Wycliffe stared out the window of the twenty-story office building in Denver. Though the magnificent Rockies lay before his eyes, his focus was turned inward, reliving the attack on the detention center in New Mexico. What a magnificent day. Though people had mocked his self-serving title before, now he was an underground hero.

So why were the men in this conference room being so obstinate? Couldn't they recognize greatness when they saw it? He supposed General George Washington might have experienced a few moments like this before emerging triumphant. These people were blind, that's all. He shouldn't hold their handicaps against them.

His eyes refocused on the outside world. How odd, planning a military campaign in a fancy urban office building in the heart of civilization. They should be bivouacked somewhere in those mountains in a log cabin or around a campfire, dressed in fatigues, not shirts and ties. He had grudgingly given in to the ridiculous dress rules that Marvin Haggard insisted upon.

The President of the Harvest Savings & Loan was a stickler about how his people dressed. He couldn't have an obviously important visitor come in looking like Timothy McVeigh. Not only was that offensive, but it would blow their cover. There was a time and a place for everything, he always liked to say.

Wycliffe turned back to face the group sitting anxiously around the expansive conference room table. He had to hold back the sneer that wanted to take over his face. Control. The general was all about control. A master. He strode imperiously back to the head of the table.

"Gentlemen. I see we have trust issues. Not surprising, I guess, given our different backgrounds and experiences. I suggest, therefore, that before we proceed further in trying to iron out our differences that we conduct a joint training exercise. Let's have each of our armies show what they've got. Not a competition, but an evaluation. I'm sure each group has strengths and weaknesses. Let's see what we have and then figure out the best way to put the pieces together synergistically so as to eliminate weaknesses and promote strength."

That seemed to break the impasse and the group quickly agreed, albeit with some trivial, tiresome details that only nitwits would care about. Or at least that's how General Wycliffe perceived it. Now that the 'what' and 'when' was decided, that left only the where.

A distinguished, middle-aged man cleared his throat and raised his hand. Up to this point, the man hadn't said a word. The show of respect immediately found favor with the General.

"Yes, what is it?"

"I'd like to offer my ranch as a potential site for the joint training exercise," the man said evenly. There was an air of confidence about the man that General Wycliffe liked.

"And you are?"

"Oh, sorry, I got here late after the introductions. I'm Alan Morrison, and I have a ten-thousand acre ranch outside Colorado Springs. There are some back ways onto the ranch from the north and the west that are in remote areas. No one would see us gathering there."

The murmur amongst the other attendees seemed to be favorable toward the idea and the man. Wycliffe was quite astute in reading body language, and saw the respect the others had for Morrison.

"Is that fine with everybody?" he asked as his eyes scanned each face. Everyone signaled their agreement in various ways.

"All right, then. In two weekends from now on Mr. Morrison's ranch. I'll get together with him and work out the details. If you'll all leave your private email addresses with me, I'll send you a map and further instructions. Do I have a motion to adjourn?"

After the meeting, Wycliffe huddled with Morrison in the far corner of the conference room as the others milled about chatting aimlessly about nothing of interest. The general would never understand why people wasted so much time and energy on useless conversation.

"Would you be so kind as to tell me a little bit about yourself," Wycliffe asked Morrison while staring straight into the man's eyes. "I like to know who I'm dealing with."

"Certainly," Morrison replied, holding the general's penetrating gaze to a standoff. "I'm the founder and CEO of Morrison, Peabody & Franklin. We've been quite successful in the computer and Internet markets, but I can't abide what the one-world government is doing to the free-market system. I don't have any military expertise, but I do have a lot of money that I'd like to invest in what you're proposing."

That certainly tweaked the general's interest. Alan Morrison was also an astute reader of human beings and saw the approval rise in Wycliffe's otherwise emotionless eyes.

"Yes, well we certainly need financial backers," the general stated as he broke eye contact to retrieve his iPhone. Truth be told, he'd found Morrison's unblinking gaze unnerving. There was a strength there that Wycliffe appreciated, but which also raised a wariness. Too many men of money thought they should run things without knowing anything. All he was interested in was Morrison's ranch and his money.

The general fiddled with the iPhone, trying to open up the contact list. "Here, allow me," Morrison offered, and relieved the general of the device with which he appeared quite uncomfortable.

"See, this is my field, but I can assure you that I have no illusions about having any military smarts. That's your field and you're the expert there," Morrison said as he quickly thumbed in his contact information. Then he pulled down a Google map of his ranch and wrote out directions.

"So when would you like to come out and see my humble abode?" he asked as he handed the phone back to the clearly relieved general.

"How about tomorrow afternoon?" Wycliffe proposed. Morrison agreed, shook his hand, waved to the others, and quickly left.

Wycliffe was quite taken with the man. This could be the financier he'd been looking for. If Morrison was true to his word and stayed out of the general's hair, this could work out really well.

Chapter Fifteen

W hen Pastor Gabriel and Rabbi Abraham awoke the following morning, they stared with wondrous eyes at one another. "You too?" Abraham asked.

Gabriel nodded, still too flabbergasted about his long dream-vision to speak.

Abraham got up from the couch, stretched his aching body, rubbed his long grey beard and sighed deeply. "It looks like we've got quite a lot to do."

Gabriel looked up at his partner. If he had to be one of the two witnesses, not an assignment he'd sought or desired, he was more than pleased to have Abraham as his cohort.

"Yes, it does. We'll have to compare notes, but I didn't sense any timeframe about all the events I saw," he finally said in a quiet voice, as though the walls had ears.

"No, I didn't either," Abraham agreed in a similarly conspiratorial tone.

"What did you make of the sackcloth? Do we really have to dress like that?" Gabriel's eyes pleaded with Abraham to say no.

"Well, I'm afraid I must say yes, but *me darf nit zein shain; me darf hoben chain,*" Abraham said and laughed.

"*¿qué es eso?*" Gabriel responded in kind.

"Ah, yes, forgive me for the Yiddish. Let's see, how can I say it in English? *You don't have to be pretty if you have charm.*"

Gabriel snorted. "Well, that leaves us out."

"Seriously, though, I do think we need to dress the part. Unfortunately, I've had some experience with that." Abraham sat down, clouds of sadness descending upon his face.

"Sackcloth and ashes for mourning?" Gabriel asked gently.

Abraham nodded, lost in thoughts, feeling once again the devastation of losing his two children to terrorist bombs. "Several times. Once personal, two or three times when Israel was going through difficult times."

Gabriel shuddered. "Isn't the goat hair itchy?"

'Hmm? Oh, yes and no. Yes it is, but the more modern garments aren't so bad, unless you're doing penance, then it has to be as rough as it gets. But you do get used to it after awhile."

"You're scaring me, Rabbi, like you're really thinking we're supposed to dress like that."

"Well, maybe just when we're conducting business," Abraham said, a sly look crossing his face.

"Business?"

"Sure, like prophesying, or shutting up the skies so they don't rain, or turning water to blood, or calling fire down from heaven. That's our job description, isn't it?"

Gabriel shook his head and had to laugh in spite of his uneasiness. "So you think we're actually going to do all those things?"

"That's what the Good Book says, doesn't it? You do believe in God's Word don't you?"

Gabriel looked back up at Abraham, sensing something of a rebuke behind the kind exterior. "Of course I do. I just have trouble believing that it's going to be us doing those things."

Abraham sat down next to Gabriel on the cot and put his arm around his beloved brother. "I know it's not easy. But given the first joint vision that led us here and now the dream-vision we apparently shared last night, I think we'd better start getting used to the idea. Besides, it's not us, it's Jehovah working through us. As long as He leads the way, we'll be all right."

Gabriel sighed, knowing Abraham was right. "Okay, so what do you think Adonai is saying we should do next? Stay here awhile longer to pray and meditate or jump into action?"

Abraham stared off into space, recalling the vivid vision. "I believe we're supposed to begin our prophetic mission in the streets of Jerusalem, soon. And yes, dressed in sackcloth and ashes. So let's pray together."

As their voices rose in Hebrew and an unknown heavenly language, the floor and walls began to vibrate. Unbeknownst to the two witnesses. Majoralis Alessandro came running down the stairs. When he opened the door, the room was bathed in bright light. He covered his eyes, unsure whether the two apparitions were the pastor and rabbi or angels. He fell to his knees and wept.

With his eyes closed against the brightness, Alessandro thought he could hear a choir in the background. The shaking grew more intense, and then gradually quieted down. The light dimmed and Alessandro opened his eyes. In the middle of the room, the pastor and rabbi were still kneeling in silent prayer. Standing over them was one like the Son of Man.

"You are my witnesses on earth. I now anoint you with heavenly oil, the fullness of the Holy Spirit."

Alessandro watched as two white doves descended upon each of their heads and remained there even as the Son of Man faded from view.

Chapter Sixteen

Reverend Michael Braintree and his wife Bonnie came running out of the cabin bedroom to see why Jesse and Francine were screaming and crying. When they saw the couple rolling around the floor, with Fran screeching loudly, their first reaction was that she was being abused by the much larger and older Jesse. Perhaps they were still influenced by the beating Rev. Braintree had received the previous night at the restaurant.

As the two Braintrees started moving in to rescue Fran, they stopped when they realized she was laughing hysterically, not crying or screaming for help. Jesse saw them staring down and turned Fran over to face them as well. In between intermittent bursts of hilarity, Fran was able to get out her joy about accepting Jesse's marriage proposal.

When Jesse and Fran rose to their feet, they went to hug their two guests, but the minister and his wife recoiled and held out their hands instead. After the quick, awkward handshakes, Fran asked Rev. Braintree if he could perform a marriage ceremony immediately.

The nonplussed minister looked outright shocked. "How long have you known each other?"

"We've worked together for about five years," Fran answered quickly. "For the last few weeks we've been on the run together from the Feds."

"Have you had sexual relations?" the stern-faced minister continued.

Francine looked over to Mrs. Braintree for help, but she simply scowled back.

"No we certainly haven't," Jesse jumped in, offended by Braintree's haughty attitude. "We're committed Christians who, by the way, rescued you from the mob, remember?"

The minister blinked rapidly as he recalled the terrifying attack. He realized that he was still in a state of shock. Not that his viewpoint about casual sex had changed, but his already uptight attitude had become hostile and defensive.

"Yes, I do remember, all too well," Rev. Braintree finally said after a long pause. He breathed deeply and let the air out slowly, feeling the tension in his body loosen just a bit.

Jesse and Fran waited politely as they saw the elderly man continue the struggle to regain his composure.

"Okay," the minister exhaled again, "let's start all over. I'm not in the habit of marrying people I know nothing about. While I certainly appreciate what you've done for Mrs. Braintree and me, I cannot and will not violate my strong conviction that all couples, particularly those unknown to the minister, should go through a minimum of three counseling sessions to determine whether they fully understand the divine commitment they are making."

Jesse looked over at Fran who seemed crestfallen. Then he turned back to Rev. Braintree, his eyes pleading for mercy. "The problem is, we have to leave tonight to meet up with another group also on the run. Then we're going to disappear into the hills as we make our way west. We'd really like to be married before setting out on that trip, because who knows when we might have another opportunity?"

An odd look played out on the minister's countenance as he turned and looked over at his wife. Even as he addressed Jesse, he continued to look at Mrs. Braintree. "I don't think it's a good idea for us to remain in the area either. That mob knows us, where we live, our church, our friends. There would be no possible way for us to avoid them. I'm too old for all this. Should have retired years ago."

That brought the hint of a smile to Mrs. Braintree's otherwise stony face. Encouraged, the minister plunged ahead. "So, if it's all right, we'd like to go with you. That way, I can get to know you two better and perhaps perform a wedding later on, one that your friends could attend as well."

Fran's whole attitude changed instantly and she began leaping up and down, clapping her hands. "That would be wonderful," she cried out gleefully. She took a step toward Rev. Braintree, intent on throwing her arms around his neck. Then she stopped abruptly, remembering the futility of her first attempt. Instead, she thrust out her hand and shook the minister's hand vigorously.

Jesse sighed in relief on the one hand, but immediately began to worry on the other about having to transport and care for two elderly people on what would most likely be a grueling journey through harsh territory. In truth, though, he had already felt uneasy about leaving them here. The Christian owner of this cabin retreat could hide them for awhile, but that was no sure deal.

"We plan on leaving within the hour. You won't have time to retrieve any of your personal possessions," Jesse warned the Braintrees sternly. He realized how quickly they had reversed positions and tried to rein in his annoyance at the minister's attitude.

The minister again looked at his wife as he addressed Jesse. "Yes, we realize that. We've been in a rut for quite awhile and have talked about how we might escape the tedium of our last years together. Perhaps this is God's answer to our prayers."

Mrs. Braintree looked fearful and skeptical, and yet she nodded assent ever so slightly.

"You won't be able to take your car, either," Jesse further advised. "Your sedan wouldn't be able to traverse the difficult roads we might be faced with. You'll have to ride in our jeep."

Both Braintrees nodded agreement.

"Okay, then, let's pack up and get out of here," Jesse urged. The Braintrees had precious little to pack. Fortunately, they were in the habit of carrying a goodly amount of cash, never having gotten used to buying things with plastic. As children of depression era parents, they had no debt. It was painful to leave behind their home of nearly thirty years, but the thrill of adventure was beginning to quicken their stultified arteries.

The jeep had already been laden down with supplies accumulated on the trip out west. Fortunately, it was a larger model with a decent back seat. The frail, elderly couple only took up two-thirds of the seat, so Jesse was able to stack up their supplies next to them.

Soon they were on the rural highway headed north, moving slowly with the lights turned off. When they had proceeded several miles away from Pinos Altos, Jesse turned on the lights every once in a while to search for the dirt road Jerome mentioned. Of course, it was possible the unmaintained dusty trail might not be marked with a sign.

"There it is," Fran called excitedly, shining her flashlight at a wooden, apparently homemade sign. "Cherry Creek Lane."

There were a few houses and trailer homes scattered along the initial portion of the dirt road, which became bumpier and rockier the further they went. Progress was slow without headlights, but Jesse wasn't taking any chances at this stage of the game.

The road looked like it was petering out as they climbed yet another small rise. Jesse stopped on the crest, turned on the headlights and got out to shine his flashlight around the barren area. Fran got out too, and was startled when a bulky body lumbered up the side of the hill.

A slight scream crossed her lips before she realized it was Jerome. The scream turned into a yelp of joy as she scrambled down the hill, tossed her flashlight aside and leaped into his strong arms. "We're getting married," she squealed, even as Jesse was trying to shush her.

"To who?" the ever slow hulk asked, genuinely surprised.

"To Jesse, you big lug," Fran scolded playfully, and kissed him on the cheek.

A flurry of introductions and explanations followed as the disparate group came together in the camp that Jerome, Sue, Brandon and the Harrisons had made down in the gully. It was a festive evening that grew quite late before the fire was doused and lanterns were turned off.

Rev. and Mrs. Braintree lay together in the double sleeping bag Jerome provided, staring up at the stars, holding hands. They were definitely off the treadmill now.

Chapter Seventeen

The next morning, Blaine awoke feeling hung over, though she'd only had one glass of wine with her room-service dinner. She usually jumped out of bed charged up for immediate action. As she pushed her aching head and lethargic body through the morning rituals, she couldn't get a handle on her jumbled emotions. She should be ecstatic to be the Global Czar's chosen spokesperson. It must be the dustup with Patrick that was stirring up the muddy waters.

She moved quickly through the lobby before anyone had the chance to accost her and ignored the several people who called out her name. She plunged into the waiting limo and breathed a sigh of relief as the driver closed the door behind her. When the limo pulled away, taking her to the Papal Palace for breakfast with Pope Radinsky and Alexis D'Antoni, her pulse finally began to quicken in anticipation.

After being escorted to the Pope's private dining room, she was greeted like a queen by the two most powerful men in the world. At once, the heady rush she'd felt yesterday in their presence returned and lifted her spirits back up to loftier heights than she'd ever experienced before. The conversation was witty and intelligent, with clever banter thrown in to spice things up a bit.

Breakfast was sumptuous and plentiful, but contained no calories according to Alexis. The rapport Blaine had with these two men she'd only known for less than a day was quite remarkable. It seemed as though they were on the same wave length all the time. Heady stuff indeed.

As the wait staff descended to clean up, Blaine was escorted into the adjacent study, arm in arm with the ultimate in nobility. As they seated themselves in the comfortable wing chairs, Alexis leaned forward and looked deeply into Blaine's bright blue eyes, past the tinted contact lenses. She felt as though he had entered her very soul.

"I hope you've considered and will accept our offer to be the spokesperson for the Global Governance Committee, because we have immediate need for your services." D'Antoni's velvety voice was soothing and inviting. She could also feel the warmth of the Pope's gaze shining love and admiration upon her.

Patrick was an idiot, she decided. No, perhaps you had to experience this in order to comprehend it. She'd try to be more understanding next time. "Of course I will," she finally exclaimed. "I'd be foolish not to accept the offer of a lifetime."

"Great," Alexis grinned. "But you haven't even asked about salary or benefits or where your office is and how big it might be."

"It's such an honor to even be offered this position. All the rest is simply icing on the cake," Blaine gushed.

"Well, let me assure you that your salary and perks will reflect the significance and importance of your position. But let's get down to business right away, because we want to announce the full implementation of the Universal ID Banking System later today, and we'd like for you to make the announcement," Alexis said as he leaned back into his chair.

"Wow, you don't waste any time throwing me to the wolves," Blaine laughed, delighted to see action right away. What a coup. *Wait till my fans see me now!*

Alexis and Radinsky smiled benevolently. She was closer to the truth than she knew.

She quickly called her boss at CNN to resign, and held her ground in spite of increased inducements to remain with the cable network. Then she worked closely with the acerbic Richard Jefferson, going over all the details of how the Universal ID system would work. At first, they each rubbed the other the wrong way. Jefferson had no respect for non-technical blowhards, especially blonde twits. Blaine was not used to being treated with disdain, but when she was, she attacked like a tiger.

In between the sparring, Jefferson became quite impressed with Blaine's prodigious memory and high intelligence. In return, Blaine came to appreciate Jefferson's incredible genius. By the end of the study session, these two unlikely allies strode side-by-side onto the temporary stage that had been erected in St. Peter's Square. Alexis and Pope Radinsky watched from behind tinted windows in the Papal Palace.

The press conference, though hastily scheduled for mid-afternoon, was nonetheless well attended by media representatives from all over the world. Having already come to Vatican City for the previous day's dramatic doings, many had stayed overnight just in case there were further developments. Sticking near the Global Czar was always good policy.

When Blaine strode majestically to the podium in her new stylish dress, the press actually applauded and roared their approval. Not only was one of their own now elevated to such lofty heights, but Blaine's sheer beauty and confidence made her seem more like a movie star than a mere spokesperson.

When the hubbub subsided, Blaine launched into her carefully prepared presentation. At the end, she introduced Richard Jefferson and was pleased that he stuck to the plan and didn't digress into unnecessary technical details. As he stepped away from the microphone, Blaine came forward to take questions, supremely pleased with her first official announcement.

Shouted questions from throughout the crowded plaza created a roar of unintelligible gibberish. Blaine smiled tolerantly, knowing what it was like to be on the other side of the fence. She pointed at Manny from Fox News, not wanting to show any bias toward her old CNN family.

"So, Blaine, congratulations and all that," Manny blurted hurriedly. "But isn't what you've just introduced here the dreaded 'mark of the beast?'"

Blaine was immediately thrown off stride. "Mark of the what?"

"Surely you're aware of the Biblical prophesies that warn Christians against receiving the so-called 'mark of the beast' on their foreheads or hands. And that's exactly what you've proposed here today, RFID, or radio-frequency identification chips, to be implanted into people's hands or foreheads, without which no one can buy or sell anything."[29]

A clamor arose from within the press crowd. Arguments against such preposterous accusations erupted into shoving matches and eventually broke down into fistfights. The Swiss Guards charged into the crowd to protect the few like Manny who voiced concern over the Universal ID System.

Blaine, flustered and confused, took advantage of the mayhem to scoot offstage and disappear back into the Papal Palace. Alexis and Radinsky exchanged knowing smiles. René moved up behind them with a smug look of satisfaction rippling across her countenance.

Chapter Eighteen

The fight between Reaper and Ryan was more of a symptom than a problem, Pastor Wally concluded after listening to various accounts from witnesses and the two participants. These were difficult times for Christians, especially when they were confined underground with all hopes of a normal life gone out the window. That was another problem, no windows. Cabin fever was spreading.

Of course, there was the underlying issue of two robust males competing for the most attractive female in the hideaway. Reaper was used to getting what he wanted. In the gang lifestyle, women were virtual slaves to be shared by the alpha males. He would need some reprogramming, a process Wally had begun in other areas and was seeing progress. Now he'd have to shift focus for awhile.

Ryan, on the other hand, was a former boxer and bouncer with a quick temper. How serious he was about Tara remained to be seen. The bigger problem was that he never backed down from a challenge and was used to resolving problems with his fists.

In both cases, learned behavior needed to be readjusted while also dealing with the strongholds and demonic influences that had built up in their lives. If they were willing, Pastor Wally knew from experience that they could be set free by the power of the Holy Spirit and the shed blood of

Jesus Christ. *This could also become another chapter in my book, The End of Bondage,* Wally noted to himself.

Jermaine had asked him to write up his case studies in such a way that the principles and techniques could be applied in the other hideaways and remote camps. Everyone was quite impressed with the breakthroughs that most of the Havenwood1 residents had attained under Pastor Wally's application of sound Biblical doctrine. Even the skeptics had been won over.

So for Pastor Wally, the bigger issue was how to deal with the burgeoning symptoms of cabin fever without jeopardizing the safety of the residents. He asked to meet with Abby and Jermaine to present his recommendations. They agreed to meet with him immediately, also sensing that things were amiss.

After Wally explained the background of the situation, the ever-practical Abby immediately asked for his recommendations. Wally smiled to himself. He'd already learned how Abby ran things and was pleased that he knew to come prepared with practical remedies instead of just diagnostics and theories.

"Despite the ever present dangers of detection," Wally began, "we need to get our people out and about. They need sunshine, nature, vistas and open fields to counteract the cabin fever."

"Yes, I agree Pastor Wally, but that's impractical around here," Abby said gently, not wanting to deflate the typically over-optimistic balloon their pastoral leader liked to float.

The prepared pastor plunged on. "You're absolutely right. That's why I'd like to recommend that we take small groups of our residents out to the remote camp in the Blue Ridge Mountains. Give each group a few days to bask in nature's glory before we send out the next group and bring the previous one back home. We can use our All Seasons

Van as cover, like we're off to a job with everyone dressed in work coveralls."

"Well, now," Jermaine jumped in, "that might be just what the doctor ordered."

Abby thought deeply for awhile, rolling the pros and cons around in her mind. "If we can avoid detection, I think that's a marvelous idea. Perhaps we can send the van out right after dark."

"Yes, that would work. They can pretend they are headed back from a job, if anyone were to pull them over," Jermaine added.

"We need to start doing this right away," Abby decided. "Winter's not too far off, so I'd like to cycle everyone through the camp before we get any heavy snows."

"Yes, and I can see some additional benefits coming out of this," Jermaine said, as he got up to pace the room. Wally was pleased and fascinated to watch them run with his idea.

"The folks out in the camp don't have cabin fever, but they do feel isolated and removed from civilization. We could also cycle some of them back through here as well," Jermaine said as he began to make circles around the conference room table.

"Good idea," Abby agreed. "Then we might also wind up trading people who are more suited for one place or the other."

"Yes, and we can do some cross-training to expand skill levels that are missing or inadequate in each location," Jermaine added, starting another circle.

"Plus, our guys and gals might be able to form new relationships. That could boost the social atmosphere in both places," Jermaine said, somewhat excited to think that he might still meet that special someone before his time on earth was done.

Chapter Nineteen

Pastor Gabriel and Rabbi Abraham decided to journey to Jerusalem as soon as possible. All their clothes and traveling gear were back in the hotel in Rome where they'd left them that fateful morning. The room was probably under watch for their return, so they'd need to acquire some new things before they could make such a trip. Fortunately, Gabriel had some cash and his credit cards. Abraham had always eschewed any form of debt, so all he had was some meager bills.

Majoralis Alessandro suggested an alternative approach. "A good friend of mine is the Abbot of a monastery in the southeast section of Rome, the Abbey of Casamari. I sometimes go there on personal retreats. They are Cistercians, in name an order of the Catholic Church, but in practice governed by the so-called Rule of St. Benedict. St. Benedict is considered by many to be the father of Western monasticism. He wrote a book of precepts for monastic living that has stood the test of time for over 1,500 years."

"And what, pray tell, does this have to do with us?" Rabbi Abraham prompted. He'd learned the hard way the Major's tendency to launch into long stories.

"Well, I think you should go there and get outfitted in their wonderful habits," Alessandro continued enthusiastically. "They are sometimes called the White Monks because their habits are pure white which they sometimes overlay with a black scapular, or apron, making them look more like penguins to me."

"Why would they allow us to wear their habits?" Gabriel wondered.

"When I tell the Abbot that you are the Lord's anointed end-time emissaries, he will welcome you with open arms."

That proved to be quite accurate. Alessandro drove them down to the monastery himself in the church van. Gabriel and Abraham ducked down onto the floor to avoid detection. It was uncomfortable, and probably unnecessary, but they didn't want to be captured at this early point in their new careers.

Not that they doubted God's Word which said they could consume their enemies with fire that proceeded from their mouths, but they weren't anxious to test those powers quite yet. Indeed, they'd had an animated, yet congenial, disagreement over how such powers might actually manifest. Gabriel thought it was probably symbolic imagery, while Abraham favored a literal interpretation.[1]

The Abbot, alerted in advance by Alessandro, greeted the two fugitives like royalty. He gathered them quickly into the monastery, gave them the habits and scapular to wear, Then he took them on a brief tour. The abbey was a beautiful sight, with its delicate columns, vaulted ceilings, small stained-glass windows, and a lovely cloistered courtyard.

"We Cistercians rebuilt this former Benedictine monastery between 1203 and 1207 A.D. The emphasis of Cistercian life is on manual labor and self-sufficiency. We practice austerity and common prayer. Our gardens sustain us as do the donations of those who come to hear our Gregorian chants."

The Abbot chuckled and whispered, "We even have a website where people can listen to the chants online, but don't tell the Pope."

Ushering them back inside, the Abbot pointed out that only twenty monks now lived in the monastery, "although we have founded new monasteries in Ethiopia, Eritrea, Brazil and the USA, and oversee 19 other monasteries."

Alessandro bid the two witnesses adieu with fond embraces and prayers for safety and success, "although I know that our Father will accomplish His purposes through you as long as you remain committed to Him."

Gabriel and Abraham enjoyed the modest meal eaten in silence and thanksgiving, but even more so, the time of common prayer and chanting. Several tourists and local visitors attended the open meeting, so the two pulled hoods up over their heads.

Later, as they turned in for the night in the guest room that housed two bunk beds, Abraham observed, "I truly think Alessandro heard from the Lord. These habits and the papers the Abbot provided will enable us to travel through customs."

They both thanked God profusely as they prayed together and prepared for the morning's journey.

*****

That same night, a convoy set out from the temporary camp in the foothills north of Pinos Altos, and began an arduous journey on back roads that wound around west and then south toward their destination, Silver City, New Mexico.

Little Walnut Road lived up to its name, a small dirt trail with scattered walnut trees. It was frustrating to the entire troop to be going so far out of their way, but the likelihood of trouble with the vigilantes of Pinos Altos mitigated their discomfort.

When the convoy finally snaked through Little Walnut Village with their lights off, they prayed that no one would notice, or if anyone did, that no one would call the authorities. Fortunately, they managed to get through without any apparent disturbance other than some barking dogs.

As they broached the outlying streets of Silver City, the partial light of early dawn guided them to a small motel on the outskirts of town that had been recommended by the Christian owner of the cabin retreat where Jesse and Fran stayed. The motel was operated by an Indian family who were Christian converts.

For proprieties's sake, Jesse bunked with Jerome while Sue and Francine shared a room as did Brandon and James Harrison, leaving Trudy to oversee the Harrison's cranky four children. Rev. Braintree and his wife stumbled into their room totally spent, physically and emotionally. Sleep came easily to everyone after the hard journey, especially given the renewed sense of safety they felt after escaping from Pinos Altos.

However, a frantic knocking on their doors woke them up in startled fear. Various members of the Indian family quickly alerted them that they'd received a tip from a Christian friend on the police force. Jesse's Land Rover was spotted in the parking lot by a friend of the vigilantes, and a SWAT team was gathering that very moment to swoop in and arrest them all. Bogus accusations of theft and fraud had been scripted by the police chief in Pinos Altos.

Everyone piled into the three vehicles in their sleepwear, haphazardly throwing their baggage inside. The caravan squealed away from the curb. The Indian owner thrust a hastily drawn map into Jerome's hands and pointed him west and then south on local streets through the poorer Hispanic areas. They went under Route 180 and proceeded slowly through several barrios until they got on Route 90 South and sped off for I-10.

Each wondered whether an APB had been issued for them. Should they stay on the Interstate and put some real distance between them and their tormentors, or get off onto back roads? As they proceeded west on I-10 at the speed limit, sirens jangled their nerves until they saw the police cars and ambulance headed east, passing by on the opposite side of the highway. It wasn't until they crossed over into Arizona that they began to relax.

Chapter Twenty

News of the Universal ID System rippled across the globe into virtually every civilized corner. For the most part, people accepted it as an inevitable follow-up to the turmoil of the past and the need to maintain the fragile peace established by the Global Governance Committee. The Committee had done a good job preparing the public for this eventuality with lots of prior publicity extolling the many benefits of such a system.

Reduction in fraud, instant purchasing, containment of drug cartels, gun control, elimination of counterfeiting, regulation of banks, control of financial markets, and the suppression of illegal immigration were all touted as advantages of a universal identification system. Those who stood up against the system for privacy or religious reasons were ridiculed, ostracized or worse.

In the end, reason won out. The loss of privacy seemed a miniscule price to pay for so many benefits. The religious nuts had no sound basis for their objections other than obscure references in a Christian holy book that had been disproven and exposed as historical myth. These zealots would have been ignored had they only kept their mouths shut and gone along with the system. But no, they had to protest and interfere every step of the way.

Thus, public opinion polls revealed that nearly 90% of the world's population felt that the prosecution of those who attempted to undermine or subvert the system was more than justified. Reports of violence against such zealots were minimized by the media, but almost 50% of those polled felt such actions were more than justified.

Everyone was given up to three months to receive the RFID chips at one of the numerous locations that had been set up worldwide. It was estimated that no one would have to endure more than an hour or two wait. However, people rushed out in massive numbers on the first few days causing huge delays. Many ID centers even ran out of chips. The central computers were overloaded and seized up or shut down on numerous occasions.

Alexis was not a happy camper. He called in Richard Jefferson for a meeting in his finally finished palace in Jerusalem. René and Blaine Whitney were also present. For the first time, Jefferson didn't seem so smugly confident. Blaine too was nervous, only partly mollified by Alexis over the turmoil at the press conference. Although he apologized for not preparing her for the Christian rightwing backlash, Blaine couldn't escape the feeling that she'd been set up, a lamb thrown to the wolves.

Her fiancé, Patrick, had been very sympathetic over the telephone and had avoided saying "I told you so." Still, Blaine felt that her lover and mentor was not pleased about her accepting the position of spokesperson for the Global Governance Committee. Now, with Alexis fuming, Blaine was feeling more and more uncomfortable, especially with a second press conference coming up to deal with all the snafus.

"How the hell did you allow this to happen?" Alexis snarled, before Jefferson even had a chance to seat himself.

"How could I possibly have known that a quarter of the population would turn out in the first three days?" Jefferson snapped back, a severe tactical mistake.

"It's your job to know," Alexis roared. "That's why we pay you the big bucks!"

"You're being unreasonable," Jefferson replied, a nervous tic starting up under his right eye. "With a three-month window, we felt our ten-percent estimate was more than safe."

Alexis turned and stared out the window of his brand new palace office. A small smirk crept onto his face. He looked out upon the Dome of the Rock and the Jewish Temple nearing completion. Here he was finally ensconced in the heart of God's holy city. Soon he would trample on its heart to complete his full takeover.

When he turned back around and stared at Jefferson, Blaine could feel his rage. It terrified her. "René, Mr. Jefferson has been your responsibility, has he not? I leave him in your capable hands to take care of this situation." His cold, hard voice brought out goose bumps on Blaine's arms.

René gave Richard her best come-hither smile and opened the office door for him. He breathed a sigh of relief and gratefully exited. He had sampled René's charms before and was hoping to do so again. She, however, had something else in mind.

Blaine watched them leave and then realized she was now alone in the office with the very scary Global Czar. How had things turned around so quickly?

"Blaine, my dear child, please sit back down."

Blaine did so, not having known she'd stood up.

Alexis too sat down across the coffee table from her. "As I said before, I indeed am truly sorry that we neglected to fully prepare you for your first press conference. Things were simply happening too fast, and I thought you needed to spend what little time there was with Jefferson to understand the ins and outs of the system."

His voice and manner had become conciliatory and caring. Blaine wondered how he could so easily change gears.

"Now, for your next meeting with the press tomorrow, we have a bit more time and you're already up to speed on the technical aspects of the system," Alexis continued in a calm, appeasing tone.

Blaine felt her fluttering heart settle down and began to relax. This was going quite a bit better than she'd imagined.

"So, this time, we're going to focus on the intangibles. Although the real fault lies with the public who behave more like lab rats than human beings, we want to come across humble and contrite. However, while accepting the blame and responsibility, we also want to shift it to the ineptitude of Richard Jefferson."

Alexis watched Blaine's reaction carefully. She was a wild card in the mix. Having not come up through the ranks of the Illuminati with all the training, programming and demonic infestation that entailed, both the Pope and René had warned him against employing her in this important position.

However, Alexis felt strongly, and Lucifer agreed, that the rewards far outweighed the risks. By preempting the press with one of their own, by taking the world's most recognized and beloved face on television, they were guaranteed instant approval for the second-most controversial aspect of their overall plan. If this went well, and they were able to control and manipulate Blaine, then perhaps she'd be able to handle the foremost and final piece of the puzzle.

Blaine wanted to defend Richard of whom she'd become quite fond, but she sensed correctly that this wasn't the time or the place. She would seek to change their minds at a later time. Finally she nodded in acceptance. "Yes, I see your point. It's always good to have a scapegoat."

Alexis beamed. *Gotcha!* "A scapegoat, yes, quite so. Now, I have an important meeting in a few minutes, so I'd like for you to work with René today to prepare for the press conference tomorrow. Though she lacks your charm, she's a master manipulator. You'll find her insights quite useful."

Blaine almost shuddered. René gave her the creeps. But sooner or later she'd have to learn how to deal with her since she seemed to hold such a high position of influence within the global government. Blaine wanted to find out exactly what René's official job was, since it didn't appear on any of the organization charts that Blaine had seen as yet.

Chapter Twenty-One

General Wycliffe showed up at Alan Morrison's ranch house right on time, just as he always did. He considered timeliness among the most important personal attributes. His keen powers of observation had taken in all sorts of information on the long winding drive leading up to where he now stood before a sturdy oak front door.

Clearly Morrison was both wealthy and understated. While the ranch was meticulously maintained and the ranch house impressive, nothing was ostentatious. There was a quiet air of efficiency that Wycliffe liked and respected.

Surprisingly, Morrison answered the door himself. "Come in. Right on time. I appreciate that."

"Yes, so do I," the general replied and smiled enigmatically.

Morrison pointed the way toward his study off the front hall and followed Wycliffe inside, imperceptibly shaking his head. *What a pompous jerk.*

As they sat in the large, comfortable room with its western motif, Morrison knew exactly what he was getting himself into. He'd carefully watched Wycliffe throughout the meeting in Denver and quickly assessed his characteristics, good and bad.

Although Morrison knew he wouldn't like the man, he felt that the tin-star general was the best choice among available options to head up the western militia. Some of the others he'd met were smarter, better tacticians, certainly more likable. However, they were not as predictable or reliable as Wycliffe would be. The very qualities Morrison liked the least were what would enable him to successfully manage the general without his realizing it.

After Morrison had inquired about libations and sent his cook off to fetch the freshly-made coffee, he began the discussion. "General Wycliffe, I think that you're clearly the man to run our militia. What can I do to help you?"

Wycliffe straightened up and leaned forward. "Not to beat around the bush, it would be your financing and the use of your ranch for training that would be of most use."

"How much money are we talking about?"

The general paused to receive his steaming hot mug of coffee from a grizzled old man who grinned incessantly. Wycliffe mumbled a thank you, and leaned away from the caricature straight out of a western movie. He was surprised that Morrison would retain such a person. That's why he could never run an army.

After taking and savoring a sip of the excellent coffee, Wycliffe set the mug down on the side table. This was the moment of truth. He'd contemplated several strategies in advance, not really knowing who he was dealing with. Now he made up his mind to take the middle approach.

"In order to develop the size militia we need here in the West, and equip them properly, we're talking in the neighborhood of $100 million," Wycliffe said evenly, masking his apprehension.

"Is that all?" Morrison exclaimed and laughed. "I was figuring it might be more like $500 million!"

General Wycliffe's eyebrows shot up before he got them back under control. Clearly he'd underestimated the man. But no harm done. Perhaps it was best not to shoot for the moon right away.

"Well, of course, we're talking about just the initial outlay to establish the militia. Afterwards, there would be ongoing costs depending on what we actually use the militia for," Wycliffe said carefully.

"Yes, of course. Well, that's all very satisfactory. Would you like me to transfer those funds into your account today?" Morrison offered, sitting back in his chair, sipping his coffee, appearing as though such sums were mere pocket change.

"Oh, no, that won't be necessary," the general said, not wanting to appear overly anxious. "We still need to get formal approval of my leadership from the other members of the committee."

"Don't you worry about that, general. I can guarantee that they will back you," Morrison said confidently. Wycliffe wondered what leverage he held over the others.

"I appreciate your confidence in me," Wycliffe said sincerely, his dreams now assured of becoming a reality.

"So let's get on with the second purpose of our meeting," Morrison said as he stood and went over to one of several large bookcases. Opening a wide drawer beneath the shelves, he pulled out a set of topographical maps and then spread them out on the large table up against the far windows.

General Wycliffe followed him over and stood beside Morrison who waved his hand over the western portion of the ranch as depicted in the topmost of several drawings.

"As you can see, this area butts up against the foothills of Mt. Cutler near South Cheyenne Canyon. The foothills provide cover for the rear. I have a landing strip built over here with several planes at your disposal. We can either fly troops and supplies in, or they can come via either of two back roads over here and there," Morrison pointed out.

Wycliffe took a closer look. "How many civilians live in the area?"

Morrison flipped over the top map. Underneath was a more detailed map of the area in question. "The homes, outbuildings, unmarked roads and trails are indicated by the symbols define in the table down below."

The general leaned over even closer. "This small ranch over here, that could be a problem."

Morrison chuckled. "I don't think so. The owner's my son."

Wycliffe pointed at Cheyenne Lake. "You don't have direct access to the lake, do you?"

"No," Morrison admitted. "But there are a couple of streams and catch basins. I'm in the process of building two larger catch basins connected to a water treatment plant."

Wycliffe stood up sharply and looked at Morrison. This was almost too good to be true. "It seems as though you were anticipating using your ranch for just such a purpose."

Morrison laughed. "Well, I didn't know exactly what it would be used for, but the good Lord assured me that it would serve a major end-time function. I just didn't know what until you showed up."

The general stared uneasily at Morrison. "I don't think God is much involved in all this. I hope you're not an unstable religious zealot."

Morrison reached over and laid his hand gently on Wycliffe's shoulder. "Don't worry, general, I'm not a nutcase and I won't allow my beliefs to interfere with your militia. Nor will I try to convert you. So how about we take a helicopter ride and survey the landscape?"

Wycliffe was somewhat reassured, but he made a mental note to keep close tabs on Morrison.

Chapter Twenty-Two

With the internal ruckus back under control and plans for alleviating ongoing tensions in place, Pastor Wally and Juanita met for the second time to discuss Biblical warfare lessons. Both were a lot more comfortable with each other after the previous session had gone so well. It appeared that God joined them together especially for this task, with each of their gifts and experiences meshing perfectly.

"So, picking up where we left off before we were so rudely interrupted," Pastor Wally joked, glad the crisis that had interfered with their first meeting had also turned out so well. ""Let's continue to look at victories and defeats in the Bible to see what to do and what not to do."

"Okay, let's skip the small talk and jump right in," Juanita agreed, and drifted off thinking about her once missing, now found, yet still far away husband Brandon. He was never one for small talk either. When they first started dating back at Grambling State University, all their friends said it wouldn't last. She was too gregarious while he was too studious and quiet. Instead, they fooled everyone and had a great marriage.

Great, except for one detail. No children. One miscarriage and one stillborn. The hemorrhaging and subsequent hysterectomy left her barren and depressed for several years, during which Brandon was a stalwart friend and companion.

Their love matured during those years even as their lives became filled with meaningful purpose. Brandon became a high-level manager at Health & Human Services; she a prayer leader for Pastor Gabriel.

They were both raised in Christian, but broken families. They each dedicated themselves to the Lord during those barren years, and both believed they wouldn't have gotten through the darkness without Jesus. While Brandon never denied his faith, he didn't shout it from the rooftops like Juanita did. Because of her passion, a mutual friend introduced her to Pastor Gabriel and the rest, as they say, was history.

"Juanita? Are you okay?" Wally prodded gently.

"Huh? Oh, sorry. I got to thinking about Brandon. I miss him so much," Juanita said as she came out of her reverie with tears running down her cheeks.

"Hey, no problem. I can't even begin to imagine what you've been through. You handle it like a real trooper. Most of the time it doesn't seem like it bothers you, so we tend to forget about your tough situation," Wally said as he rose and held Juanita as she began to sob.

"Let it all out," the pastoral counselor encouraged. "He's safe now and I believe you'll see him again sometime soon."

Wally held her until she'd cried it all out. "Thank you so much," Juanita said softly. "I try so hard to be strong for everyone else that I forget to attend to my own needs."

"Well don't ever do that again," Wally scolded in an exaggerated tone and wagged his finger at her.

Juanita laughed heartily. "Okay, Doctor Freud, I promise. Now, can we get down to business? I haven't got all day you know."

Wally laughed too and then summarized what he'd been saying when Juanita had disappeared into the past. "I thought it was quite instructive how King David defeated

106

the Philistines two times in a row, but in two different ways. First, he inquired of the Lord whether he should go up against them and was told to do so and won the battle.[30] Then, the second time the Philistines attacked Israel, David once again asked the Lord if he should go out against them and the Lord said no."[31]

"Isn't that when the Lord used the mulberry trees?" Juanita remembered.

"Yes, indeed. The Lord told David to circle around behind the Philistines, and wait until they heard the sound of marching in the tops of the mulberry trees. The Lord made it sound like there was an enormous army, and the Philistines fled before David in a panic."[18]

"So, as we were discussing last time, the Lord doesn't necessarily do things the same way. That makes it imperative that we always seek His guidance first," Juanita concluded. "Jesus never healed the same way twice. One time He healed a blind man by just touching the eyes, another time he put mud on the eyelids."

"Right, and we have to be prepared for the Lord to do things in ways we don't expect. We can't put him in a box," Wally agreed. "There are no formulas; we have to be totally dependent on Him."

"The hardest time to remember that is when things are at their worst," Juanita noted, recalling several instances in her own life when she felt something had to be done instead of waiting on the Lord. Once, that resulted in being in the wrong place at the wrong time. If she'd only stayed at home, she wouldn't have been driving around desperately trying to find her friend's lost child. She didn't see the stop sign, totaled her vehicle and put the other driver in the hospital. The Lord had told her she was supposed to stay at home and pray, but she'd wanted to do more.

Wally waited a few moments when he saw Juanita drift off again, and then continued when she returned to the present. "Another example of the different and even bizarre ways the Lord brought about victory was when Samaria was besieged by Ben-Hadad, the king of Syria. The people of Israel were starving to death, prices for basic food supplies were astronomical. But Elisha prophesied a word from the Lord that by the next day, prices would be back to normal. No one believed him, of course, and the King of Israel even wanted to chop off his head.[32]

"Now there were four leprous men at the entrance gate to Samaria who were also dying of starvation. They knew if they went inside the city, they would die there as well, so they decided to surrender to the King of Syria, who might kill them but who also might feed them as captives. So at twilight, they crept out to the Syrian camp and found that no one was there. The Lord had caused the Syrian army to hear the sound of many chariots and horses during the night and they fled in a panic, leaving behind all their supplies. So the Lord kept His word when all hope seemed lost and no rational way could be seen out of their predicament," Wally concluded.

Juanita sighed. "The Bible says nothing is too hard for the Lord, and that even we can do all things through Christ who strengthens us. Why, then, don't we rely more on Him?"

"Human nature, I suppose," Wally answered.

'More like the sinful nature we inherit in this fallen world," Juanita clarified, and Wally nodded his assent.

"It's like no one in King Saul's army would stand up to Goliath," Juanita continued. "They were afraid because they saw the situation only through their own eyes. But then the little shepherd boy, David, comes along and he knew that God was big enough to take on Goliath through anyone. He volunteered, and the whole Philistine army was routed as a result."[33]

"Right. And another example was when King Sennacherub's army besieged the Israelites and King

Hezekiah was distraught, but prayed to the Lord. Then the prophet Isaiah received a word from the Lord that, because Hezekiah had humbly prayed, He would cause the Assyrian army to go away. This seemed impossible, but then an angel of the Lord went forth and killed 185,000 of them, so they departed and returned home to Ninevah."[34]

Wally leaned forward earnestly. "And I love the story of Saul's son Jonathan who went to spy on the Philistine camp with his armor bearer, saying *'nothing restrains the Lord from saving by many or by few.'* The Lord had given him a sign, so they boldly showed themselves to the garrison who said to come up there, the sign he was told to look for. They defeated the twenty guards and then there was a great earthquake, causing great trembling and confusion amongst the Philistines who were then driven off. If Jonathan hadn't been obedient and believed the Lord, none of that would have happened."[35]

Juanita shook her head. "Who knows how many times we weren't obedient or didn't even hear the Lord and missed out on a great blessing or opportunity?"

"Wow, when you put it like that, it's staggering to think how much different and better our lives might have been had we heard and followed the Lord's leading," Wally agreed and sat back to contemplate that for awhile.

This time it was Juanita who politely waited till Wally's eyes refocused and looked over at her. "What about examples of what went wrong when people didn't hear or obey the Lord?"

Wally beamed "Good question. And one I'm prepared to answer."

He sifted through his papers, and pulled one out. "To summarize, we have Saul who was twice disobedient. First when he didn't wait for Samuel to do the burnt offering,[36] and then when he didn't kill Agag and kept some of the spoils of victory.[37] As a result, he lost his anointing as king which was later given to David."

"That's why the Lord didn't want Israel to have an earthly king in the first place, because only He is the King of Kings and Lord of Lords," Juanita declared emphatically.

"Amen to that," Wally agreed, and then went to the next item on his list. "Another example is when King Ahab didn't listen to the prophet Micah who told him he would die if he went out to war against Syria. He chose to go ahead in disguise, but of course it did him no good when a 'random' arrow found and killed him."[38]

Juanita could only shake her head in horror at the great price that had been paid over history by God's people not listening to or obeying Him.

Wally's eyes scrolled down the extensive list until he found what he was looking for. "A different kind of example is the story of King David and Bathsheba. He was supposed to go out to war with the troops, but for some reason stayed home. That's when temptation comes, through the doors of disobedience. He saw Bathsheba, desired her, slept with her and then arranged to have her husband Uriah killed to cover up his sin. As a result, the Lord took the child that was fathered in sin."[39]

"And let's not forget about Samson," Juanita chimed in, "who allowed Delilah to shear his hair and then lost his strength because that violated his Nazarite vow."[40]

They both sat back for a few moments, somewhat drained from the enormity of the positive and negative lessons.

"I suppose we should take a break before we get into spiritual warfare," Wally recommended gently, not wanting the queen of warfare to feel put off.

Juanita smiled tenderly at him. "I agree, there's only so much a body can take at a sitting. If you think you're a bit worn out now, wait till we really get into it. So let's wait another day or two until we're freshened up for battle."

Chapter Twenty-Three

Rabbi Abraham and Pastor Gabriel took deep breaths to calm their fidgety nerves. As they stood off to the side, they could see security and police forces scrutinizing all the people in virtually every key area of the terminal at Rome's Leonardo da Vinci (Fiumicino) Airport.

"Well, we got past the guards at the entrance, so perhaps these monk habits will get us past all the others," Abraham reasoned hopefully.

"There's a lot of them," Gabriel sighed nervously. "They might have let us inside in order to entrap us, rather than scaring us away outside."

Abraham glanced around once more. "You know, we're probably going about this in the wrong way. If God has ordained us to be the two witnesses, and I reluctantly admit that it looks like He has, then why don't we just leave it in His hands to protect us? After all, it's His prophesies that must come to pass, and He is not a liar."[41]

Gabriel turned and stared deeply into Abraham's glowing eyes, transformed by those life-changing moments in St. Peter's Square. He wondered whether his own eyes had that new luster. "Yes, you're undoubtedly right. All we need to do is follow His leading and not worry about all the rest. If we're identified and captured, then that must be part of His plan."

"Precisely," Abraham whispered excitedly. "We both felt led to go to the monastery, to wear these habits and to accept these false ID papers. And now we've both agreed that we're supposed to take this flight to Jerusalem, so let's just proceed in confidence rather than fear."

"Yes, God would not want His representatives slinking about fearfully," Pastor Gabriel agreed. "After all, His Word says '*For God has not given us a spirit of fear, but of power and of love and of a sound mind.*'[42] So we need to start operating that way."

Abraham nodded vigorously. "Our doubts and fears were not of God, but of ourselves. We're still not fully believing that we could possibly be those witnesses. Instead, we must say, '*In God I have put my trust; I will not be afraid. What can man do to me?*'[43]

Now Gabriel was also nodding excitedly, the hood at first shaking and then falling back off his head, exposing his now famous face for all the police to see. "Lord God Almighty," he began to pray, "forgive us our doubts and fears and fill us with Your Spirit. Into Your hands we commend our souls. We will follow wherever You lead and do whatever You tell us to do."

With that, Abraham defiantly threw off his hood and they both strode confidently forward and got in line at the security checkpoint, holding their boarding passes they had printed online back at the monastery. They had no luggage but small carry-on bags. They took their shoes off as instructed, flashed their tickets and papers, and passed on through with nary a sideways glance from the various security personnel.

As they strode down toward their gate, not one person even glanced at them. It was so unusual that they stopped and turned around in a tight circle, scanning the faces of all the people and officers. Not one eye focused on them, even in their monk garb. Clearly God had His hand over their eyes.

When they checked in at the gate, the agent saw them, processed their ticket, gave them their seat assignments, all without any curiosity or hesitation. Perhaps it wasn't the eyes that God blinded, but their minds. The two witnesses enjoyed a relaxing flight with no one in the middle seat between them. They sipped their soft drinks, nibbled on the snacks and slept peacefully.

Strolling down to the customs inspection area of Ben Gurion Airport in Tel Aviv, they did feel a twinge of anxiety, but steeled themselves in the Lord and remained confident that things would continue to proceed smoothly here as they had in Rome. There seemed to be even more security than usual, Rabbi Abraham thought, but kept it to himself.

Unbeknownst to the two travelers, Alexis D'Antoni had already figured that the witnesses would return to Jerusalem, since that's where all the serious end-time strategies would play out. He had given his troops orders to stop anyone even remotely resembling the world's most wanted fugitives.

As a pair of well-armed IDF soldiers and their growling dogs approached, Gabriel and Abraham stood motionless, expecting, hoping that the soldiers would simply pass right by, but they didn't.

"Show us your passports," the lead soldier demanded.

After they had done so, he examined them and returned them with a sneer. Meanwhile, the dogs were sniffing and snarling at the two apparent monks, pulling hard against their leashes.

The two soldiers fought to restrain the dogs and exchanged a glance and a nod of agreement. The lead soldier then delivered the rehearsed message. "The Global Czar, Alexis D'Antoni, welcomes you to Israel, and requests the honor of your presence at his new palace in Jerusalem tomorrow. A limousine is waiting outside, which will first take you to the King David Hotel. In the morning, the same limousine will pick you up at eight o'clock and bring you to the palace where you will have breakfast with his highness. You will not want to miss this breakfast meeting, because Mrs. Tezla Cohen will be there as well."

Abraham's heart skipped a beat and he grabbed Gabriel to keep from falling over. *Oh, God, my precious Tezla. They have taken you.*

"Follow me," the lead soldier commanded and led the way. Gabriel guided the ashen-faced rabbi as the second soldier followed closely behind, continuing to restrain his growling dog.

The two witnesses sat quietly as the limo made the thirty-mile drive to Jerusalem and threaded through the crowded streets of the old city section that Gabriel remembered from his previous visit. But instead of the fish market above which Abraham lived, they arrived at a magnificent landmark hotel, majestically overlooking both the old and new sections of the holy city.

Only after they had been escorted to their suite and left alone did Gabriel finally speak to his disconsolate partner. "This must all be part of God's plan, otherwise we wouldn't have been unseen in Rome but captured here."

Abraham looked up from the chair nearest the door. It seemed to Gabriel that Abraham had aged a decade or more in just the past hour. Gabriel's heart went out to him as he thought about his own wife, Carmelita. Was she still safely tucked away in the hideaway? Or had the long arms of the Global Czar plucked her out too? He thought not, since the soldier had only mentioned Tezla.

"Do you think this room is bugged?" Abraham said softly, sadly.

"I'd assume so," Gabriel replied as he looked around the plush suite. "But let's not worry about that. Let's continue to believe that God is going to watch over us to do all that He has indicated in His Word."

"Yes," Abraham sighed, and sank into the chair. "But I didn't read anything about Tezla in the Good Book. What's to become of her?"

Chapter Twenty-Four

René told Blaine to meet with her the following morning after she'd dealt with Richard Jefferson. Blaine called Patrick and told him about the scary meeting with Alexis. She was getting nervous about him and was beginning to regret her hasty decision to become his spokesperson.

"What's more, now I have to work with René. She is one creepy lady," Blaine sighed and took another sip of wine. It was 12:45 a.m. in Jerusalem. What a pain it was dealing with the time difference between Jerusalem and New York where it was now 5:45 p.m. yesterday.

"This is all so hard to comprehend," Patrick said as he pulled on his suit jacket. The star anchor of the evening news with the highest ratings by far, patted down his tie and double-checked his carefully coiffed hair.

"Not that I don't believe you," he added quickly before Blaine could take offense. "But his public persona is so smooth, so rational, so together, that it's hard to understand this other side of him."

"That's what's so hard to deal with. He's like a Jekyll-Hyde personality. One minute he's charming and charismatic, the next he's a raving maniac," Blaine slurred as she slurped the rest of the wine.

"Well, I imagine he's under a lot of pressure," Patrick offered, touching up a spot on his cheek that the makeup artist had missed.

"Yeah, I guess that could be it," Blaine agreed uncertainly. She hoped that was the case.

"So when can you take those days off he promised you so you can get your affairs in order and move some of your stuff back there?" Patrick wondered, checking the time once again.

"I was afraid to ask him, he was in such a mood," Blaine admitted.

The knock on the door told him it was time to get to the set. "I love you, sweetheart. And I can't wait for you to get your cute little tush back here, but I've got to go."

Blaine sighed. "Love you too, honey. I'll ask him about it tomorrow. Actually, later today I guess," she stammered and returned his phone kiss.

She clicked the iPhone off, laid back flat on the bed and stared at the ceiling. She wasn't sure she even wanted to see the Global Czar tomorrow. Then she remembered her meeting with René in another seven hours and shuddered. Fortunately, the wine took over and guided her into blissful oblivion.

She awoke with a start, out of yet another nightmare. She tried to remember the awful dream. Something about vampires. She glanced at the clock. Three a.m. Another night of disturbed sleep. She felt plagued by unseen forces that disrupted her sleep each night. But that was idiotic. It was all in her own mind. The supernatural realm of religion and metaphysics was a myth born of a human need to explain away their own insecurities.

So yet again, she began the painful probe of her own mind. What was back there in her unconscious that was coming to the surface in response to the stress of her new job? A brief image of her drunken father smiling down at her flashed by. She shivered and pulled up the covers.

No, not now. She'd go there another time, when there was peace in her life. She didn't need to be stirring up long-buried memories just when she was coping with her most difficult challenge. No, she had to get hold of herself. She was a star. She was beautiful, intelligent, successful, strong. She simply would not allow all of this to get to her. It was probably all due to the wine. She'd have to stop drinking before bedtime, she resolved.

She spent the remaining hours in restless sleep and struggled out of bed feeling totally spent. This was getting old fast. She was used to being the pepper pot in the morning, not the wet blanket. She willed herself down to the exercise room, pushed herself through her normal routine on the treadmill and step machine, drank a lot of coffee, dressed, called her driver, and got to her enormous palace office just before eight o'clock.

Blaine found René waiting inside, sitting in her chair, sorting through the folders that had been neatly stacked on the marble-topped desk.

"What are you doing?" Blaine snapped at René.

"Hmm? Oh, just passing the time until you got here," René said, as though it was perfectly normal to violate the sanctity of someone else's office and paperwork.

Already thrown off, Blaine slammed her briefcase down on the desk as René slowly rose from the chair and strolled over to the window. Blaine didn't see the little smile of satisfaction René erased before turning back around.

"So, shall we begin?" René asked, her voice smooth as silk. Blaine looked up at her and almost did a double-take. René was dressed in an almost transparent blouse with the shortest, tightest skirt imaginable. Even for the sexually liberated Blaine, it was way too much. Who was this woman?

What was her role? How could she be such an important part of the global administration?

Blaine looked away again and straightened the folders on her desk, this time missing an evil smirk.

"Okay, I'm ready," Blaine answered. "But where's Richard?"

"Who? Oh, yes, Jefferson," René answered innocently. "He died suddenly last night. I guess the pressure got to him."

"What? Dead?" Blaine's head was spinning. She slumped down in her chair.

René sidled over behind Blaine and began to gently stroke her long blond hair. "This isn't the place for weaklings," she said softly.

Somehow René's gesture of caring touched Blaine. She closed her eyes, desiring, needing comfort. René's hands felt so good, so warm on her chilled face. When those hands began to wander further, Blaine bolted up and pushed René away.

"What do you think you're doing? I'm not like that, not that I feel it's wrong, but….."

"But what?" René purred.

"But it's not my style," Blaine stated lamely and backed away from René who laughed gleefully.

"Oh, well, it was worth a shot," René said, shrugging her shoulders. "So I guess we'll just have to plan the boring old press conference, then."

Blaine nodded bleakly and pulled the Universal ID System folder out of her briefcase.

Chapter Twenty-Five

The caravan pulled wearily through the triple-posted entryway with the elegant wooden sign overhead confirming their arrival at Trinity Ranch. The cross and fish symbols on the sign were refreshing and reassuring. Jesse was driving lead and pulled off to the side of the well-maintained dirt road and waited for the two other vehicles to pull up behind him.

Jesse got out and spread his topographic map on the hood of the jeep. The engine warmth felt good on his hands, with the autumn temperatures announcing winter was not far way. He glanced at his handheld GPS unit and compared the coordinates against those Alan Morrison had given him over the cell phone.

"Why are we stopping?" Jerome whined as he came up behind Jesse. "This has got to be it."

Jesse held back the sharp retort that fell dead on his tongue. He knew they were all tired, stressed-out, hungry and irritable. And he knew that many of them hadn't appreciated his insistence that they take back roads and country highways instead of the Interstates. Conditioned by his FBI training, Jesse was nothing if not over-cautious.

Brandon sidled alongside Jesse and put his arm around his shoulders. "Congratulations, big guy, we did it. You got us here without incident."

Jesse looked up and smiled gratefully. Turning to Jerome he said gently, "I just want to make sure that there aren't any forks in the road ahead. People tend to make most of their mistakes when they're close to their objective and let their guard down."

The Harrison kids had disembarked and were running around wildly, screaming at the tops of their lungs. James Harrison opened his mouth to scold them yet again, and then realized this was the perfect place and time for them to let off some steam. No neighbors were in sight, and this way they'd be calmed down a bit when they finally met the mysterious Alan Morrison.

Rev. and Mrs. Braintree smiled at one another and held hands, too tired to climb out of the Jeep, but thrilled to have survived the journey. Sue, Francine and Trudy Harrison huddled off to the side. The men glanced over nervously, wondering what the women were cooking up.

Just then they heard a loud engine and the thwapping of a helicopter's rotor blades. With some trepidation, they all as one squinted west toward the setting sun and watched as the chopper closed in and settled down to the ground some distance away. Dust and small debris were scattered around as the helicopter slowly wound down.

Trudy yelled frantically to the children to get back to their vehicle immediately, fearing a projectile as much as a possible enemy. But the chopper was far enough away that none of them got sprayed. As the dust cloud settled, a grinning middle-aged man came trotting toward them dressed in jeans, a plaid flannel shirt and a cowboy hat.

Despite Trudy's pleas, the children ran to meet the first cowboy they'd ever seen up close. Morrison grabbed the two smallest kids and swung them around evoking shouts of glee.

Shedding their worries, the rest of the adults, sans the Braintrees, hurried over to greet their benefactor, who warmly welcomed them to his ranch like they were long lost friends.

As they were completing all the introductions, a pickup truck came rolling to a stop. A younger cowboy leaped out and hustled over to the large group standing in the middle of the dirt road.

"This here's Wayne Crosby, the head cowboy of the Trinity Ranch. In fact, he's the one who really runs things here. They just let me pretend I'm in charge. He'll lead you back to the ranch house," Morrison explained giving his ranch hand a warm grin.

The gang trooped back to their vehicles and fell in behind Crosby's pickup truck. They were all surprised at how long it took them to reach the ranch house. Off to one side they saw a huge herd of Black Angus chomping away at the sparse vegetation, some resting under the shade of scattered trees. A large field of late corn lay ripe for the picking off to the right. Closer in, white pole fences marked off several corrals where many horses chewed at the grass or stood looking over at the passing vehicles.

It was the stuff of movies and dreams for most of the urban easterners, especially the kids who couldn't wait to explore the vast foreign landscape. Although much different in scope and topography, the horses nonetheless brought a tear to Brandon's eyes as he remembered his own little horse ranch he'd shared with Juanita.

Several men and women greeted the newcomers and quickly escorted them to their guest rooms in the expansive, two-story ranch house. They were all surprised to find closets full of western wear in more or less their appropriate sizes. Jesse didn't let on that he'd described the group to Morrison in their last phone conversation.

Soon the urban cowboys trooped down to a massive dining room where two large tables were set up for dinner. They could see two cooks just outside the windows, laboring over what looked like an enormous metal tube lying sideways with the top quarter cut open. Racks of steaks, foil-wrapped potatoes and corn-on-the-cob sizzled, sending streams of pungent smoke skyward.

The delightful aroma stirred up all their appetites and they feasted shamelessly on the piles of hearty food. Apple pie a la mode completed their trip to culinary heaven. They'd grown quite tired of fast food, trail mix and protein bars on the three-day journey from New Mexico.

Everyone was so nice to them, treating them all like royalty. After dinner, the children were allowed to wander around outside under the watchful eyes of a young couple. Sue wondered if one of them was a Morrison offspring.

The adults retired to the large family room across the wide hallway. When they were all seated, Alan Morrison began to answer many of their unspoken questions.

"Up until now, we've used this land only as a working ranch. We're known for our fine cattle, horses, turkeys and corn. Because of the increased scrutiny and control of the Global Governance Committee, I've turned over the operation of my computer/internet company to some trusted people to continue running without overtly resisting the dictates of the one-world government."

Morrison looked around to make sure everyone was following him. "I'm now devoting all my energy and assets to mounting counterattacks against this ungodly, devilish New World Order. According to the Bible, we will not win this war. Revelation 13 says that the one-world government will be victorious until, that is, Jesus returns. It goes on to say that the two beasts, the anti-Christ Alexis D'Antoni and Pope Radinsky the false prophet, will 'war with the saints and overcome them.'"[44]

The guests shifted in their seats and a few mumbled angrily. It was always difficult to digest that Christians could not always be victorious. Surely, there must be another way of interpreting these Scriptures?

"I know what you're thinking," Morrison continued after the grumblings died down. "The Bible also tells us that we can be overcomers,[45] even 'more than conquerors.'[46] So how can these two disparate views be reconciled? The answer is that we can still win battles within the 'gross darkness'.[47] But God's overall plan will come to fruition in order to allow sin to come to its fullness[48] before this old earth is wiped out and the new heaven, the new earth and the new Jerusalem are established by Jesus Himself."[49]

"Hallelujah!" Francine called out. "Bring it on, the sooner the better."

The Braintrees shifted uncomfortably. End-time discussions were not their cup of tea.

"So, to repeat, we will not change the course of history and prophecy, but we can win individual battles," Morrison emphasized. "What are the spoils of victory? Souls for the Kingdom of God. In the short time we have left, we want to save as many people as possible from an eternity in hell. I hope this ranch will become one of several worldwide centers for revival."

A greater buzz now coursed around the room. "What are your specific plans?" Brandon asked.

"Even before I knew all of you were headed this way, I had begun to establish a high-tech computer lab to counter the government's Universal ID System as well as to infiltrate their other systems so that we can stay a step ahead of them," Morrison answered and then smiled at Francine. "I was wondering who was going to run this system and was praying for God to bring someone here to do so. Now I see that He has."

"She's the best!" Jerome exclaimed, with other voices adding their confirmation.

"You can count on me," Fran volunteered enthusiastically

"I'd also like for Jesse to head up all of our non-military counterinsurgency efforts," Morrison added, and looked over at him for a response. Jesse nodded his acceptance, anxious to get back to doing something positive instead of running like a fugitive.

"You said non-military," Brandon interjected. "That implies that you've got some militaristic plans as well?"

"Yes indeed," Morrison answered, "and I'm glad you're the one who asked. Remember General Wycliffe?"

"Of course," Brandon answered. "I owe him my life. So do the Harrisons and Sue."

"Well, General Wycliffe has agreed to form a larger military group by combining militias from all over the west," Morrison announced. "That means we can attack more detention centers to rescue illegally incarcerated Christians as well as defend our hideaways and remote camps."

"Wow, that's great!" Jerome proclaimed. "Can I join your army?"

Morrison laughed, appreciating the support from this large, strong man. "Well, it's not really my army. I'm financing it, but the operations are being entirely run by General Wycliffe. I'll introduce you to him when he returns later this week."

Morrison saw that the group was starting to reel from their long, arduous trip, the huge meal and his own dramatic announcements. "One more thing, and then I think you should all get a good night's sleep in a real bed. We are also building a massive underground facility here that will dwarf any of the hideaways. This is where all the computer equipment will be and where we will house the souls we save. Enough of it is complete so that you can all move there tomorrow."

"But why can't we stay here in the house with the nice comfy beds?" Jerome grumbled.

"Because, you'll be a whole lot safer there," Morrison answered and then laughed. "Besides, the beds there are even more comfortable."

Chapter Twenty-Six

Abby was growing restless. Now that the exchange of people between the hideaway and remote camp was underway, things had settled down and there wasn't much for her to do. She knew that Pastor Wally and Juanita were working their way toward a spiritual warfare course that might change the nature of how they were functioning, but she was becoming impatient.

Also, the announcement of the Universal ID System and its three-month deadline to receive the RFID chip or not be able to buy anything, had thrown her off stride. Sure, they had a good supply of food and essentials on hand, but it certainly wouldn't last the required three years or so, the timeframe of Pastor Gabriel's interpretation of when the pre-wrath rapture would occur.

Jim had gotten to know his new wife much better now that they had been able to live together at the hideaway for awhile. Although they had to share their room with Wally and Michelle, their privacy arrangements had given them sufficient enough time together to develop a sound foundation for the marriage.

Jim knew that something was bothering Abby and he also knew why she wasn't saying anything about it. She was loathe to bring up her own personal concerns as leader of Havenwood1 lest she cause any negativity to flow down from the top. She took her leadership role quite seriously, perhaps too seriously, to her own detriment.

For Jim, this whole period had been one of renewal and refreshing. No job, no responsibilities. As a new Christian, he had been studying hard to show himself approved" as the Bible says.[55] As a former demonized Illuminati conspirator, he was continuing to meet with Pastor Wally for personal counseling. But he too was starting to get itchy to do something. It was beginning to feel a bit weird to be so relaxed.

So Jim finally took Abby aside after she'd briefed and sent out the day's evangelism teams. "How are things going on the spiritual front?" he asked as they settled down on a sofa in the lounge.

"Pretty smoothly for the last few days. The Lord used us to save dozens of souls and send them to our camp in the Blue Ridge Mountains. But I'm still getting over losing two whole teams last week. I know there are losses and casualties in a war, but it's still hard getting used to," she replied, sensing that Jim had other things on his mind.

"Yes, it is, and it's especially hard on you because you care so much about these people," Jim observed tenderly. "In fact, if you didn't care so much, I wouldn't be a Christian and we wouldn't be married."

Abby reached over and stroked Jim's hair. "I'll take some of the credit, but it took a lot of courage to make all the changes you had to go through."

Jim cleared his throat and Abby sat back in the couch and waited to find out what Jim really wanted to talk about. She too was getting to know her husband and love him even more.

"Okay, well, I was thinking, uhm, that you were, you know, getting a little.. a little antsy," Jim finally got it out and blushed a bit.

Abby almost laughed at his discomfort but limited herself to a comforting smile. She couldn't help but recall the man he once was: obnoxious, overbearing, hedonistic, sexist. And now here he was blushing and stumbling because he didn't want to hurt her feelings. *Praise You, Jesus!*

"I guess you could call it that," Abby admitted carefully.

Jim leaned toward her, becoming more animated. "Well, so have I, but probably for different reasons."

When Abby didn't respond, he continued. "While your reasons and mine might be different, I think the underlying cause might be the same."

Abby leaned forward and kissed him on the cheek. She had been waiting for this day, and perhaps it was at hand.

Jim didn't really understand Abby's loving reaction so early in the conversation, but certainly appreciated it. "As for me, it's an outgrowth of what I was saying in our last group meeting. While I needed this quiet time to study and heal, I'm getting tired of sitting on my hands and watching the world being taken over by the devil. I want to, need to, get out there and do something. Take a stand for the Lord."

Abby pondered that for a moment. "Yes, I guess you're right, we do share an underlying need. I wouldn't have put it quite like that, but yes, I have been getting 'antsy.' I'm itching to do something but I don't have the slightest idea what."

Jim was getting excited and had to stand up and walk around a bit. Fortunately no one was in this small lounge this morning. Most people congregated together in the two larger lounges to watch the latest news on TV and discuss things together.

"When Alan Morrison told me what he was doing out west, my first thought was that I wanted to move out there where the real action is." Jim looked over and saw that Abby was both shocked and hurt.

"What, you don't think we're accomplishing anything here?" said the hideaway's leader, unable to cover up her disappointment that her husband thought so little of what she did.

"No, no, that's not what I meant," Jim said quickly and rushed back over to take Abby's face in his hands. "You've done a great job, but now it's time for something new, something bigger. You've been in training for greater things."

Abby's eyes widened. She hadn't thought of her underlying restlessness in those terms. She thought it was a fault, a deficiency of character that she couldn't be content as the hideaway's chief. Could it possibly be that the Holy Spirit was stirring things up?

"You've got this place running on all cylinders and Jermaine is twiddling his thumbs. While he's in charge of all the hideaways and remote camps, that doesn't keep him busy all day. I think he should take over here to free you up for something new."

Abby was stunned to think that what she'd thought of as a mild case of boredom might result in something big and new and exciting. She realized she was holding her breath. "Exactly what do you have in mind, my darling husband?"

Jim stood back up, unable to contain himself. "Alan Morrison said he would fund us to do the same thing here in the east that he's doing out west." There, it was out. Instead of feeling nervous, he felt relieved to have it all on the table.

Abby leaned back again, lost in thought. Jim was absolutely right. They had both been in training, and now it was time to put all that experience to greater use. Her heart was filled with joy. She'd been waiting for her husband to be ready to take over being the spiritual head. She still wanted to exercise her leadership skills and didn't need a boss, but their marriage had been missing something and this was it. Now they were ready to fulfill their potential together, in harmony with each other and according to Biblical principles.

Chapter Twenty-Seven

Rabbi Abraham awoke early in the morning feeling somewhat better. He had spent several hours in prayer and reflection last night before he'd finally been able to fall asleep. He rose, pulled back the curtains and let the sun stream in over him as it rose over the tormented capital of God's Kingdom on earth.

His spirit stirred with the warmth of the sun, thinking that the Son was also rising over him from the east, the 'Bright and Morning Star.' The true light of the world, not Lucifer the pretender. His blood boiled as he thought of Alexis holding Tezla in captivity. Well, it was time to see how much power God was giving to his two anointed witnesses.

When he opened his bedroom door he could smell the delicious aroma of freshly brewed coffee. Gabriel was on his knees, his arms spread wide, the sun shining on his glowing face. It seemed the Holy Spirit had them on the same wavelength this morning, a good sign.

Abraham poured himself a cup of coffee and retreated back into his bedroom, not wishing to disturb his colleague. As he closed the door, he had to chuckle to himself. Who would ever have thought that his closest associate would wind up being a Pentecostal, Hispanic-American pastor. Mysterious ways indeed.

With his heart brimming over with love, he thought of his precious Tezla. She had been hurt so much by their children's death, then his miraculous conversion to Christianity and the resultant rejection of their friends, family and Synagogue. Now, once again, she was suffering because of him.

"No, my friend, it is because of Me," said a voice near the window. Abraham snapped out of his reverie and glanced over at the light beams that nearly blinded his eyes. In the midst of the bright light was a shadowy figure of a long-haired man in a white robe.

Abraham put the coffee down and sank to his knees. "Lord, I am Your humble servant."

"Do not despair, Abraham, over Tezla or anything to come," Jesus said in a soft voice that somehow seemed to fill the entire room.

"As you say, my Lord," Abraham answered, overwhelmed.

"There will be difficult times, but always remember that I am in control over anyone who calls on My name. What is it to you if I choose to bring Tezla to her reward sooner than you'd like? Hasn't she suffered enough? To die in Christ is gain, not loss. Do you not know that you shall be with her in all of eternity after this brief moment is over?"

Abraham felt ashamed over his lack of faith and under-standing. He began to weep.

A hand reached out from the sunbeams and covered his aching heart. "Do not be ashamed my son, it is a difficult path you must walk. You will make mistakes. You will rise to the heights of love and sink to the depths of despair, but one thing will remain constant. The One True God will be with you always, whether you see Him or not, whether you feel Him or not. What might seem like a tragedy to you might in fact be a glorious victory. Do not judge. I alone am Judge. Seek only Me. Seek only to know Me and My will."

Abraham closed his eyes and felt the most incredible love filling his spirit, soul and body. His tears of fear and regret morphed into sobs of unrestrained joy. He immersed himself into the One who held his heart in His hands.

"Abide in Me as I abide in You," the voice whispered in his ear and then withdrew.[51]

Gradually Abraham returned from his journey deep into eternity. He felt as though he were a different person. He couldn't quite put his finger on it, but the world seemed to have changed. He supposed it was his outlook that had changed.

He rose to his feet and stumbled back out the bedroom door just in time to almost bump heads with an exuberant Gabriel. They both reared backward in shock at the glowing face of the other. "You look like Moses,"[52] Gabriel exclaimed and then they roared in laughter.

Gabriel quickly summarized his own encounter with Jesus. "He gently rebuked me for my 'little faith' and then held me in His arms. I felt pure love and joy like never before. It was glorious!"

"Isn't it amazing that He can be with us in different ways at the same time? We always say that He is omnipresent, but that's just a concept until you experience it directly," Abraham observed.

"Yes, you're absolutely right. He really means it when He says He is always with us,"[53] Gabriel agreed. "But it's up to us to know it and act accordingly."

"Speaking of acting, we need to get ready because the limo will be ready for us shortly," Abraham said as he turned to go back into his room to shower and dress.

Their faces were still glowing slightly as they rode in the limousine through the congested streets to the Global Czar's new palace. Abraham was anxious to see where Alexis had built his blasphemous palace. Would it be in the southern shadows of the Temple Mount where archaeologists believe King David's original palace was located?

But no, the limo had turned to the north and then proceeded eastward along Via Dolorosa, the street where Jesus carried the cross on the way to his crucifixion, Gabriel recalled. The limo then turned onto Derech Sha'ar HaArayot to the north of the Temple Mount, finally turning right onto the grounds of the Mount on HaMelech Faisal.

There stood the new palace in all its gleaming self-importance on the northwest corner of the grounds. It towered over the Dome of the Rock, with a massive obelisk much like the Washington Monument sitting incongruously atop a replica of the Taj Mahal in place of the traditional dome. What kind of twisted statement was the Global Czar, the anti-Christ, trying to make?

They drove past the reflecting pond out front, and then around to a side entrance where they were greeted by an Asian man in an all-white Nehru suit with its distinctive stand-up collar. Very mixed signals, Abraham decided.

Gabriel wandered off onto the large front portico past several of the many stark white columns and looked out over the grounds toward the Dome of the Rock and then out over Old City Jerusalem. He was amazed to simply be standing on what was once such holy ground, seeing first hand in one place the symbols of Christianity's Jewish roots, the incursion of Islam and the desecration of the Universal Religion.

Nehru tapped him on the shoulder. "We need to go. It is not a good idea to keep his highness waiting."

Gabriel turned and looked into the man's eyes and saw only the blackness of demonic possession. Before the man could react, Gabriel commanded the demons to "depart in the mighty name of Jesus Christ." After a long piercing shriek and a few convulsions, the man collapsed and lay limp on the white stucco floor.

Abraham came running over and watched with Gabriel as the once rigid, expressionless, robotic body curled up and cried softly. They gently lifted the man to his feet.

Gabriel checked his eyes and saw they were clear. "You are free now. Free to do as you wish, go where you will."

The man looked around as though seeing things with new eyes. ""Where will I go? What will I do?" he asked warily. "Yes, I can feel the freedom, and it is wonderful. But I have no family, I have no place to go. May I stay with you?"

Gabriel's eyebrows rose in question as he looked over at Abraham who hesitated and then nodded. "Yes, you can stay with us for as long or as short a time as you wish, for you must always remember that you are free," Gabriel said, thinking that perhaps they could use someone to help out logistically.

Suddenly the man leapt at Gabriel, throwing his arms around him, hugging him tight. Gabriel let him hold on for a few moments and then tenderly lifted his arms off and held him at arms length. "What is your name?"

"Aadideva Hermawan Suryatama, kind sir."

"Uhm, can we just call you Aadi for now?"

"Oh, yes, kind sir."

"What does your first name mean, Aadi?"

"It means 'highest god' in Sanskrit, kind sir."

"Really. Well, I want you to know that there is no higher God than Jesus Christ. He is the highest God, the God above all gods. It is He who has set you free, not me. See that you worship only Him."

"Oh, yes, kind sir. I will, if you will only show me how to do so."

Abraham put his arms around Aadi. His eyes were moist and his heart gladdened to see another soul added to the Kingdom. "You can worship our Lord Jesus Christ wherever, whenever, however you wish, just as long as you declare him to be your Savior."

"Oh yes, kind sir, I do so declare. I will serve Him and only Him forever!"

"One more thing," Gabriel interjected. "Please call us by our names too. This is Abraham and I am Gabriel."

Aadi was stunned. "I cannot do that, honored sirs. It would be disrespectful."

"Well, then, you can call us Rabbi Abraham and Pastor Gabriel if that makes you feel better about it."

Aadi nodded vigorously. Then his eyes turned fearful. "But what about the Global Czar? He will be furious!"

"Don't you worry about him," Abraham said as he guided Aadi back to the side entrance. "You just leave him to us."

Upstairs, Alexis D'Antoni was indeed fuming, venting his anger and frustration on René. Poor Tezla sat in the corner terrified, clenching her hands, gritting her teeth. She had so looked forward to seeing her beloved husband again, but she feared for his life at the hands of this monster who raged on and on.

Suddenly the door to the dining room opened and there stood Abraham grinning broadly, one arm around the shoulders of a young, handsome Asian lad. D'Antoni stopped in mid-rant and stared unbelievingly at this strange apparition.

"Get your arm off my servant!" Alexis screamed at Abraham.

"He's ours now, or I should say he's Jesus Christ's servant now," Abraham said, and stared hard at the Global Czar, daring him to try and reclaim Aadi.

Alexis glared back for awhile. Gabriel could almost see D'Antoni's mental wheels churning through numerous scenarios until Alexis finally looked away and strode down to the head of the table upon which breakfast was laid out.

"Yes, I see that the traitor has betrayed me," he said as he turned to face them once again. "But I have so many more, it means nothing to me if you steal one of them. They are, as you say, a 'dime a dozen.' But what I do have, is your wife, Abraham." The Global Czar gave him a sinister smile.

Abraham glanced over at his precious wife who sat wringing her hands as though in a stupor. "You may have thought you had her, but we're here to take her back," Abraham said as he began to move toward Tezla, who was still sitting in the far corner of the large room.

Before he advanced more than a few paces, several doors opened revealing numerous white-clad Asian men pointing Uzi's at him. Abraham came to a sudden stop, paused and straightened up "In the name of Jesus Christ I dismiss all of you. Be gone!"

Abraham swept his arm around the room. The armed servants fell backward and the doors closed sharply.

"Quite a display, most impressive," Alexis sneered. "But you're still not getting Tezla."

"On no?" Abraham strode purposely over to his wife. This time there was no further interference. Still Tezla continued to wring her hands, looking up worriedly toward Alexis.

"Tezla, my love, it's me, Abraham. Can't you see?" he wondered as he held his arms out to her.

Tezla heard his voice and looked around right past him, sweeping the room with her eyes, searching for him. "Have you blinded her, you son of Satan?"

Alexis chuckled as though he knew something no one else did. "No, my good man, I haven't laid a hand on her, nor have any of my henchmen."

Abraham couldn't stand it anymore. He lunged for Tezla and his hands went right through her. Back and forth we waved his hands through her body, but she batted not an eyelash.

"What kind of trick is this?" Abraham turned and demanded of Alexis.

Before the Global Czar could answer, Gabriel piped up. "It must be a holographic image."

"Aren't you the smart one," Alexis gleamed. His face became covered with a black rage. "If you two don't do as I say, I will have her killed, make no mistake about it."

Abraham looked down at the image of his wife. Apparently she had a TV screen and could hear and see Alexis, but not him. "My darling Tezla, forgive me, but I put you now in the hands of our blessed Savior."

He then glowered back at Alexis. "As for you, Lucifer's child, we will do nothing except what Jesus shows us to do."

D'Antoni's countenance became engorged in blood red fury. "We will torture her, cut her fingers off, gouge out her eyes, pull her apart by her limbs!"

Abraham continued to gaze lovingly, sadly, upon Tezla's image as she recoiled in horror. "Good-bye my love, I shall miss you until we meet again in Heaven."

Were his eyes deceiving him? Another figure in a white robe appeared in the holographic image and reached down for Tezla. Even as her physical body slumped in the chair and then fell forward onto the floor, it appeared as if the angel of the Lord lifted her spiritual body to his chest and ascended up through the ceiling out of sight.

All Alexis saw was Tezla's lifeless body lying on the floor. "Noooo!" he screamed, losing his presumed leverage over the witnesses.

"I should call down fire down from Heaven and consume you on the spot, you worthless piece of garbage," Abraham fumed.

René, who had been watching the entire episode from a divan up against the far windows, slowly rose and slinked toward Abraham looking as cool and collected as Alexis was apoplectic.

"Surely you know that you can't do that," she purred, her lips turned slightly upward in contempt. "Or else how would all the prophecies in your Bible about the anti-Christ come to pass?"

Abraham's emotions had drained him to the core. He despaired over losing Tezla in this world, but rejoiced that she was now seated in Heaven with the Lord. His mind, though, had short-circuited and was unable to respond to René.

Gabriel stepped forward and stood face to face with René. "Oh Mother of Harlots, how I wish you were not protected by prophecy too. You do well to believe the Scriptures, for they say that the ten horns of the beast you ride will eat your flesh and burn you with fire.[54] I look forward to the day I see you fry."

Before the shaken harlot could regain control of herself, Gabriel tenderly guided Abraham out the door, signaling Aadi to follow.

Chapter Twenty-Eight

Pastor Wally and Juanita sat down together in the small conference room stunned. Abby had just announced to the whole underground community that she and her husband Jim were embarking on a new venture. Jermaine would be taking over as operational head of Havenwood1 in addition to his responsibilities as overseer of all the hideaways and remote camps.

"What do you think about all that?" Wally asked Juanita.

She got that faraway look, closed her eyes, and hummed a little. Wally knew to wait as she communed with the Holy Spirit. When she reopened her eyes, they had a twinkle and a sparkle Wally hadn't seen in some time.

"This is a good thing," she pronounced. "A very good thing. It's just what we need right now. While you and I prepare to launch a spiritual warfare offensive, Jim and Abby simultaneously will be creating a physical counterpart. The Lord is quite pleased that we are in tune with His perfect will."

Wally digested that for a few moments. He realized that his initial disappointment upon hearing the announcement was due to a personal sense of loss. He and Michelle had grown quite close to and fond of Abby and Jim. The thought that they would be leaving the hideaway also created a concern that Michelle might revert to her anxious ways, with her best friend and mentor departing. What couple would they room with now?

Then he chastised himself for his lack of confidence in his wife. She'd had some major breakthroughs, thanks to the Lord. Now was not the time to doubt her, or the Lord. If this was His will, then He would help them to iron things out.

Juanita watched as Wally's face went through several subtle changes. She thought she knew what was troubling her pastor. Her pastor? Had she given up on Pastor Gabriel? No, she quickly realized. Just like Wally was coping with Jim and Abby leaving, she'd had to give up on her beloved pastor returning to shepherd his flock. Gabriel had been called to higher things. She might not ever see him again.

That, of course, got her thinking of Brandon. She was delighted that he was safely ensconced out west on Morrison's ranch. But what now? Should she join him out there? What about her leadership responsibilities back here? He, though, was anxious to participate in Morrison's anti-government activities.

Wait a minute! This morning's announcement changed everything. Brandon could come back here to help Jim and Abby replicate what Morrison was doing out west. That would resolve all her problems. She refocused her eyes, saw Wally watching her with a grin on his face, and realized that she had a big smile on her own face.

Before they could say anything about what they were thinking, there was a quick knock on the door and then Michelle burst into the room, practically giddy. Wally's eyes widened in amazement.

"Sorry to interrupt, but I just had to tell you the good news," Michelle blurted out in excitement. "Abby told me that Jermaine and Tara are engaged and will be married before Jim and Abby move out. Then they'll be our new roommates!"

Well now, Wally thought as he grinned back at his wife. *The Lord has indeed taken care of things. What a fool I am to doubt Him.* "That's great!" he said to Michelle as he got up to hug his wife. She had changed so much. He needed to let go of the old Michelle, and truly believe that these changes were permanent.

After Michelle left, all Wally and Juanita could do was shake their heads in wonder. "Well, I guess we should get started," Wally finally said, although it was hard to switch gears.

"I thought perhaps I could bring up some of the key spiritual warfare Scriptures, and then you could elaborate on how you've experienced them in real situations. Perhaps then we can develop a list of do's and don'ts."

Juanita simply nodded, still caught up to some extent in her own thoughts.

"The two most prominent verses that speak directly to spiritual warfare are Ephesians 6:12 and 2Corinthians 10:3-4," Wally stated and again Juanita nodded her agreement.

"And, I feel that Mark 16:17-18 and Luke 10:19 are required to tell the entire story," Wally concluded.

"No, not the *entire* story," Juanita suddenly came to life. "But those lay a good foundation."

"Yes, you're right, of course. I do get a little carried away at times," Wally admitted, not at all offended. He knew Juanita was the expert and had actually been concerned that she wasn't speaking up enough.

"So, here's what I conclude when I look at those verses: there is definitely a war going on; it is not physical, but spiritual; therefore, the weapons of our warfare must also be spiritual and they come only from God; Jesus gives us His authority over demons and over *all* the power of the enemy (Satan); to cast the demons out and heal the sick."

Juanita laughed. "That's the most concise summary I've ever heard. Good job. But I think we'll need to elaborate some when we teach the class." She winked to let him know she was joking.

Wally appreciated their new relationship. The fact that they could tease each other a bit showed they were getting more and more comfortable with one other.

"Yeah, I suppose we should do that. We'll read all the Scriptures, then I'll give my summary and you can talk about some of your practical experiences in applying these verses."

"Oh, yes, I've had experiences. Lots of experiences, good and bad."

"What do you think you've learned from those experiences?" Wally asked, and then sat back looking forward to hearing what really happens out in the world.

Juanita got up and began to pace, as was her modus operandi for prayer. "The first thing I learned early on is that demons are indeed real, and they are not to be trifled with. They have certain powers, but mostly they are sneaky liars."

"That's certainly confirmed in Scripture," Wally agreed. "There are eighty verses in the New King James version that mention demons, so they are certainly real. The King James Version sometimes calls them 'little devils' because they are fallen angels just like their master, Satan, who is the 'father of lies.'"[55]

"Yes, and that's mostly how they achieve their objectives, by whispering lies into our unconscious minds in such a way that we think it's our own thoughts," Juanita concurred, beginning to really warm up.

"What's more, they come disguised as 'angels of light,'[56] making themselves out to be the good guys, and then leading us down a primrose path into a thicket of thorns," Juanita added disdainful. "So many people believe in angels nowadays, but they don't differentiate the good from the bad."

"So, the battle is mostly in our minds?" Wally asked, never having quite thought of it that way before.

"For the most part," Juanita answered. "The strongholds that 2Corinthians 10:3-5 talk about are all in our minds. That's why it says we should cast down every argument, or imaginations, that the devil exalts above the knowledge of God and, instead, bring every thought captive in obedience to the Word who is Jesus Christ."

"But what about the strongholds that the enemy creates on earth? I've heard that we need to tear those strongholds down too," Wally asked.

"Ahh, yes, that's a very key question." Juanita stopped pacing around the table and stared off into space. "Early in my warfare career, a group of us used to go around to areas we thought were particular strongholds of the enemy, like abortion clinics, high crime districts, even bars. Not only didn't we see much in the way of results, but we noticed that, one by one, each of us or our families were getting sick, having accidents, losing jobs and having miscarriages."

Tears came to her eyes as she recalled losing both of her babies before they were born. "Then we read John Paul Jackson's book, *Needless Casualties of War,* and finally understood what was happening. The Bible says Satan is the "prince of the air," meaning the spiritual realm. Until Jesus returns, we do not have the authority to wage war in what Jackson calls the 'second heaven,' the first being the earthly realm, the third being where God resides to which we return when we die."

"The second heaven? I don't quite get it," Wally admitted, truly puzzled.

"It works like this: we can war against Satan and his demons as they affect people, but not against the devil's strongholds in the spiritual realm. That's why those Scriptures you summarized say we can cast out demons and heal the sick, because they are affecting people. When it says we can trample the demons in Luke 10:19, the analogy is earthly, that is trample on the ground as they affect us or other people. We have authority in the earthly realm over all the power of the enemy, but in the spiritual realm, Satan is still prince."

"But what about the 'principalities... powers... rulers of darkness... and spiritual hosts of wickedness in the heavenly places' that Ephesians 6:12 talks about?" Wally protested.

"Only as they affect people," Juanita reaffirmed. "When I went back to study that verse in greater detail, I also took a look at the verses immediately before and after it. We must always look at verses in context, not in isolation. That section starts off talking about the armor of God that we're supposed to wear. Why? Because it says we 'wrestle' against these principalities and powers. Wrestling is a personal act, hand to hand combat in the earthly realm."

Juanita could see that Wally was digesting this so she waited a few moments before she went on. "Then, after we have all our armor on, we're not told to go out and attack, but rather to just stand! That used to bother me a lot. I wanted to go out and take it to the enemy. But instead, we're called on to just stand. It uses that word, stand, three times in nine verses, so I think we need to pay attention to that."

"Another indication that those verses are referring to close-in combat is the Hebrew word for sword. It's not the word for the long sword we usually think of, but rather for their short sword, or dagger, that would only be used to stand and defend oneself," Juanita finished with a rush, and then sat back down.

Wally contemplated it all for awhile. "So we can only defend ourselves, not attack?"

"Yes, we *can* attack. Verse 17 says that, after we've put on the armor, we should not only stand, but pray always in the Spirit with supplication for the saints. You see, we don't have to go anywhere physically. Our prayers can touch people all over the world. We can combat the enemy in China, but only as it directly affects people, or people groups."

"Wow, that puts a whole different slant on things," Wally sighed. "It sure is a big help to me, and to all the people here, that you've had so much experience and studied this so closely. But I think I need a break before we continue."

Chapter Twenty-Nine

Another late night at work, more drinking back at the hotel, and then the obligatory midnight call to Patrick. Blaine didn't mind the work so much when it consisted of research and answering questions from the media, either on the phone, by email, instant messaging, Twitter or live at press conferences. What she did mind, was her boss, Alexis, and especially his sidekick René. She was still afraid of them, but now she also sensed there was something wrong with them.

"I don't know, Pat, but I think there's something fishy going on here," Blaine slurred.

"Oh, come one, honey. You're just overworked, over-stressed and homesick. You miss me, that's the main problem. Come on, admit it," Patrick cajoled, even as he examined himself in the mirror. He had a new junior partner tonight and she was a real looker.

"No, don't dismiss me like that," Blaine complained. "You're trivializing what I'm feeling."

Patrick stopped his self-examination. He was treading on dangerous ground. Too many landmines around. She could explode at any moment. But, then again, she's never sounded like this before. Beaten down. Not on top of things. Typically, if she didn't like how things were going, she'd get angry and then browbeat everyone around her, so what should he say now?

"Are you there?" Blaine prompted, knowing that Patrick often slipped off into his own self-centered world.

"Yes, honey, I'm still here. I was actually trying to think through your situation," Patrick explained. "On the one hand, I could say 'I told you so' about taking this job, but on the other hand, now that you're there, I'm truly surprised that you sound so beaten down. Normally you'd be in heavy-duty attack mode by now."

Blaine's emotions jumped in a number of directions. Instead of reacting to them, she just watched them go by. Perhaps that was the wine, or maybe Pat was right. She certainly wasn't herself. Where was the Blaine who was so driven for success that she'd run over anyone in her way? How was it that Alexis and René dominated her so easily?

Patrick had braced himself for Blaine's expected retort, but there was only silence. He'd purposely tried to push her buttons. That there was no response at all was actually quite worrisome.

Blaine hesitated to state how she really felt. She could barely acknowledge it to herself. She was at her wit's end. She had to get it out. "Pat, I think there's something really, really evil about Alexis and René. I even feel like there's an evil presence here in my hotel room. That's why I haven't been able to sleep at night."

Now that was a shocker to Patrick. Normally, he would be the one to bring up the supernatural, half in jest, but half open-minded about it all. Raised by atheists, his rebellion had been to dabble in New Age and Eastern religion. It had a certain appeal, but when his career took off he had no time for such pursuits, except to annoy Blaine with various metaphysical theories.

Patrick glanced at his watch. Still a little time before he had to break in the new chick. "I think that's just the wine talking, honey. When push comes to shove, I don't really believe there are evil forces in the world, no devil, no demons, no goblins and ghosts. Those are either figments of our imagination or attempts to explain what we don't understand."

Blaine was prepared for Patrick's disbelief. She'd known all along that's how he really felt. She'd also known that he liked to tweak her and stir things up. Truth be told, she too enjoyed the give and take, the banter, the charged atmosphere that got their juices flowing.

But now she was serious. She felt like a scared little girl, once again worrying about monsters under the bed. A brief vision of her drunken Dad climbing in bed with her to protect her from the monsters flashed by. She waited till it was gone and breathed again.

"I don't know how to explain it, Pat. You know more than anyone else how opposed I've been to believing there was anything beyond what we could see or touch. Logic and science are my gods. But there is something going on within me and around me that defies logic. I can sense it, even though it doesn't make sense."

Patrick jumped on her slight retreat. "You're right, you're not making sense. You know it. Maybe your hormones are out of balance? Maybe you're coming down with the flu? "

Blaine sighed. It was no use. She couldn't make sense of it, so how could she even begin to try and describe it? Maybe she was going crazy? That was the most likely scenario, now that she thought of it. She'd allowed Alexis and René to get into her head and now she was all twisted up like a pretzel.

She was barely cognizant of the remaining conversation and good-byes. It was actually a relief to get off the phone with Patrick. Yet another change. But he was never there for her when she needed him. Up till now, that hadn't been very often, so it wasn't that big a deal. They only clicked when she was on top of her game.

Maybe it was time to cut her ties with him? Find someone she could really talk to, who wouldn't turn tail at the slightest introspection. Somehow, that made her feel better. She finished up the bottle of wine, changed into her nightgown and turned off the light.

She was exceptionally tired. Surely she'd sleep well tonight. She drifted off quickly but awoke with a start about an hour later. *What was that? Someone is in the room!*

Blaine grabbed frantically for the light switch and finally fumbled it on. She blinked rapidly against the light, but couldn't see anyone. For the first time in her life, she wished she had a gun. She sat in bed and listened for awhile. All was quiet. She got up slowly and walked out of the bedroom into the living room area of her hotel suite, turning on the light with a switch near the door.

She looked around quickly. No one there. She went over to the little kitchen. Nope, no one. Just her jangled nerves. She started back for the bedroom when something out of place caught her eye. The book she'd been reading while waiting to call Patrick was on the floor. She'd left it on the coffee table right next to her briefcase. She was sure of it. But then again, maybe she did have too much wine.

She put the book back, left the living room light on, got back in bed and slept fitfully until another noise brought her awake with a jolt. This time she was absolutely certain she'd heard something. She ran out the bedroom door into the well-lit living room and stopped short. Now her briefcase was on the floor, its contents scattered haphazardly across the floor as if the briefcase had been flung.

Her nerves jangled furiously. She checked to make sure the front door was latched and bolted. It was. She checked around again, even looking inside cabinets and behind curtains. Definitely no one there. This was getting out of hand. Wine-induced imaginations? Hallucinations? No more sleep for poor Blaine Whitney.

Chapter Thirty

During the short break, Wally cleared his mind by turning on the news on the lounge television set. Idly he wondered how they were still getting TV reception. Since the nation had gone all digital a few years back, it couldn't be antennas, and he felt sure they didn't have cable out here in the middle of the woods. Then he remembered seeing the satellite dish in a remote clearing on top of an adjacent hill. Oh the wonders of technology. But how soon before the Universal ID System became established and cut off their clandestine TV and internet reception?

As though the newscaster was reading his mind, the screen displayed a rehash of CNN's coverage of the latest Blaine Whitney press conference. Wally had always detested the way beautiful women were thrust into the forefront of the news, many of whom could barely manage eighth-grade English. Blaine, though, had been a clear exception. Smart, witty, courageous. Her beauty had become an afterthought.

But now? Why had she signed on to become the Global Czar's mouthpiece? Wally understood that she was ignorant of D'Antoni's true colors, but it still hadn't made sense to him that she would trade objectivity for blatantly biased blather. Wally heard little of what she was saying in response to the many shouted questions about the initial problems with the new ID system, but was drawn to the harrowed, haunted face that had seemingly aged several years in just a few weeks.

Hmm. Perhaps she was getting a firsthand taste of the life-draining alignment with the forces of evil? Had she been a wicked person to begin with, she would have found such an association invigorating. Since that obviously wasn't the case, the inherent evil of the devil's minions was wearing her out as they sought to flush out any remaining goodness.

A quick switch on the screen to a major airplane disaster jolted Wally back into the present. With thoughts of somehow reaching out to Blaine playing in his mind, he wandered down to the small conference room to see if Juanita was back yet. In truth, she had never left, plunging instead into prayer about all the new plans being hatched out west and now here in the east as well. And, of course, about Brandon whom she hoped to see again real soon.

Wally opened the door, tiptoed inside, sat down and waited politely for a few moments until Juanita stopped pacing and mumbling. A deep sigh, then Juanita sat down, thoroughly drained. She always gave all of herself to the calling of prayer. If she didn't work out so assiduously physically, she'd never have been able to compete so hard spiritually.

Thoughts of Blaine Whitney still dominated his mind, so Wally asked, "Given that we war against the devil as he affects people, but not out in the spiritual realm, how would you pray for someone who was under severe demonic attack?"

Juanita cleared her mind of lingering personal concerns and focused on Wally. Clearly, something specific, someone in particular, was on his mind. Since he hadn't offered who, she wouldn't push him about it, but rather treat the question as a teachable moment. *Guide me, Holy Spirit. Show me what he needs to know, and then show us how to turn this into classroom material.*

A lot of Scripture came flooding into her mind, so she took another moment to sort it all out. Wally couldn't help but smile a bit watching her, understanding now what went on within this woman who had been so hard to figure out initially.

"Well, first off, I would pray protection over her," Juanita began. *Her? How did I know it was a her? Michelle? No, she was just here all charged up. Who then?*

Wally was taken aback. Did Juanita know who he was thinking of? Of course, the Holy Spirit knew, so perhaps she did.

"Psalm 91 is a great place to start," Juanita continued, "specifically verses three to thirteen. Surely He shall deliver her from the perilous pestilence... Under His wings she shall take refuge. His truth shall be her shield and buckler... A thousand may fall at her side, and ten thousand at her right hand, but it shall not come near her... No evil shall befall her, nor shall any plague come near her dwelling. For He shall give His angels charge over her... In her hands they shall bear her up... and she shall tread upon the lion and the cobra. We declare these truths over her, Father, in Jesus' glorious and mighty name."

As Juanita prayed, Wally kept speaking the name, Blaine Whitney, inside himself, all the while wondering why she was so heavy on his heart.

"Then, I would prayerfully encourage that person to 'Submit to God, resist the devil, and he will flee from you,'[57] while also declaring over her, 'No weapon formed against you shall prosper.'[58]

Wally decided he should tell Juanita who he was thinking about so they could agree about her in prayer, recalling Jesus' admonition that wherever two or three agree on anything on earth in His name, His Father in Heaven would bring it to pass.[59]

Juanita was quite surprised to find out who the subject of her prayers had been. But it wasn't anything new to her, praying for people she didn't know personally when the Holy Spirit laid it on her heart. Most times, you never knew why, you just prayed. Nor did you usually hear about the results. She remembered one time being awakened suddenly with the urge to pray for the Vice President in the early morning hours only to see on the morning news that he'd suffered a severe heart attack, but survived and was doing all right.

"So, what else would you pray for her without knowing specifically what's going on?" Wally asked.

"Well, first I would ask the Holy Spirit what to pray, and am doing so now," She responded, and closed her eyes for a few seconds. "Father, I pray in the name of Your precious Son, that you would help Blaine to 'cast off the works of darkness and put on the armor of light,'[60] and that it's 'not by might nor by power, but by My Spirit, says the Lord of hosts.'[61]

"Show her, Father, that it was 'for this purpose the Son of God was manifested, that He might destroy the works of the devil.'[62] Teach her that 'the thief does not come except to steal, and to kill, and to destroy, but that You have come that she might have life, and have it more abundantly;[63] that in this world, she will have tribulation, but to be of good cheer, because You have overcome the world."[64]

Yes, Father, in Jesus name, I agree with these prayers, Wally said silently, knowing that the Holy Spirit can read our minds, but not the devil or the demons.

"Thank You, Holy Spirit, for leading and guiding me in these prayers. Thank You Father, for Your Word, and the manifestation of the Word, Your Son and our Savior, Jesus Christ. We commit Blaine Whitney to You. Help her, Lord, teach her Father, save her Jesus. And reveal to her the truth of Your Word about those who she now works for: "And I saw the beast, the kings of the earth, and their armies, gathered together to make war against Him who sat on the horse and against His army. Then the beast was captured, and with him the false prophet... These two were cast alive into the lake of fire burning with brimstone. And the rest were killed with the sword which proceeded from the mouth of Him who sat on the horse.'"[65]

Juanita was once again pacing furiously in circles around the small conference table. "Yea, though Blaine walks through the valley of the shadow of death, she will fear no evil for You are with her. Your rod and Your staff, they comfort her. You prepare a table before her in the presence of her enemies.[66] And she will overcome them by the blood of the Lamb and by the word of her testimony, and she will not love her life unto the death.[67] Indeed, we declare according to Your Word that Blaine Whitney shall arise and shine, for Your light has come! And the glory of the Lord is risen upon her. Though gross darkness may cover the earth, and deep darkness may cover her, You will arise over her and Your glory will be seen upon her."[47]

Once again, Juanita collapsed into the chair, totally spent. Wally still had his eyes closed. He could feel his heart, his very spirit, still reaching out to Blaine. Though he had no further words, he felt that somehow the Holy Spirit was reaching out to Blaine through him all the way across the ocean. He kept the channel open until the feeling slowly dissipated and was finally gone.

When Wally opened his eyes, he saw Juanita watching him with tears in her own eyes. "I think the Holy Spirit has finished putting this course together for us," she said softly.

Chapter Thirty-One

When Brandon heard that Jim and Abby were going to start up CIA-East, he was ecstatic since it meant he could participate *and* be with his wife Juanita for the first time in a long time. Moreover, he thought Jim's name for it was hilarious. The former CIA director had dubbed the new efforts to resist the Universal Directives of the one-world government the "Counter Insurgency Agency."

Alan Morrison agreed to fund an eastern version of the complex he was creating on his ranch in Colorado. Jim and Abby spent a week at the ranch studying the setup and discussing how and where to establish a similar operation back east. Land acquisition would be the biggest problem. Although the three-month deadline to comply with the Universal ID System was still in the future, large-scale purchases already required government approval. Banks had to report any transaction over $10,000.

Morrison accompanied Jim, Abby and Brandon back east and immediately began contacting former Christian friends who he thought might possibly own some large tracts of land. He was discouraged at first by how many of them were simply capitulating to the "new ways," as one former friend said. Although he didn't tell them of his specific plans, most of his friends were aghast to even speculate about resisting the one-world government.

Biblical arguments fell on deaf ears. Warnings against accepting the "mark of the beast" were either laughed at or sneered at. Morrison couldn't understand how believers could pick and choose which parts of the Bible to follow. The discouraged financier and erstwhile leader of the counter-insurgency met with Jermaine to discuss the possibility of using the remote camp in the Blue Ridge Mountains, but fairly quickly discarded that option because of the difficult terrain and the danger to the now three-thousand people hidden away in the mountainside retreat.

Juanita called everyone together for a prayer session. "If this concept is of the Lord, and I believe it is," she began, "then I believe that He will open the door for it to happen in His perfect timing. But we have to have our eyes and ears ready to recognize the door when it opens, because it may not happen the way we expect."

Following the intense prayer meeting, Morrison spent some time getting to know the leaders of the hideaway that he'd funded, but never visited before. Pastor Gabriel and Jermaine had been his only personal contacts till the "westward ho" group arrived at his ranch. Morrison was a doer, so the waiting was difficult. He kept in touch with CIA-West daily, receiving updates from Jesse and Fran about the construction of the underground counter-insurgency headquarters and computer center.

Morrison also spoke with General Wycliffe about the ongoing recruitment and training of the enlarged militia group, although getting details from the tight-lipped leader was like pulling teeth. However, it did seem that things were running smoothly, albeit expensively. Fortunately, Morrison had caches of cash that the government knew nothing about, and he was determined to use every bit of it fighting against the devil's plans.

As it often happens with the Lord, a door opened before anyone knew what was happening. Tara's evangelism team rushed back into the hideaway all excited with an elderly gentleman in tow. "Hey, everyone, I want you to meet Mr. Avery Jackson. Not only did he rededicate himself to the Lord today, but he says he wants to come and live with us and will turn over his entire bank account to us!"

Jermaine rang the bell that he'd hung near the entryway to welcome new members into the Kingdom and everyone cheered. No one thought much about Mr. Jackson's bank account because he was a disheveled man in dirty clothes. His gray, kinky hair was long and unkempt, and his albino eyes peered out from beneath bushy white eyebrows, accented by pasty, reddish-brown skin. He was most certainly an unusual looking man.

It turned out that he was as eccentric as his appearance suggested, but in a delightfully funny way. He soon had everyone laughing and feeling good. There really wasn't any room for another hideaway resident, but Mr. Jackson didn't want to go out to the remote camp, saying that "them there mountain alligators are just hankering for a taste of albino hide."

Several groups said they didn't mind having him as a fifth person in their small, four-person room. They drew straws to see who would get to have this peculiar, enchanting man as their new roommate. Jermaine pulled a spare cot out of storage along with a small bureau and squeezed it into the tight living quarters of Ryan O'Donnell who was busy regaling the older gentleman with his own tall tales.

The following day, Mr. Jackson asked if they could go to his bank and retrieve his "fortune" so that he could give it to the Lord. Jermaine and Ryan got one of the dilapidated but functional vehicles from the hidden section of the half-collapsed old barn, and drove Mr. Jackson back to Fredericksburg on Route 1. It was slower than taking I-95, but there were reports of random inspections along the interstate as the government tightened its grip on the whereabouts of its citizens.

Mr. Jackson kept them laughing the whole way, pointing them onto a residential street off Germana Highway, also known as Plank Road. They took the street all the way to the end, while Jermaine and Ryan scoured the area for a bank. It seemed quite unlikely that it would be off the beaten track amongst the upscale dwellings. Jermaine had already decided that they were on a fool's errand, but didn't want to upset Mr. Jackson, so he turned onto Altoona Drive as directed, and drove to the end of the street where it abutted open, wooded land.

As Jermaine and Ryan shook their heads in disbelief, the elderly man bolted from the front passenger seat and headed confidently toward and then down a ridge, waving for the two skeptics to follow. More to protect Jackson from the environment and himself, they hurried after him, amazed at how agile the old coot was. When they caught up to him in a small hollow, he was pulling a shovel out from under some thick bushes.

"Let me handle that for you," Jermaine offered.

Mr. Jackson handed him the shovel and then scooted off further down the swale. He rooted around some other bushes for awhile and then stepped back with a big grin on his face. "Here she be, fellas. Dig her up and give her some air," Mr. Jackson said with a twinkle in his eye.

Jermaine shrugged at Ryan, suppressed a smile, and began to dig at the designated spot. He thought he'd go about a foot deep and then express his condolences to Mr. Jackson that someone must have taken his treasure. Just before he was about to stop digging, the shovel clanked against metal. Jermaine cleared away some more dirt with the shovel, and then he and Ryan began clawing at the loose ground with their bare hands.

Jermaine lifted a small metal box out of the hole and gave Mr. Jackson a quizzical look of surprise. What in the world did the old geezer have in the box? It was latched, but not locked so Jermaine pulled it open and saw a pile of greenbacks.

"That's my bank, yessirree, snug as a bug in a rug," Jackson hooted and danced a little jig.

Jermaine flipped through the large denomination bills and quickly estimated that there was over one-hundred thousand dollars. *Will wonders ever cease!*

"The best treasure is always on the bottom," Jackson crooned in a hauntingly beautiful voice.

Jermaine reached under the money and found an old, yellowed document. Opening it carefully, he read with a gaping mouth that it was the deed to a 5,000 acre plot of land in the Shenandoah Valley.

Chapter Thirty-Two

A fter the standoff with Alexis and René, Abraham, Gabriel and Aadi returned to the King David Hotel on foot, a time of therapeutic unwinding. Abraham silently thanked the Lord that Tezla was home with Him now, and no longer in the spiteful hands of the Global Czar. There was little conversation until they were settled back in their suite with a room service lunch ordered and on its way.

It was hard to stop Aadi from waiting on them as a servant. "Aadi, please, we are not royalty, nor are we your masters. The Bible says to worship only God, not angels and certainly not men," Abraham finally had to tell him sternly.

"As you wish, kind sir. But what is it that you have for me to do or be?" Aadi was genuinely puzzled.

"Our only desire is that you become what God planned for you to be from before you were even a seed in your mother's womb,"[68] Abraham said. "And you can drop the 'kind sir' business, too, okay? Call us by our first names."

"Oh, okay…. Abraham. But how could God have known what was to become of me before I was born?"

"Because He's the Creator of all things! The only reason that things don't turn out as He planned is because of our own hardheadedness. We're stubborn, don't listen and usually fail to obey." Abraham explained.

"So, how do I find out His plan for me?" Aadi asked, plaintively seeking his place in this strange new world.

"We pray and ask Him," Gabriel interjected. "So let's do so now. We too need to find out what to do next."

So they did until they were interrupted by the room service waiter. As they sat at the table, Abraham gave thanks for the food and then gave Gabriel a quizzical look. They were getting used to receiving the same messages and images.

"What did you see my friend?" Abraham asked when he observed the deep frown creasing Gabriel's face.

"Too much," Gabriel finally answered with a sigh. "I saw that we were witnessing to large groups of poor people all around the earth. That was the good part. Then I saw much violence directed at these ethnic groups."

Abraham nodded. He too had seen similar images.

"What about me?" Aadi asked as he closely examined the insides of his hamburger.

"Didn't you hear or see anything?" Gabriel asked in return, holding back a smile as he watched Aadi sniffing at the meat.

"Yes, but I think it must be my own imagination, because surely I could never be so learned as to give speeches to large crowds of people." Aadi carefully extracted the lettuce, tomato, cheese and pickle, and then set the bun and burger off to the side.

Abraham and Gabriel exchanged glances again, and nodded in agreement.

"Well, Aadi, God actually tends to choose the most unlikely people, like Abraham and me, to do his work because He likes to use the foolish things of the world to confound the wise.[4] That way He gets all the credit, not us. At any rate, Abraham and I also saw that you will be preaching to the poor as well, so that means you're to become our apprentice."

"Apprentice?"

162

"Yes, it means we will teach you and train you to be a preacher for the Lord God Almighty," Gabriel said, and then laughed as he watched incredulity spread across Aadi's always expressive countenance.

"Such a thing is too marvelous to even contemplate," he finally gasped and looked down humbly at his food.

"Are you a vegetarian or do your beliefs prohibit you from eating beef?" Abraham inquired gently, wanting to get Aadi's mind off the grandiose plans the Lord had for him.

"Yes, a vegetarian is what I am," Aadi pronounced proudly, grasping at something solid to define himself.

"Can I order you something else, then?" Abraham asked.

"You order for me? Your world is upside down and hard to grasp," Aadi sighed.

They began training him immediately. Aadi proved to be an apt and eager student. More importantly, he seemed to be a gifted orator, surprising even himself. Gabriel explained that spiritual gifts are like that, sometimes lying dormant until just the right time.

Gabriel longed to contact Carmelita, but didn't want to do anything that might compromise the hideaway and her safety. He was certain Alexis was holding Sir William's hand to the fire to encourage him to find Carmelita, so he contented himself to daydream about her and pray for her.

It wasn't too long before Abraham and Gabriel both felt a strong unction to take Aadi back to Indonesia and begin to minister. Both were feeling somewhat stir crazy in the hotel, so they took an extra day of prayer to be certain it was God's plan and not their own restlessness fueling the fires.

When they felt certain it was the Holy Spirit leading them to go, they asked Aadi to turn the tables and teach them about Indonesia. At first, he was reluctant and embarrassed, but he gradually warmed to the task when it became apparent that Abraham and Gabriel were quite serious about learning all they could about the first country they would go to for ministry.

Although Aadi had grown up in a lower-class family of fishermen, he had studied hard in school and earned a scholarship to a small university where he majored in history. It was his high grades and linguistic capabilities that propelled him to become a translator, which led to an assignment with Alexis who immediately took Aadi under his wing.

Indonesia, Aadi explained, is perhaps the most diverse and complicated nation on the face of the earth. There are around 300 ethnic groups, 742 different languages and dialects among the 250 million people living on the 17,508 islands that comprise the transcontinental country. Once diverse in religion as well, Islam was now the declared religion of over 86% of the population, making it the world's most populous Muslim nation.

Aadi had been a Hindu before his recent encounter with Jesus. His family came from Bali, east of Java, the predominant Indonesian island. On Bali, over 90% still followed a blend of Shivaite Hinduism and their own animist traditions. Animism is one of the most primitive religions, believing that everything has a "soul," called an "anima" in Latin, including animals, plants, rocks, mountains, rivers, stars. Each "anima" is a powerful spirit that can help or hurt them, including the souls of the dead, the "ancestors."

For thousands of years they deified animals, stars, idols of any kind, and practiced witchcraft, divination, and astrology. They used magic, spells, enchantments, superstitions, prayers, amulets, talismans, and charms in their worship ceremonies and within the home. *No wonder Aadi was so demonized,* Gabriel realized.

Soon, the trio was on their way to Bali, each wondering what lay in store for them. Gabriel was concerned about the violence he had seen in his visions, not so much for himself and Abraham, since they were under God's prophetic wings, but for Aadi and his people.

Chapter Thirty-Three

Blaine Whitney's world had turned completely upside down. From an abrasive, overconfident, strong-willed, free-spirited woman of the world, she had become a fearful, overwrought, stressed-out recluse. Although she was still able to put on an act for her Global Governance bosses, the media and her viewers, she otherwise hid out in her hotel suite, ate room service food and slept with the lights on and a pistol under her pillow.

But in the midst of the darkness and confusion, she had seen a light of hope. The avowed agnostic, who shunned all things spiritual and believed only what her own senses or scientists could confirm, had experienced a glimpse into another world. After yet another tormented night of fitful sleep, with things literally going bump in the night, she had undertaken some internet research.

Poltergeists! She had poltergeists!! Or so the various websites said. Still the skeptic, she had to be sure. So, she made an inventory and took digital pictures of the positions of all her things. "If you damn poltergeists are for real, I challenge you to come and do your thing tonight," she called out and curled up in bed with her hand on the handle of the gun. She realized a bullet meant nothing to a ghost, but it made her feel better.

Sleep was a long time coming, but finally around two a.m. her heavy eyelids closed. About half-an-hour later, several loud bumps shocked her immediately awake. She pointed the pistol at the open bedroom doorway. And blinked several times to determine for sure that the lights were indeed going on and off in the living room. As she rose cautiously from the bed, the bedroom light switch shut off.

Blaine screamed and ran out into the living room in time to see two kitchen cabinet doors swing open and shut several times, each bang sending chilling tremors up her spine. "Okay, stop! I believe you're real, so enough with all the theatrics," she cried out.

Suddenly, everything became still and quiet. She walked around and saw that one lamp had been pushed off the table next to the couch, a book lay on the floor, and a pot had been knocked off the stove.

Blaine's mind was in turmoil, her emotions on the edge of a dark precipice. She couldn't deny what she'd seen, but it was still hard to accept. Firing up her laptop, she plunged back into cyberspace to learn what she could about ghosts and poltergeists. As her mind engaged in doing what she did best, her emotions began to calm down.

There seemed to be several different camps of opinion that she organized into three groups. The first were the Satanists and witches who actually sought connection with these dark spirits; the second were the New Agers who embraced angels and saw all things spiritual as good and beneficial; the third group were the religious types with their cautions and warnings about not consorting with demons and unclean spirits.

She certainly didn't want to get into witchcraft and sorcery; that seemed too weird and felt downright scary. The New Age blather felt good, sounded nice, but did she want to make friends with a poltergeist? She was too angry with it to consider such a prospect. She could, of course, simply ask for a new room or even switch hotels. However, was the spirit attached to her or the room? According to some websites, it could be either.

The religious stuff was all over the place. Some said spirits and ghosts were nonsense and nonexistent. Others said they were real, but have nothing to do with them. A smaller group said that Jesus gave us power over them. The very name Jesus gave her the willies. Her limited Catholic upbringing left her with the impression that He was always looking over your shoulder waiting for you to make a mistake, then wham! Guilt and shame, presumably cured by some Hail Mary's. Thanks, but no thanks.

So, no immediate solution, but she felt less crazy knowing there were so many people who apparently had experienced similar phenomenon. Blaine made herself a cup of Earl Grey tea and contemplated awhile. Since no one said these poltergeists were dangerous, perhaps she'd take a middle approach and not exactly befriend it, but at least tolerate it and not be afraid. Maybe when it saw she wasn't fazed by it any longer, it would simply go away and find someone else to haunt.

Though she was quite tired, she actually felt lots better mentally and emotionally, so she showered and dressed, ate a quick breakfast and went off to work early. When she returned that evening, a couple of books were scattered around and the hall light was on. She laughed. "Oh you silly poltergeist."

After eating her take-home Chinese food, she read for awhile, got sleepy early, went to bed and slept soundly until a loud crash startled her awake. This time it was the bedroom lamp that had been pushed off the nightstand, the ceramic base shattering into many pieces. She was angry, but held her tongue. After cleaning up the mess, she was wide awake. Since it was closing in on two a.m., she'd only have to wait a little while until she could call Patrick after his nightly newscast.

However, she wasn't sure she wanted to talk with him. Their last conversation had been unpleasant and uncomfortable. Here she'd thought he was the one open to spiritual things, but when push came to shove, he was just a poser. Plus she'd glimpsed more of his self-absorption. Usually, he was the one with the problems that needed sorting out and loved her attentiveness to his needs. But when the shoe was on the other foot, well, he just wasn't there for her.

While she waited, she logged on to the internet and, with the special ID and password Patrick had given her, brought up the live stream of his broadcast. Her mouth popped wide open when she saw his new partner, a blond bombshell who bore a close resemblance to Blaine. However, although she was quite well-spoken, she was not assertive like Blaine, but rather fawned over Patrick who positively glowed from the attention.

She quickly logged off, sat back on the couch and closed her eyes. What was it about her and men that never seemed to work out? First her father, then Ray, then…. Her father? Blaine's nerves fluttered. Images rushed into her mind. She tried to shut off the flood as she always did, but for some reason, this time they kept on coming. She began to sob convulsively as the bitter truth sank into her consciousness for the very first time.

Chapter Thirty-Four

Jermaine, Morrison, Jim and Abby pored over maps they'd printed off the Internet of the Shenandoah Valley. Off to the side on the large conference room table was a report from the assessor's office that confirmed Mr. Avery Jackson as the sole owner of the 5,000 acre tract of land in a remote southwestern corner of Rockingham County, Virginia.

Using the GPS coordinates on the report, they had now pinpointed the area and saw from the Google Earth maps that it was isolated, difficult to reach, with no other facilities in the area. The fact that it was not much further southwest from their remote camp in the Blue Ridge Mountains made this tract almost too good to be true.

"I can't believe that this perfect location for our eastern Counter-Insurgency Agency was buried like treasure in a metal box by that old coot, Jackson," Morrison said as he shook his head in disbelief. "There's gotta be a catch to this. It's in the middle of Federal land, for goodness sake!"

"Yes, but this report indicates it's been 'grandfathered' since it was in the possession of the Jackson family for many generations," Abby pointed out.

Morrison simply sighed. He was a pragmatic man who didn't like things that couldn't be explained. "And you mean to tell me it's just a coincidence that this man shows up just at the time we're looking for just this kind of land? What if it's a trap by the Feds to lure us out into the open?"

Juanita laughed. "What is it about Jehovah Jireh you can't comprehend? This is just what we prayed for. He owns the cattle on a thousand hills.[69] The whole earth is His footstool.[70] Nothing is too difficult for Him.[71] So let's just be grateful and get on with it!"

Jermaine nodded in agreement. "This is the time when God is going to do great things to help His children cope with the gross darkness that covers the earth. As the darkness grows, so will His light shine all the brighter, and it's shining on this little corner of the earth, so let's follow His lead."[47]

"Okay, I guess I'll stop second-guessing things," Morrison agreed. "I guess it's like the manna that miraculously fed the Israelites in the desert,[72] and the water that came out of the rock.[24] Still, it's hard to believe."

"Well, let's get Jackson in here so he can tell us a little more about this land and what's the best way to get there," the ever-practical Abby suggested. Jim set off to retrieve him.

Jim looked in the central, common areas of the hideaway, and then knocked on his bedroom door. Ryan answered and said he hadn't seen him in awhile. They both then probed every corner of the hideaway, but no sign of Jackson.

"Did he leave?" Ryan wondered.

"Let's check with the external guard," Jim suggested, and they rushed outside. Dmitri adamantly claimed that no one had come out the entrance all morning.

Jim returned to the meeting greatly puzzled. The group sat in quiet contemplation until Juanita suddenly exclaimed, "He must be an angel. The Bible says that sometimes we'll entertain angels without knowing it."[73]

Everyone's eyes widened in astonishment. Could it be true? Had God answered their prayers through an angel? The circumstances and Jackson himself were certainly enough out of the ordinary to see the possibility.

"I wonder if we would have received the land had Tara not witnessed to him?" Abby wondered aloud. "And, if we hadn't welcomed him into our midst, we might have lost out on this wonderful gift!"

That was a sobering thought. Each began to think over their lives where perhaps they had not responded in the right way to one of God's messengers. How might life have been different then?

"Well, maybe he'll simply turn up somewhere," the skeptical Morrison said, "but let's get going and see this place before we get too far ahead of ourselves."

Morrison borrowed the helicopter from the eastern office of his Internet business in Arlington and flew the group out to the property. As they perused the landscape from above, it was apparent that this was a perfect location, almost too perfect.

Heavily wooded, mountainous terrain had just enough flat areas off the beaten track to land small aircraft, build underground facilities, and bivouac a large militia. Morrison pointed out where they could build a ranch house, barns and other structures that would give the appearance of a working operation.

"In fact, it will be functional. We'll hire some solid Christians to run the place just like it was a ranch," Morrison declared as he set the chopper down on a ridge overlooking a valley below.

They could see a rough, unmaintained dirt road that led to the valley from the west, with another even rougher track that meandered off into the hills to the north. As Jim scanned the opposite ridge with his binoculars, a hint of movement caught his eye. He focused in and, to his amazement, there was Mr. Avery Jackson waving to them.

171

"Look!" Jim called out, pointing at the ridge and handing the binoculars to Abby.

"Oh wow! It's him," she confirmed.

"How did he get here?" Morrison wondered, scratching his head, his brow creased in wonder.

"The way all angels do, I guess," Jermaine said as he waved toward Jackson.

"Wow, he just disappeared," Abby said incredulously, scanning the ridge line with the binoculars. "Right before my eyes. He was there one second, then poof, gone."

Chapter Thirty-Five

Blaine Whitney was as miserable as she'd ever been. Her spirit had been broken. By Alexis and René, by Patrick, by the damn poltergeists, but mostly by her father. Now that the memory dam had burst open, there was nothing left of her. She realized that her whole life, her very personality, had been driven by an unconscious need to rise above the guilt and shame she'd always felt, but never understood.

Where to turn to now? Certainly not Patrick. She shuddered at the thought, realizing he looked somewhat like her father. She had no other friends. No one to confide in. No one to seek comfort from. She was all alone with her demons and poltergeists, her only companions.

Blaine chuckled ruefully, poured more wine and continued her pity party. Something was clawing at the back of her mind, trying to get out. With her defenses down, she couldn't hold it back. Instead, she sighed and let it spill out. A jolt of surprise caused her to bolt upright on the couch, knocking over the wine glass. Fortunately, it only held a few loose drops that she wiped up with one of the many tear-stained tissues piled off to the side.

Now where did that thought come from? Bible.com? Why would she think of that? Had she seen it on her previous Internet search? She didn't think so, but the urge to check it out was almost overwhelming.

She shrugged her shoulders, grabbed her laptop, fired it up and pointed her browser to www.bible.com. With not a little trepidation, she steeled herself for all the "thou shalt nots" that Christians always hit you over the head with. Instead, the home page seemed to reach out and grab her. As she followed the various links, there was talk of a Jesus who loved everyone and forgave mistakes out of compassion. A Holy Spirit who was a comforter and helper. A Father who wished that no one would be sent to hell, but that all would be saved through His Son.

Normally, even that message would have fallen on deaf ears, or would have sent her into a fit of rage. Whether it was the terrifying circumstances, lack of sleep or something else, she didn't know, but she felt an urge to contact them. They were located in Arizona. It would be late afternoon there. With trembling fingers, she called and was able to explain her predicament. They gave her the name of a contact right in Jerusalem, and then prayed with her for quite some time. She felt lots better afterward.

Since it was now nearly five a.m., she ordered breakfast, called in sick, and waited till nine to call a Rev. Boris Wainwright. His secretary answered, said the minister was in a counseling session and would call back in an hour. Blaine fidgeted nervously, second-guessing herself, chiding herself for getting involved in such foolishness. She picked up the phone several times to say never mind, but hung up each time. She felt as though something was drawing her in this direction, something good, not malevolent like this annoying poltergeist.

When the hotel phone rang, it startled her and she knocked it off the side table, then scurried to pick it up and apologize for her ineptness. The deep, calm, reassuring voice on the other end put her immediately at ease. She explained the situation in her best journalistic manner, sticking to the facts, giving a false name.

Rev. Wainwright chuckled kindly on the other end. "Only a poltergeist? Most of my clients should be so fortunate. I know they can be quite irritating, but they are really nothing more than a nuisance."

The warm, confident voice soothed her. She wanted to, needed to, meet with this man, to tell him her troubles and cry on his shoulder. But maybe that was inappropriate with a reverend? After all, the priests were all so stiff and formal.

"Are you still there, my child?" the kindly voice inquired.

"Oh, yes, sorry, I was just... thinking."

"Ahh, yes, thinking is good sometimes. Other times not. I find that if I do it too much, my head hurts."

Blaine laughed for the first time in a long time. "I'd like to talk with you about my situation. Do I come to you or do you come to me?"

"Well, unless you intend to bring your guests with you, perhaps I should come there and tell them where to go," Rev. Wainwright suggested with another good-natured chuckle. He agreed to stop by that afternoon.

She wished he could come right away, but of course he must be a busy man, so the afternoon would have to do. As she cleaned up, she found herself humming. She was quite surprised to find that she was feeling somewhat optimistic. It made no sense at all to her logical, dominant left brain, but her instinctive, creative right brain was lapping it up.

Blaine paused to think about it. She could already feel a difference in her mental processes. Cold hard facts were not sufficient any longer. There was a broader mosaic within which to evaluate these facts. She couldn't quite put her finger on it or define it, but somehow it felt right.

What had opened this once closed portion of her mind? Was it simply that she'd taken down the dam that had been holding back conscious recognition of her abusive father? Or was something more going on? Again, the facts weren't enough, so she shrugged and let it go. Even that was a change from the tigress who never let anything go.

The rest of the morning passed pleasantly enough considering all the circumstances. She caught up on the news and cleaned out her backlogged email account. When the knock on the hotel door finally came, she was pleased to see that her nerves had calmed down enough to keep her from jolting once again.

When Rev. Wainwright was seated and sipping iced tea, he gazed upon the expectant Blaine a few moments. As a topnotch interviewer, Blaine knew that look. The minister was debating something within himself, so she held back her eagerness and tried to sit still.

Her journalistic mind studied the man's appearance. He was older, but not elderly. A bit plump, but not fat. A jolly face with a grey-flecked beard. Something like Santa Claus if the Christmas icon lost some weight. Although his façade was encased in humor, there was a seriousness and intelligence below the surface that gave Blaine confidence in him. She found herself wishing she'd had a father like this man.

Finally, she could see the shift in Rev. Wainwright's eyes. "I believe honesty is the best policy," Wainwright began. "So I think you should know that I recognize you. However, I am not one of those who gets star struck, nor do I hold it against you."

The twinkle in the minister's eyes was more important to Blaine than his words. She simply nodded an acknowledgement and waited for him to continue.

"I suspect there is more at play here than the parlor tricks of your pesky guests," Wainwright continued. "So, I'd like for you to tell me what's really going on in your life. You see, the devil needs some open doors through which to afflict us. Sometimes it's a result of the things we've done. Sometimes it's what others have done to us that leaves us open to attack."

Blaine had not planned to talk about her father. She'd barely had time to acknowledge the frightful memories herself. But it seemed that the reverend had picked up on it somehow. A sign? Well, she'd leave it for last and see how she felt then. So, after gathering her thoughts, she began a surprisingly concise, well-organized synopsis of her life.

Rev. Wainwright watched and listened carefully. More importantly, he kept himself in a prayerful attitude, ready to hear what the Holy Spirit had to say.

When Blaine finished her life summary, leaving out the childhood torments, she sat still, hands folded in her lap, sad eyes cast downward.

"What about your childhood, Ms. Whitney. I sense something dark and evil there," Wainwright said, his eyes revealing a great depth of empathy and compassion.

So Blaine took a deep breath, continued to stare down at her hands, and slowly touched ever so lightly on the dreaded nightmare that had turned out to be real.

Rev. Wainwright held up his beefy hand. "That's enough, dear. I get the picture. You don't need to relive all the trauma."

He sighed, gazed off into the distance, a tiny tear trickling down his cheek. Then he turned back to look at Blaine with tender, loving eyes. "That's a lot for anyone to deal with, especially a young child. With the Lord's guidance, I can help you with all your problems, if you'll allow me to do so. But for now, let's get rid of these pests."

Blaine simply nodded. She was too far gone emotionally to respond.

"First I need to give you a little background so you'll understand what I'm going to do," Rev. Wainwright said as he sat forward in his chair, rubbing his hands together in anticipation.

"Poltergeists are nothing more than demons, fallen angels, low-level ones at that.[74] They are specifically trained

177

to harass us with silly tricks. They cannot harm us. The intent is to scare people, which opens the door to spirits of fear, higher-level demons that have also been tormenting you."

Blaine again just nodded. Though it appeared as if she might not be listening, her well-trained left brain was recording and processing the information.

"All angels, fallen or otherwise, are under the jurisdiction of Jesus Christ, the Son of God."[75] Wainwright waited to see how Blaine would receive that statement. She flinched, but didn't say anything.

"I know that you are not a believer, Ms. Whitney. For now, that's not necessary. In Jesus' name, I have the authority to rid you of these poltergeists and to ensure that they do not return. The only thing I need you to do is declare out loud that you do not want these things bothering you any more."

Blaine looked up at the minister with red-rimmed, hollow eyes. In a soft whisper, she said, "I most definitely don't want these poltergeists bothering me anymore, ever again."

"Good. Now, in the mighty name of Jesus Christ, I command all you poltergeists to leave and never return. I also command all spirits of fear to leave as well."

Rev. Wainwright rose, took out a bottle of anointing oil, and walked over to the front door. With his index finger, he dabbed anointing oil on the door posts and lintels. "Just as the children of Israel were saved from the angel of death with the blood of the lamb,[76] I anoint this door with the oil of the Holy Spirit and the blood of Jesus Christ, the Lamb of God, and declare that demons, you may not cross the blood-line into this room anymore."

He then proceeded to similarly anoint the walls and windows. When he was done, he sat down again across from Blaine and looked upon her as though she were a wounded bird. Blaine felt the love pouring out upon her, which overrode all the questions and doubts about the strange rituals he just performed.

Rev. Wainwright stood to go, but Blaine saw pain in his eyes. She didn't know about the daughter he'd lost to a pedophile at the tender age of seven, nor the son who'd died in a car crash just after he turned eighteen. His only children. The source of his pain, the catalyst for his salvation and ministry.

"You will not be harassed any more by those poltergeists, but the spirits of fear will not give up so long as those doors remain open within you. After you've had a chance to digest all this, if you'd like to get rid of all your baggage, I would be delighted if you'd call me again."

Blaine had much she wanted to say, questions that needed answers, but her mind couldn't get her mouth in gear, so she simply mumbled "Thank you," and watched as the minister let himself out.

She sighed and looked around. Everything looked the same except for those spots of oil. She noticed that some had been made in the shape of a cross. There was a sense of peace that hadn't been in this hotel suite since she'd arrived. Blaine breathed it in and hoped it would last through the night.

Chapter Thirty-Six

As time inexorably marched on toward the deadline for receiving the RFID chips in order to buy or sell anything, anywhere, at any time, construction on CIA-West was completed. Francine had the computer center up and running well in advance, and had hacked her way into the Universal ID Banking System. She'd seen how to circumvent the ID checking software with a subtle but effective ploy.

After the scan of the hand or forehead was made, the coded information was sent wirelessly to the nearest of thousands of servers scattered across the globe. Six massive satellites had been launched into orbit to handle all the billions of daily transactions. Fran's first thought had been to manipulate the data stream when it was first received by the servers, but after playing around with that awhile she realized it would be better to intercept the data on the satellite before it was beamed to the central mainframe in Brussels.

There were only two satellites serving the North American Union, so the western and eastern CIA units would interact separately with the nearest satellite. Then, when null (i.e. blank) data was received by the satellite, indicating the absence of an RFID chip, she reprogrammed the outbound transmission to resend the data for randomly selected RFIDs from legitimate purchasers from the prior day. The transactions would then be credited to that person's account.

She then realized that the possibility existed of randomly selecting a tapped out account, and the transaction would "bounce" like the old-fashioned overdrawn check. So, in the trillionth of a second required, she had the satellite check the random account first, switching to another viable account if the first one was no good. Then, the day before the deadline, she finished the cleanup work on the servers, erasing the spurious satellite transmissions and all evidence of her intrusion on the servers.

When she told Morrison about her plan, she admitted to feeling a little guilty about tapping into other people's accounts. "It's like stealing, isn't it?"

Morrison thought about it a moment and then a big grin spread across his face. "A Bible verse came to mind: *the wealth of the sinner is stored up for the righteous.*[77] Anyone who goes along with the 'mark of the beast, is complicit with wickedness, so I think this principle holds, especially in these end-days where many will be killed for refusing to accept the RFID chips," he said.

That made Fran feel better about it, so she asked for volunteers to be the first persons to try out her scheme to circumvent the enemy's system. Many hemmed and hawed but no one volunteered, so Fran herself marched confidently out of the underground computer center, borrowed Jerome's Land Rover and set off for Denver. When Morrison found out she'd gone, he was furious and worried that his computer genius would be hoisted on her own petard.

Rather than make some innocuous little purchase, Fran decided to stock up on a whole list of things she thought the underground community needed. Clearly, the men had initially stocked the place So Fran went to a grocery store for kitchen staples like flour, oil, spices and powdered milk. When she'd filled her shopping cart with other supplies, she boldly presented herself at the checkout counter, held out her wrist that had been pierced as though a chip had been inserted, and casually glanced around at the other checkout lines.

This was the first day that every consumer had to comply. While the ID system had been operational for a month or so, only the early recipients of the "mark of the beast" had tried out the system. Early crashes and wrinkles had pretty much been worked out. Now, many nervous "first-timers" were fidgeting in line, but Fran looked as though she didn't have a care in the world.

"You're good to go," the checkout lady said and began to scan her purchases. There was quite a celebration when she returned as the triumphant heroine. A huge underground party was joined by all the hideaways, remote camps and the few people out at CIA-East. That facility was only partially built, but the pace was fast and furious, building on the lessons learned on the western campus.

Jim and Abby were staying in the first completed underground section. Brandon commuted weekly from the hideaway, staying with Juanita on the weekends. It took a little while for the two of them to reconnect. So much had happened, and in many ways, Brandon was a different person. He was stronger, bolder, and more outspoken than before his capture, incarceration, escape, attack on the detention center, and leading the Harrisons to safety.

Juanita was used to being the boss, the talkative one, the spiritual leader. Brandon bristled now under those same conditions. As he asserted himself, Juanita grew distant. In a way, it was a blessing that he was away during the week. On the weekends, they met with Pastor Wally for counseling. Gradually, they were able to strike the right, Godly balance built on a foundation of love and trust (which Wally asked permission from them to discuss in detail in the book he was developing entitled, *The End of Bondage*.)

Jim and Abby had gone through a similar transition, successfully navigated with Pastor Wally's help and the Lord's love and compassion. Now they stood as role models for Brandon and Juanita. During the week, Brandon would discuss his frustrations with them. They were able to show him how childhood patterns had created strongholds in his mind. Some of those had come down along the way on his adventures; others were causing friction with Juanita.

They prayed with him that those mindsets which were built on ungodly foundations would be torn down and every one of his thoughts would become captive and obedient to Jesus Christ.[78] When those strongholds came crashing down, so did Brandon. He thought he was having a nervous breakdown, but with the love and patience of those around him, he was able to climb to a higher psychological and spiritual plateau.

The key strongholds turned out to be bitterness and resentment. His mother had been a lot like Juanita. When his father left the family behind, she had become an iron-willed sergeant. Looking back, he could see how that was necessary with three sassy boys to raise. While Brandon always loved and respected his mother, he'd chafed under her heavy hand in his teenage years.

That learned behavior (passive aggression, Pastor Wally called it) had continued in his relationship with the wife he loved and adored. He'd hold back, allow her to fill the vacuum, then resent her for doing so. However, he sublimated it so that it would come out in different ways, such as forgetting her birthday, working late when he didn't have to, going out with the guys a little too often.

The "root of bitterness" he learned was a particularly nasty beast that eventually consumed the carrier as well as those around him.[79] Brandon came to realize that only Juanita's strong relationship with the Lord had enabled her to overlook and overcome the resentment and bitterness that

Brandon didn't even know he had. Such strongholds become havens for demons as well, so it was a double-whammy. He'd been undermined by his own "stinkin' thinkin," with the little devils fanning the flames of discontent.

By the time CIA-East was up and running, so were Brandon and Juanita, with a new, stronger relationship. The only issue that remained was where would they set up permanent residence, at the hideaway or in the new CIA facilities? They both agreed with Pastor Wally that they'd let the Lord decide, since He knew the future and, therefore, what would work out best.

After much prayer and meditation, Brandon felt he'd had an idea that he thought was from the Lord, but he wasn't sure, since he was not used to operating in the spiritual realm. "I feel that I need to stay full time at CIA-East to help Jim and Abby get it up and running, but then I saw a brief image, vision I suppose, of Juanita leading prayer meetings at the hideaways, the remote camps, and the Counter-Insurgency centers. We need her spiritual leadership in all those places. So, after the CIA is running smoothly, we could travel together out to the other hideaways and camps to help them too."

This struck an immediate responsive chord in everyone they conferred with. After one last group prayer session, that's what they decided to do. Juanita was so proud of her husband for taking the lead and showing the way, and she looked forward to working with and training new prayer warriors and intercessors around the country. Now that the Havenwood1 spiritual warfare course had been developed, other locations had already been clamoring for it.

She and Pastor Wally had started trying to write it all up into a cohesive course, but somehow it hadn't felt right. The give and take of the classroom environment was so important in communicating experiential knowledge, so this would also enable Juanita to take the warfare course out to all the other locations. She felt excited and renewed, and had no qualms about leaving the Havenwood1 prayer group in Tara's capable hands.

Chapter Thirty-Seven

Alexis, Pope Radinsky, René and Blaine convened for an all-day meeting to review the status of the Universal ID System and to make plans for the next six months. The Pope and the Harlot were blathering on about numbers and details that were of no interest to the Global Czar. René was now in charge of the technical people with Jefferson having been eliminated from the equation. Surprisingly, René had a Masters in Computer Science from MIT and had made a fortune early on in the social networking market.

She had then turned her attention to the personal side of social networking, using her money, brains and body to rapidly climb into the inner circle of global finance. Alexis called her the "networking queen." Pretty good for the daughter of a no-account dad and a waitress mom from Altoona, Pennsylvania. Nothing was out of reach for René, except Blaine whom Alexis was closely studying.

Something had changed over the past few weeks. Since he'd first hired her as the spokesperson for the Global Governance Committee, he'd watched her go from a roaring lion to a basket case to….. Well, that was the question, really. What had she become? Alexis had never seen such a rapid cycle of personal change and found it fascinating. He didn't care what became of her one way or the other. She'd already outlived her usefulness. The instant credibility she'd given them was no longer needed, so was she now a liability?

While Radinsky and René babbled on unrelentingly with trivial nonsense, Alexis saw that Blaine was only partly paying attention, taking down a note or two every once in awhile, then lapsing back into an all-consuming reverie. But it wasn't worry or distraction that seemed to grip Blaine. Instead, it seemed like she disappeared to an internal island of peaceful rumination. Alexis needed to know the nature of that island.

Was she in love? His background check indicated an on-again, off-again relationship with Patrick Dewey, the news reader on some major network or other. His operatives said nothing had changed there, perhaps even cooled somewhat. Most likely, though, it was a result of the visits of a Reverend Boris Wainwright. Alexis had his people run a background check on Wainwright. A Christian counselor. If Blaine was turning to Jesus, he'd have to do something about it. Many interesting alternatives came to mind, but he'd hold off a little while until he had a better handle on the situation.

"Blaine, my dear, you seem somewhat distracted today. Is there something I can help you with?" Alexis asked, his practiced smile obfuscating all the internal machinations.

Blaine looked up, perplexed. She realized she hadn't been paying much attention. Rev. Wainwright had given her so much to think about. She wasn't quite ready to become a Jesus freak, but was surprised to find herself leaning in that direction, against every principle she'd stood for, against all logic. When she attempted to resist, she found herself agitated. When she gave into it, there was peace. Peace or logic, that's what it came down to, she decided.

All conversation had stopped. Blaine saw everyone looking at her quizzically. She sat up, straightened her skirt and blouse, brushed back her hair, took a deep breath and got ready for the interrogation she knew was coming. Rev.

Wainwright had said he was followed and she assumed her hotel suite was bugged. That's why she paid for a second room in the hotel where she met with Wainwright.

"I'm sorry I drifted off," she apologized. "Too much detail puts me to sleep." She glanced over at René who was staring daggers at her. Blaine simply smiled back sweetly.

"I too am bored with such banalities," Alexis concurred, striving to establish some new common ground. He hoped he could save her. Perhaps it was time for her to get initiated into the Luciferian religion. If she was getting spiritual, a major change, then she might be open to where the real power lay.

"Yes, but it's my job to know these things when I face the media." Blaine turned to Pope Radinsky and René. "I'm sorry I wasn't paying attention. That was quite rude."

René looked at Blaine sideways. She too was noticing major changes in Blaine. From René's standpoint, she had ground Blaine down and chewed her up just as she planned, leaving Blaine a basket case. At that point, her pretty rival should have slunk off for good. Instead, she was making a comeback, but as a changed person. Curious. Very curious.

Taking their cue from Alexis, René skipped the tedious details and gave a cogent summary. Overall, she said, the ID system was working well. A few glitches here and there. Several hackers had been caught and were going to be publicly prosecuted as a warning to others. Some RFID chips had failed, all from one manufacturer who, René said coyly, was no longer in business.

Before René could jump off onto any more rabbit trails, Alexis quickly changed the subject to what was really on his mind. He turned to Radinsky. "So how is my holographic statue coming?"

The False Prophet sat up straighter, a smug expression on his face. He was dressed casually, detesting the regalia he had to wear most of the time while pretending to be a real

Pope. He was looking forward to the day, not too far off, when he would simply be the Exalted Ruler of the Universal Religion. Then he could be himself. But first things first, and Alexis, child that he was, must always come first.

"Not only is it coming along well, it is finished, tested and ready for implementation," Radinsky announced proudly.

Alexis was suitably pleased, but Blaine looked confused, so Radinsky turned his attention to her. "A holographic image of the Global Czar will be projected into the center of every major city from special satellites covering the entire globe. It is a moving image, very lifelike, which will convey different messages as circumstances warrant."

Blaine was stunned. "Wow. That's amazing. Why haven't I heard about it before? When is it to be implemented?"

"Oh, we still like to have our little surprises," Alexis beamed.

"We are scheduled to do a live test next week here in Jerusalem, New York City, London and Tokyo," Radinsky explained. "Then, if that goes well, we'll roll it out region by region over the next month, so we need to alert the media as soon as possible. I'd be pleased to spend some time with you going over those details you detest so much."

Blaine blushed, feeling a bit chagrined at her earlier statement. She was glad that she wouldn't have to spend any more time with René, or even Alexis for that matter. The two of them were just too creepy. She hadn't gotten to know Pope Radinsky all that well, but he seemed like a good person. Perhaps he could give her some spiritual guidance.

Chapter Thirty-Eight

The trip from Jerusalem to Bali had been long and arduous. Travel restrictions were becoming more and more cumbersome as the Global Governance Committee strove to contain the world's population. Until all the RFIDs were functional with their built-in GPS units, only "necessary" travel was allowed. Afterward, the massive computers would know where everyone was at all times.

Abraham, Gabriel and Aadi had gotten caught up in the system several times along the way. Apparently, it was Alexis himself who approved their movements, even without receiving their RFID units. They made it to Bali just before the deadline, but were told that they must receive their chips there. Abraham and Gabriel, of course, knew they would never receive the "mark of the beast," but their new protégé Aadi didn't understand the implications.

After flying over Java, west of Bali, they landed at the Ngurah Rai International Airport in Tuban, an isthmus just south of Kuta, the center of tourism near the southern resort beaches. Aadi had family all over Bali, and Balinese ancestry was an important cultural dynamic. So Aadi proposed that they start visiting his extended family on a northward route until they could find available accommodations for the three of them.

"Believe it or not, but I am somewhat famous here due to my relationship with the Global Czar," Aadi explained as they took a taxi a short distance into the district just north of the airport. "I am sure that we will be able to secure transportation and housing for free."

Aadi didn't want to embarrass his mentors, but he was quite aware that they had just about run out of money. Gabriel was loathe to contact his wife Carmelita or his Havenwood associates, for fear of exposing them to the authorities. Abraham was simply tapped out, never having had much in savings. They were completely dependent upon God and Aadi from here on.

After passing several ritzy hotels and resorts, the cab dropped them off in front of an impressive villa built in the "Bali style," the traditional architecture derived from two sources: Hindu influences from Southeast Asia; and building styles from the pre-Hindu indigenous people who originally migrated from Taiwan. The multilevel tiled red roofs reminded Gabriel of the Asian temples and pagodas he'd seen in the in-flight magazine on Bali Airlines.

Aadi rushed inside, leaving the impatient taxi driver stewing near the anxious pastor and rabbi. But Aadi soon emerged with his hands overflowing in local currency. He must have given the driver a good tip, because the angry frown turned quickly into a huge grin which was given with a mock bow.

Trailing behind Aadi were Uncle Wayan and Aunt Nyoman. They were the proprietors of the villa and quite wealthy, according to Aadi. The middle-aged couple nodded emphatically in agreement. English, Aadi had explained on the way over, was the common business language in Bali due to the extensive tourism industry. Aadi slipped into Balinese and appeared to be negotiating some kind of deal which, after much shaking of heads upwards and sideways, eventually was concluded with a handshake and smiles all around.

The plumpish Uncle Wayan retrieved a large bunch of keys from the bulging pockets of his expensive Western business suit, took one off and handed it to Aadi, bowed to Abraham and Gabriel, and then turned quickly to go back inside. Aunt Nyoman also turned to follow her husband, but did not move anywhere near as quickly, wrapped up tight in her traditional Balinese dress. The garment was very colorful, but quite restrictive.

"The practice of winding the sabuk as tightly as possible around the female body," Aadi whispered, "is considered essential to achieving the desired look of slimness. Only loose women wear loose clothing, is an old-school saying. But, in reality, it also constrains women physically and metaphorically."

Then he waved at his two mentors to follow him around to a side parking lot where a newish, black Mercedes sedan responded to Aadi's press of the key fob. "First I tried to get us some free rooms here, but they insist their resort was all booked up. So then they felt obliged to let us use one of their touring cars."

As Aadi sped away, Gabriel in the front passenger seat, Abraham in back, Aadi was a non-stop tour guide and history teacher. Abraham took notes because he wanted to be a good guest and not violate local customs and sensibilities. He was surprised to hear that the population of the relatively small island was approaching 3.5 million, of which 93% was Hindu. Most areas of Indonesia were now firmly Muslim, but not Bali which clung stubbornly to tradition.

In fact, that's what led to the two defining moments in Balinese history. The Dutch colonial empire added Bali to the Dutch East Indies in the 1840s and set up a provisional government on the island's north coast. They then sought to increase their control of the south in 1906 when they mounted large naval and ground assaults. They were met by an estimated four thousand members of the royal family and their followers who marched to death in a suicidal *puputan* assault rather than face the humiliation of surrender.

Bali was included in the Republic of the United States of Indonesia following World War II in 1949 when the Netherlands recognized Indonesia's independence. In the 1950s and '60s, conflict between supporters of the traditional caste system and those rejecting those values resulted in a coup attempt by the Indonesian Communist Party that was put down by forces led by General Suharto. The Indonesian army became the dominant power and instigated a violent purge in which 500,000 people were killed across Indonesia, with an estimated 80,000 killed in Bali, equivalent to five percent of the island's population.

Abraham commented that tradition and death seemed to be the predominant characteristics of Bali's history. Aadi agreed as he swung the Mercedes northward. "Yes, that's true. Don't forget the Islamic terrorist bombing in 2002 in Kuta, which we just drove through a little while ago. Two hundred people were killed. Then another attack in 2005 almost killed our tourist industry. Spiritually, we celebrate the cycle of life, but pay special attention to death with an elaborate cremation celebration."

"That's an important aspect in understanding the under-lying spiritual forces in a community or a nation," Gabriel commented. "These types of events open doors for darkness to enter and set up demonic strongholds. A culture of death, plus the worship of many false gods, leads to heavy demonization."

Aadi took in what Pastor Gabriel had to say and under-stood him intellectually, but a part of him resisted the thought that something was wrong with his homeland culture, so he kept quiet. He'd noticed a difference within himself ever since they'd landed in Bali. The blind faith in his pastor and rabbi was gradually being replaced by a growing resentment he didn't quite comprehend, so he set it aside for now.

He drove a bit out of their way into the provincial capital, Denpasar. He wanted to show his two guests that Bali was a modern nation in spite of their traditional ways. "The best of both worlds," he pronounced proudly as they passed through a downtown of office buildings interspersed with other "Bali style" buildings, including the Jagatnatha Temple, just off the main drag.

"Bali is known as the 'island of a thousand temples' and Jagnatha is just one of many right in this area," Aadi said proudly, driving up the main entrance a short way so his two guests could see the impressive building and grounds. The temple itself towered upward in narrowing stories like a pyramid, with squared-off roofs at each level.

"Every Balinese belongs to a temple by virtue of descent, residence or some mystical revelation of affiliation," Aadi explained. "Some of the temples are associated with a village or family compound, others with key geographical landmarks or areas of significance, even large rice fields. We are a very spiritual people."

On the vast, nicely landscaped grounds a ceremony was underway. "What's going on?" Abraham asked.

Aadi squinted against the glare of the sun. "We have ceremonies for almost everything, so it's hard to say at first glance."

Music and singing filled the air, while dancers in traditional dress enacted some sort of drama. "Ahh, this ceremony represents a battle between the witch, Rangda, who stands for evil, against the dragon Barong, who represents good."

Gabriel and Abraham cringed when some of the dancers seemed to fall into a trance while others seemed to be stabbing themselves with sharp knives, but they made no comments. Aadi, though, sensed their disapproval and drove off silently, his resentment deepening.

Aadi turned to the southeast, heading toward the shoreline. When Aadi turned onto a seaside road, a number of run-down huts were interspersed with well-kept but small traditional homes. Several rickety piers jutted out into the ocean swells where a surprising number of fishing boats large and small, old and older, were in the process of unloading the day's catch.

Aadi pulled up near the end of the pier. "This is my hometown, my birthplace," he said softly, his voice cracking. As Aadi got out of the Mercedes, all work on the boats and the pier stopped and all eyes were peeled at the sight of the fancy automobile. Aadi waved and called out to them, then began to run toward them where he was greeted with many hugs and slaps on the back.

After the initial excitement wore down, Aadi led several men back to the Mercedes and beckoned Gabriel and Abraham outside. When Aadi formally introduced them as pastor and rabbi, eyebrows shot up and expressions dimmed. Gabriel and Abraham could see the disapproval in their eyes. Nonetheless, the men were polite, particularly Uncle Putu.

As Aadi had explained earlier, his father died at sea during a terrible storm Afterward, his father's brother Putu had assumed responsibility for Aadi's mother and siblings. Uncle Putu led them down the street to one of the nicer homes where his mother Surya shyly awaited the return of her wayward son. Many other families were gathering around the front porch.

While it was clear that Aadi was loved, it was also becoming apparent to Abraham and Gabriel that the family was none too pleased with his leaving the employ of the Global Czar, especially for two nobodies, and most especially for a Christian and a Jew. Though they all spoke in Balinese, their gestures and facial expressions were easy enough to read.

However, they treated Abraham and Gabriel with respect. A massive feast was put together in no time. Aadi explained that usually they ate their biggest meal of the day for lunch, but in their honor they would be treated to a multi-course traditional meal that evening. Aadi also pointed out that they ate very little for breakfast, just a little "nasi goring" or fried rice with coffee.

Soon, Gabriel and Abraham were served a plate of steamed rice and a cup of soup, "bubar ayam" or chicken porridge served with "can-weh," a Chinese bread. Surya then presented them with their choice of a meat, fowl, fish or vegetable dish. Aadi encouraged his mentors to try them all. The meat, "babi guling" or roast pork was deliciously tender, while the "bebek betutu" or darkened duck was surprisingly tangy. Aadi said they really didn't want to know about the fish dish, while the vegetables were whatever was growing in their gardens, but always extra spicy, so "watch out."

Gabriel did well with the spicy vegetables, but the large gathering laughed uproariously as Abraham choked and gasped and reached for glass after glass of papaya and passion fruit juice. Instead, they thrust the "air kelapa muda" or coconut juice, his way and he found that did a much better job putting out the fire. Abraham's palate had barely calmed down when a dessert of "pisang goring" or fried banana fritters was served. The heaping stack of fritters was a welcome finishing touch.

Of course, everyone was stuffed to the gills. As some of the women and children performed various songs and dances, Abraham and Gabriel found themselves nodding off. The festivities soon wound down, and the two guests were shown into the bedroom of Aadi's two younger brothers, Kadek and Ketut. The room was small, but comfortable with Rattan-type furnishings. The two weary travelers climbed into two small beds and were quickly asleep.

Chapter Thirty-Nine

General Wycliffe stood on a ridge overlooking a valley one hundred feet below on the western edge of Alan Morrison's ranch. Behind him rose the foothills of the Rockies, casting early shadows in the early winter season. Nearly twelve hundred men and a few dozen women had just completed their final training exercise of the week. They turned as one to gaze up at Wycliffe, awaiting the signal for weekend leave.

The General felt more like Moses today, raising his arms in various signals to the troops below. His Aaron and Miriam were the male and female aides who stood beside him, ready to enact his commands at a moment's notice. Down below, Lieutenant General Alex Bernard served as his Joshua, leading the militia units through the series of exercises that served as the final exam for the newly formed Western Militia.

Wycliffe hesitated, enjoying the moment very much, and then finally gave the signal for Bernard to dismiss the troops. When he did so, hats went flying and cheers rang throughout the valley, once home to a thousand head of cattle. The General stood and watched until every last soldier had left the valley. The shadows had deepened, with temperatures dropping into the upper thirties. The two aides continued to stand at attention, focusing all their energy holding back the shivers that would most certainly earn them a rebuke if they became physically evident.

Finally Wycliffe turned, eyed his two aides sternly, before dismissing them with a "good job" that pleasantly surprised them. They did a quick about-face, and marched off in unison. The general watched them with a fondness that was new to him. Though he was never one for personal relationships on or off duty, those two youngsters had worked their way into his heart with their blind devotion and instant obedience.

Hank and Bill, his aides in the New Mexico militia, were still somewhat resentful about being replaced. Wycliffe had explained that he needed to put members of other state militias into his leadership ranks in order to mollify the other tinhorn generals. Hank and Bill were made unit commanders and should have been quite pleased with their positions of authority, but instead they whined about not being his aides anymore. Oh well, Lt. Mary McBride and Lt. Evan Holliday showed much more deference and respect than Hank and Bill ever did.

When everyone was out of sight, the general allowed a couple of tears to flow down his chilled cheeks. He was happier and more fulfilled than he'd ever been in all his fifty-six years. Two failed marriages, three estranged children, and several failed business ventures were all left behind in the wake of his rise in the militia. He'd fought against all odds to assemble and train the New Mexico militia and then gained instant hero status with the successful raid on the detention center.

Now he was truly a general over a large army that would soon give the North American Union pause. Wycliffe cared nothing about politics and even less about religious matters. His sole motivation was to finally prove himself worthy. That thought caught him up short. Worthy of what? To whom? His successful, wealthy, tyrannical father who died of a Type-A heart attack in his forties? Wycliffe sniffed his contempt for the man. His wannabe socialite mother who had no time for her only son? *Give me a break.*

Who then? There was no God, no Creator to please, he was quite sure of that. Then he understood. It was to himself that he had to prove worthy. That's all that mattered, what he thought of himself. And now he had finally done so, lived up to his own high expectations. With a sigh of contentment, he began the slow descent down into the valley and his camouflaged jeep.

He drove back toward the main ranch house to meet with Morrison, the opposite direction of all the troops who'd driven out the back way, west into the foothills onto ragged jeep trails, then a swing to the south on primitive roads until they were headed back east toward paved roads and eventually Denver. Wycliffe detested having to report in to Morrison, but he was Mr. Moneybags, so it had to be endured for the sake of the cause.

Hmmph. The cause, he snorted. A fool's errand was more like it. A bunch of Christian lunatics, Jesus freaks. Starry-eyed dreamers with no sense whatsoever of reality. The only cause that drove Wycliffe, besides his personal ambitions, were to attack a government that had no right to impose its will on him or anyone else. He didn't care if it was United States of America, the NAU, or the Global Governance Committee, no one was going to tell him how to live his life and then extract taxes from his hard earned income.

Wycliffe blamed the government for the failure of his business ventures, robbing too much for taxes, eating up his capital before the businesses had time to mature. Of course, if his father or mother had supplied him with more of their wealth, it would have been a completely different story, but no, he had to get by on an allowance like a little child. Even now, his feeble old mother still held on tightly to the purse strings. He couldn't wait for her to die.

In the meantime, he had to deal with yet another money manager to whom he must grovel, although he had to grudgingly admit that Morrison had been far more agreeable to deal with than Dad or Mom or Uncle Sam. Nor had he interfered with military matters. Still, it grated on his ego.

Morrison was on the phone when the housekeeper showed Wycliffe into the ranch house office. He strolled over to the east-facing windows and stared out into the darkness, immersed in visions of battlefield glory. He was actually disappointed when Morrison called him over.

He succinctly and unemotionally gave his report and pronounced his army ready. "So now, can we establish a target? I don't want the troops to peak and then have nowhere to go but down."

Morrison smiled enigmatically, as he did so often. It drove Wycliffe mad trying to figure out what the man was thinking. Morrison knew that the general had no allegiance to the principles which drove the rest of them, but he had talents and experience that no one else did. Morrison was also aware that many of the soldiers did not share his Christian beliefs, but were simply patriots or armed thugs.

And so, he must always be wary of the general, wary of his motives, and completely surrendered to the Holy Spirit. When he smiled, it was because he was communing with Jesus, seeing him right there in the room with them, as He promised in His Word. Jesus was the Lord of Hosts, the true Commander of this new militia regardless of what Wycliffe thought.

"Yes, the target. We've thoroughly reviewed all the options at our last meeting, so unless there is some new insight, do you have a recommendation?" Morrison finally asked, already knowing what Jesus wanted.

Wycliffe sat up even straighter, if that was possible. He knew what the target should be, but he had to convince Morrison. "After thoroughly going over every possible target from every conceivable angle, there is one that stands out for a number of reasons. We not only want to win our first battle, but we also want to accomplish something meaningful as well as make a statement. Only one of these potential targets satisfies all three criteria. We need to take back the San Gabriel hideaway. Now that the effects of the tidal wave have fully dissipated, we need a base in Southern California, and we need to take back what once was ours."

Morrison smiled enigmatically again. *Ours, he says. I financed the hideaway, Gabriel and Jermaine built it, others manned it, and none of them were named Wycliffe. Where does he get off calling it 'ours?'*

However, this is what Jesus had already communicated to Morrison through His Holy Spirit. He recalled the Bible verse that talks about how God steers the hearts of kings like a river,[80] and he remembered how often God used non-believers to His own purposes. Well, here was another example.

"Why that's a great idea," he pronounced and watched as the tightly-wound general unwound just a bit. "How soon?"

Now Wycliffe was in his element. "With the target known, I'll send out scouts tomorrow. Then, I'll get together with my unit leaders to map out a specific plan of attack, with a secondary objective of occupying the target indefinitely. Then we'll start training to implement the specific plan. That will take all next week. I'd like to attack a week from Sunday."

Morrison flinched. *Sunday? Attack on Sunday? Sacrilegious? Jesus, is this right?*

Wycliffe now observed Morrison squirm for a change. Mr. Moneybags closed his eyes, praying Wycliffe presumed. What a waste of time. The crutch of the weak, who couldn't think for themselves.

Morrison was indeed praying, but not believing what he was seeing. The Lord often answered his questions about going ahead with something or not, by showing him an image of a red or green traffic light. He saw the green light, but still felt it couldn't be right, so he asked for confirmation. His eyes bolted open when he distinctly heard the Lord's voice within his mind.

"*Was not the Sabbath made for me? And when did I change it from Saturday? Can you find that in My Word?*"

Morrison remembered a debate in his church about that very topic. It was the Roman Emperor Constantine who changed the Sabbath to Sunday when he merged Christianity with the pagan worship of the sun god, after which the very day was named.

His face had turned pale with the shock of hearing the Lord so clearly. Usually it was just a sense of knowing. "Yes, Sunday will be fine," he finally said. Wycliffe was pleased, but somewhat taken aback at what he'd just seen. Something had happened, but he had no idea what.

They said their mutually respectful, but not friendly, parting comments and Morrison walked Wycliffe to the front door. He watched as the General marched off stiff as a board in the direction of his camouflaged tent to the south, near the creek. Far be it from a general to be housed with the lower level folks down in the underground shelter. Some of the militia soldiers had opted to live on site, while others, mostly from the greater Denver area, commuted weekly.

As Morrison continued to stare off into the distance, Jesse and Jerome wandered by for an after-dinner stroll. They didn't want to disturb their host, but he saw them go by and called out to them.

"What's the morale like down below?" Morrison asked without any usual greetings.

Everyone liked and respected Morrison, but found him somewhat aloof and hard to understand. He never spoke about himself or his past, so all kinds of rumors abounded.

"Well, I guess I'd call it pretty good," Jesse answered after some thought. "What do you think Jerome?"

"It's okay, could be better," Jerome responded rather quickly. It looked like he had something on his mind. Sometimes you had to work around it to uncover the underlying thoughts.

"Why, what's the problem?" Morrison asked, genuinely concerned.

Jesse waited for Jerome to pick up the ball. "Oh, nothing really. Just the same old, same old."

Morrison was a little taken aback, not used to the way Jerome's mind worked. "You mean people are getting bored? There's been so much to do. We've had great successes in circumventing the government systems. The militia is getting ready to roll. Why would people be bored?"

Jerome looked a little chagrined, and blushed a bit. He was uncomfortable under the scrutiny of the head honcho. "Well, maybe not exactly bored," he finally answered.

Morrison held back his quick tongue. He remembered now that Jerome was a bit slow. In a kinder, gentler tone he probed further. "I'm sorry to be pushing this, but I'd really like to understand what's going on over there. I want to do everything I can to make people comfortable and happy."

"Oh, we know that, Mr. Morrison. It's not anything like that, but I got to thinking that we needed a little excitement, you know, like a party or a celebration or something like that."

Morrison looked over to Jesse for confirmation. Jesse shrugged his shoulders, not quite sure where Jerome was going.

"We can do that," Morrison agreed right away. "What kind of a celebration would you suggest?"

Jerome hesitated, stared at his feet awhile. "Well, how about, maybe something like a, uhm, wedding?"

Morrison's and Jesse's eyes both widened. Then Jesse understood. "Did you ask Sue to marry you?" he asked, a big smile breaking across his face.

Jerome looked up, blushed deeper and nodded. "And she said yes!"

Jesse rushed over and hugged the big man while Morrison grinned. *That might be just what Doctor Jesus ordered.*

Before either Jesse or Morrison could say anything more, Jerome blurted with a rush, "And maybe you should get married too!"

Jesse froze. For some reason, after his initial rush to marry Fran back at the cabin in New Mexico was rejected by Rev. Braintree, the flames of their ardor had dampened. Since then, the two of them had gone through some counseling sessions with the minister and his wife, who constantly stressed the major differences between the two and the need to be absolutely certain before making a lifetime commitment.

It gave Jesse pause given his first failed marriage. Then Fran got busy with the counter-intelligence work and the embers seemed to have cooled.

"Uhm, I don't think we're quite ready yet. But congratulations to you and Sue."

Jerome looked crestfallen, but then just as quickly his face brightened again. "Would you be my best man? And maybe Fran could be Sue's maid of honor?"

Jesse laughed in relief. "Sure, buddy, it would be an honor to be your best man. But Sue will have to ask Fran herself."

Morrison just shook his head in wonder as the two men strode off, Jesse's arm slung over Jerome's wide shoulders. What a pair.

Chapter Forty

Morrison contacted Jermaine to let him know the militia's first target would be one of the original Havenwood hideaways. When retaken, Jermaine would be in charge again of its operation while the militia provided protection. This would be a different situation than all the other ten hideaways whose location was unknown to the authorities.

Would the global army strike back after the militia's surprise attack? Morrison was sure they would, so the two discussed contingency plans for all kinds of scenarios, the most likely being a tactical retreat.

"No matter what General Wycliffe believes about the capabilities of his militia," Morrison observed, "there's no way it can stand up to the full power of the global forces. It must act as a surgical strike team, using 'shock and awe' tactics combined with the element of surprise."

Jermaine agreed, but pointed out that they had one other weapon at their disposal, one the enemy could never match. "I'll get Juanita and the spiritual warfare group going on this. The enemy will never know what hit them."

Morrison hesitated before finally deciding to voice a question, a lingering concern that had bothered him for many years. Like most people, he didn't want to ask a dumb question. And, like many believers, he didn't want to reveal a lack of understanding or, worse yet, a doubt about one of the pillars of the Christian faith.

"If God already knows and approves our plans, why do we need to pray about it? Shouldn't we just stand in faith, expecting Him to see it through to a successful conclusion? Doesn't praying about it show a lack of confidence in God? I can understand praying for guidance or to ask Him to do something He might not already have on His agenda, but if it's already His will, why pray?"

Wow, where to begin? Jermaine thought to himself as he cleared his throat to buy a little time. Fortunately, he'd been down this road many times with Juanita, so he only needed to get his thoughts organized.

"That's a very good question, one that most people are afraid to ask," Jermaine began. "It comes down to the concept of dominion. When God created Adam and Eve in the Garden of Eden, he gave them, and by extension all of humanity, dominion over the earth.[81] He handed over His authority, which means that He was no longer in charge of His creation. However, Adam and Eve handed over that dominion, that authority, to the devil when they allowed the serpent to deceive them."[82] That's why Satan could try to tempt Jesus by offering Him dominion.[83]

Jermaine paused to see if Morrison had any questions or comments, which most people did at this juncture of the discussion. Sure enough, Morrison asked, "So you're saying, then, that the devil is in charge of this world?"

"Absolutely. That's why the Scriptures say that Satan is the *'god of this age'*[84] and the *'prince of the air.*[85] Jesus, though, came and took back that authority. That's why He says, *'All authority has been given to Me in heaven and on earth.'*[86] The Scriptures also point out that God the Father *'has given Him authority to execute judgment also, because He is the Son of Man.'*[87] However, until He returns to *'restore all things,'*[88] and make *'all things new,'*[89] He will not use this authority Himself, but extend it back into this world through us, because we were originally supposed to have dominion."

"Well, that's a whole different perspective than I've heard before," Morrison noted. "So that's why Jesus tells us to pray in His name?"

"Right. Because He's the one with the authority now, but will only use it through us – that is, until He returns. That's why He said, *'Behold, I give <u>you</u> authority, to trample on serpents and scorpions, and <u>over all the power of the enemy</u>, and nothing shall by any means hurt you.'*[(90)] and *'And these signs will follow <u>those who believe</u>: In My name <u>they</u> will cast out demons; <u>they</u> will speak with new tongues; <u>they</u> will take up serpents; and if <u>they</u> drink anything deadly, it will by no means hurt them; <u>they</u> will lay hands on the sick, and <u>they</u> will recover.'*[(91)]

"But, isn't God sovereign?" Morrison objected. "Doesn't that mean that He does what He wants, that nothing happens that isn't of His will?"

"God's plan, as spelled out in His Word, will indeed come to pass, but that's in an overall sense. What happens at the individual level is up to us," Jermaine explained. "God won't act on the personal level unless activated by prayer. However, if that prayer violates His will, it will not be answered, or more precisely, the answer will be no. To pray in Jesus' name means according to His character, nature and will. That's why Scripture says, *'Now this is the confidence that we have in Him, that if we ask anything according to His will, He hears us.'*[(92)] Many people think that just by praying 'in Jesus' name' they can get whatever we want. But God is not some cosmic bellhop who rushes around fulfilling our every whim."

"Well that's certainly interesting, Jermaine. I'll have to give it all some thought and research in the Word before I can fully accept what you're saying," Morrison said, somewhat apologetic.

"Hey, that's what you should do, just like the Bereans[93] checked out what the Apostle Paul was telling them," Jermaine replied. Both of them felt a new connection between them, a sense of camaraderie that hadn't existed before.

Afterwards, Jermaine filled Juanita in on Morrison's and Wycliffe's plans and watched as her jaw became rigid and her eyes aflame with determination. "Glory, hallelujah, it's about time we went on the offensive!" She quickly assembled her prayer warriors and explained the situation. Immediately they launched into spiritual warfare.

"Lord God Almighty, Creator of the universe, our One True Father, we come to you in the name of your precious Son and our wonderful Savior, Jesus Christ," Juanita began. "Your holy Word says that the weapons of our warfare are not carnal, but mighty in God for pulling down strongholds.[78] As You already know, our Western militia, Your army on earth, is preparing to retake our San Gabriel hideaway. What was once our stronghold for You has become a stronghold for our enemy, Your enemy.

"We ask Father, that your Son, the Lord Sabbaoth, the Lord of Hosts, will go before us and prepare the way. Let the fear of the Lord fall upon the enemy and cloud their minds. We ask, Father, in Jesus' name, that Your Holy Spirit will supernaturally enlighten General Wycliffe and his troops. Give them Your great wisdom beforehand to develop the right plans, for You already know the enemy's numbers and defenses.

"We declare the Word of God over the militia that no weapon formed against them shall prosper.[58] A thousand may fall at their side and ten thousand at their right hand, but it shall not come near them.[94] For You shall give Your angels charge over them and they shall tread upon the lion and the cobra and trample them underfoot.[95] And they shall overcome the enemy by the blood of the Lamb,[67] not by their might or power, but by Your Spirit, says the Lord of hosts."[61]

Tara immediately jumped in: "Lord Jesus, precious Savior, our redeemer, our friend and deliverer, we come to You with humble hearts seeking to do Your will. We pray, Lord, that General Wycliffe hears You and follows You. We understand that he is not a believer, but You can still use him to accomplish Your purposes, just as You did so many times in Your Word. But more than that, Lord, we pray that as You use Him, his heart will open up to receive You as his Commander-in-Chief and Savior.

"We pray the whole armor of God onto General Wycliffe and all the troops so that they will be able to withstand the enemy, having girded themselves with the helmet of salvation, the belt of truth, and the breastplate of righteousness. We pray that their feet be shod with the preparation of the gospel of peace and, above all, that they take up the shield of faith with which to quench all the fiery darts of the enemy, wielding the sword of the Spirit, which is the Word of God."[96]

Ryan then picked up the mantle of prayer: "Heavenly Father, we thank You for all Your blessings and benefits, for Your ongoing protection in these perilous times. We proclaim Your Word over the militia that the battle is the Lord's,[97] and You will give the enemy into our hands, because it was for this purpose, Father, that Your Son was manifested, that He might destroy the works of the devil.[62] We declare Your Word that says You will bring the counsel of the nations to nothing, that You will make the plans of the enemy of no effect.[98]

"We ask, Father, in Jesus' name, that You enable our militia to be invisible to the enemy, and that they be covered with a blanket of protection under the shadow of Your wings, for You are their shield and buckler.[99] Let the enemy be scattered before them, and then protect them against coun-terattacks after they take possession of the hideaway. Give General Wycliffe wisdom and revelation to know whether to stay and occupy or to destroy the facility and withdraw."

Some of the other prayer warriors also spoke out their requests and declarations while others prayed silently. They continued on for hours late into the night. Then they recon-vened daily, with more specifics as General Wycliffe's plans unfolded. More than that, they individually prayed on and off throughout each day as the Holy Spirit gave them the unction. Juanita also called the prayer leaders in the other hideaways and remote camps to get their prayer groups going as well.

Chapter Forty-One

Abraham and Gabriel awoke early to the sounds of an entire village preparing for the day ahead. The women fixed breakfast and made lunches to go, the men got the boats and fishing equipment ready, while the young children were herded off to school just down the street.

They each lay in bed, refreshed but troubled. These were mostly good people, but great darkness lay like a heavy blanket over them. Both Gabriel and Abraham had seen Aadi lose more and more ground to the enemy the longer they were in this heathen country. The demonic strongholds over Bali were intense after centuries of people worshiping numerous false gods. Every one of their ceremonies opened the doors and welcomed demons into their midst on a continual basis, reinforcing and expanding their grip over the nation and its people.

After the early morning noise had subsided, Aadi knocked gently on the door and poked his head into the bedroom. Abraham and Gabriel both rose reluctantly, a sense of foreboding permeating the atmosphere. Aadi saw that something was bothering them, but couldn't figure out what it might be. He felt his lingering resentment rise up stronger, but pushed it aside.

Neither Abraham nor Gabriel was hungry, or at least not for what was offered. So they sipped the delicious locally grown, fresh-brewed coffee on the front porch and watched the last of the fishing boats disappear over the horizon. Aadi was busy running errands for his mother, desperately trying to overcome her displeasure with him. The resulting silence was soothing, as Gabriel and Abraham contented themselves with watching the ocean swells lap at the beach while the Bali version of sea gulls fluttered around looking for clams or mussels or whatever it was they ate.

Suddenly, screams and commotion poured out onto the oceanfront street from the one-story schoolhouse about a quarter-mile down the road. Aadi's mother shuffled outside, looked up the street and then plodded toward the school in her tightly wrapped sabuk. Pastor and rabbi looked at one another. Ordinarily, they would spring into action, part of the job. But here in Bali, they were considered pariahs. Would it be a breech of custom or culture for them to go see what was happening, to possibly offer their help?

And so they waited and watched from a distance. They saw Aadi come running back from someplace inland, several packages in his arms. Shortly after he disappeared into the school, he ran outside again holding a different package, the screaming, bleeding body of a young girl. Aadi ran straight down the street toward Abraham and Gabriel.

When he got to the front of the porch, he pulled up short and looked up frantically at his two mentors. "Please, heal her. You said Jesus was a healer, well we need him now or she's going to die!"

As a crowd began to form a half-circle around the porch, Jesus' two representatives walked down the five steps and examined the young girl, She was still squirming a bit, and blood continued to spurt out of several wounds. However, she was no longer screaming, but gurgling, as blood pooled in her throat and lungs.

"What happened?" Gabriel finally asked.

"One of the older boys tried to rape her," Aadi explained breathlessly. "When she resisted, he stabbed her many times before the teachers could pull him off her."

Gabriel looked over at Abraham who shrugged, with a resigned look on his face. The witnesses were back on duty. Together they placed their hands on the girl and looked up toward the heavens.

"Merciful God, blessed Redeemer, we come before You today and humbly ask that You do a miracle of healing right here, right now," Gabriel began. "Your Word says that you give us the authority and power to lay hands on the sick and they will recover.[91] So we declare over this young girl that by the stripes of Jesus, she is healed."[100]

At first, the only change was the gurgling changing to gagging and choking. The crowd began to grow restive. Then a gust of wind blew in off the water, a sweet lavender aroma filling the air. Everyone looked toward the sea, expecting to see something, but nothing was there.

They were startled when the young girl squealed loudly, assuming it was a cry of death. But instead, the girl leaped out of Aadi's arms and started jumping up and down gleefully. Everyone stared in wonder. Though her clothes were still stained blood red, all of her wounds were gone.

Slowly, the dumbstruck silence gave way to a buzz of excitement that eventually exploded in yells and screams of joy, led by Aadi who couldn't stop jumping up and down himself. The girl's mother rushed forward and swept her up, hugging her tightly, sobbing uncontrollably.

As the extreme emotions began to subside, the crowd backed away from Abraham and Gabriel, not sure what to make of it all. Abraham felt that something needed to be said, and stepped forward. "This girl was not healed by us, but by Jesus who is the Creator of the universe and our Savior. He is with us right now, right here. You can't see Him with your eyes, but you can receive Him into your heart."

The people began looking around for Jesus anyway, continuing to back away. Finally, the mother placed the girl back on the ground and led her away down the street, everyone else trailing behind. Only Aadi remained. As the crowd drifted away, they began to chatter in their native language.

"What's going on?" Gabriel finally asked Aadi, who seemed torn between staying and going.

"They're planning a ritual celebration," Aadi finally replied. "They are going to thank the forces of good for overcoming evil through the spirit called Jesus. They're simply folding Jesus into our traditional worship of all kinds of gods and spirits."

"And you, what do you think?" Abraham asked pointedly.

Aadi sighed, having anticipated and dreaded the question. "It is very difficult for me here. I know what you've taught me and have felt His power, but it's hard to completely forego a lifetime of beliefs and to abandon my people, my family as well." With downcast eyes, Aadi slunk off to follow the crowd.

Despite the impressive healing, the two witnesses still felt that same sense of foreboding. Where was the joy? Where were the converts? With nothing left to do, they refilled their coffee cups and took up their positions on the porch once again. Sounds of music and singing eventually filtered up their way on capricious winds that grew more and more violent.

In a short matter of time, the skies had turned black as the ocean swells became enormous waves crashing onto the shore. Strong gusts of wind blew debris down the street. Lightning flashed all around, tremendous blasts of thunder shook the ground.

Off on the horizon, the fishing boats lumbered toward shore, rising and then falling out of sight, only to reappear seemingly no closer than before. Aadi rushed back, ran into the house and came out with a pair of binoculars. Anxiously he scanned the horizon. "Some of the boats are breaking apart," he exclaimed, and rushed down to the pier.

Abraham and Gabriel got up to follow Aadi but were stopped in their tracks by the womenfolk who pointed angry fingers at them, apparently blaming them for the fierce storm. The two witnesses watched helplessly as the first boats finally lurched against the dock and helping hands pulled the fishermen to safety. Finally, all but two boats were secured and their battered sailors safely ashore.

Apparently two boats had broken apart and sunk. Several of the fishermen were rescued but not all. Mass hysteria was breaking out amongst the families with more pointing back toward the two presumed culprits. The heavy winds were blowing straight on shore, the waves creeping over the edge of the street, inching toward the small, vulnerable houses.

A mob of angry men began moving toward Abraham and Gabriel who fell to their knees in prayer on the porch. Shouts from the dock stopped the advance of the mob. Bits and pieces of the two lost boats began washing up on the shore. Relatives of the missing men wailed in grief into the howling wind. Then a body washed ashore. Another and another. Six all together.

The families rushed to the edge of the road and pulled the lifeless bodies out of the water. The angry mob turned once again toward Abraham and Gabriel, their black eyes intent on revenge. Abraham rose to his feet, spread his arms wide and looked up into the ferocious sky.

"Jesus, Jesus, Jesus," Abraham wailed, not knowing what to pray. Gabriel prostrated himself on the porch and cried out in his heavenly language.

Abraham's voice rose above the raucous cries of the closing mob, even above the roar of the mighty wind. "Jesus, forgive these people their blasphemy, calm the storm and raise their dead!"

Just as the leading edge of the mob reached the porch and latched onto the two culprits, the winds suddenly died. As the mob looked skyward, an invisible hand seemed to sweep the broiling clouds back out to sea, the sudden brightness of the sun blinding their eyes.

Then a roar of amazement and joy began to ratchet up like a jet engine opening wide. As the waters receded from the road down the beach, the soaked dead bodies climbed to their feet, moving at first like zombies out of a horror movie. Everyone and all of nature held their collective breath, not believing what their eyes were telling them.

Then the bodies shook free of death and began to leap and run and dance and sing and shout and laugh and cry. The mob released Gabriel and Abraham and rushed to their revived compatriots, hugging and dancing with them on the wet sand.

When the commotion began to dwindle, everyone turned as one and stared back at Gabriel and Abraham who didn't know what to expect this time. "Thank you, Jesus. Thank you, Jesus," they said quietly as they waited to see what would happen.

"Hosanna, hosanna in the highest," Gabriel praised. "Save now, save now," Abraham translated.

One by one, the once-dead, now alive fishermen, actually four men and two teenagers, began to file slowly toward the two witnesses, with the crowd forming behind them. When they arrived at the base of the porch, the six fell to their knees and bowed before Abraham and Gabriel.

Abraham cried out, "No, see that you do not worship us but the Lord Jesus Christ who healed your girl and raised your dead. But also see that you no longer worship your false idols, because the One True God is a jealous God who will no longer abide with your blasphemy. This is your last chance to receive Jesus as your Lord, your Master and your Savior."

Aadi translated quickly and a hush fell over the entire assembly of townsfolk. Then the revived six rose to their feet, raised their hands to the heavens and began to chant in unison. "Jesus is Lord. Jesus is Lord. Jesus is Lord." Soon everyone was chanting.

Gabriel spoke quickly to Aadi and then waved at Abraham to follow him to the beach. Aadi addressed the crowd and told them that they should follow the two ministers and be baptized to publicly declare their saving faith in Jesus.[(101)] This immediately appealed to a people used to marking every significant occasion with a ritual of some kind.

Abraham addressed the people as Aadi continued to translate. "This baptism symbolizes your death to the old ways and your birth into your faith in Jesus Christ. Just as these six were raised from the dead, so too will you die to all your sinful ways which will be washed away in the tide of God's love and forgiveness. Then you will arise into eternal life as a new creation in Christ."

The six eagerly went first with both Gabriel and Abraham fully immersing them in the calm blue waters. As each one came back up out of the water, ghostly demons fled out of each body. At first, Gabriel thought only he and Abraham could see them, but the astonished faces of the onlookers told them otherwise.

Aadi was the last to go. When he was raised up out of the water, two white doves flew down out of the sky and alighted on the heads of Abraham and Gabriel. A voice thundered out of the heavens. "These are my two witnesses on earth. Follow them as they follow Me."

Chapter Forty-Two

Blaine Whitney felt somewhat guilty after her last counseling session with Rev. Wainwright earlier that week. She'd neglected to tell him about her meetings with Pope Radinsky for a number of reasons. When she logically paged through those reasons, she thought they made perfect sense. Why then did she feel any guilt at all?

For one thing, she had a confidentiality agreement with the Global Governance Committee which forbade her from discussing any business that had not yet been made public. Secondly, she knew Boris, as he insisted she call him, had something against the Pope, so why enflame the fires? Thirdly, Boris might be jealous or insulted that Blaine was also receiving spiritual guidance from another source.

Besides, she wasn't rejecting Boris or his guidance. In fact, she was greatly appreciative of the help he had given her. She felt like a new person, although she'd yet to fully submit herself to Christ. Boris didn't push her, saying it would come in time. Pope Radinsky didn't push her at all about Jesus, didn't even mention His name. Instead, Vladimir, as he also insisted on being called, helped her connect with her own spiritual center. She hadn't known such peace and contentment in all her life.

In addition, Vladimir had prepared her very well for the press conference earlier that day at which she revealed the plans for the Global Czar's holographic image to be projected into four test cities tomorrow. She would never have guessed that some of the media would raise a question about whether people would be required to worship that image.[102] What a bizarre, crazy notion.

When Vladimir pointed out beforehand that this was in the Bible, she joined with him in laughing mockingly about it. Clearly, the Bible that Boris thought was "without error" was riddled with such nonsense, as Vladimir showed her. Noah's Ark, Jonah and the Whale, even Adam and Eve were simply fairy tales, good stories with worthy moral lessons, but fiction nonetheless.

She hadn't returned any of Patrick's phone calls over the past week, not wanting to hear him trash all the good things that were happening to her now. Judging from the body language on his nightly newscast, he was enamored of his new ingénue anyway. Perhaps it was for the best that they each move on separately with their lives.

For whatever reason, Alexis and René had backed off and were leaving her in the Pope's hands for now. This meant that she'd temporarily moved into the Vatican Palace. So now she had two temporary residences. She hoped she could settle down and plant roots somewhere someday soon, although she wasn't sold on living in Jerusalem or Vatican City. So she'd bide her time for now.

Meanwhile, Vladimir had invited her to a special Mass that he was conducting that evening. It was a midnight Mass for just a few selected Cardinals and Bishops who were part of some kind of inner circle. She'd declined at first, shuddering as she remembered having to sit through those boring Catholic Masses as a child. However, Vladimir assured her this would be quite different. Although conducted in Latin, he advised her not to try and understand what was going on, but rather to connect her spiritual center with the strong spirit that would be present.

At ten minutes before midnight, Pope Radinsky's aide, Mustafa, came to escort her into the depths of the Vatican Palace where, he said, they conducted these special, private services. The sanctuary was small, seating perhaps a maximum of fifty people. Tonight she saw about thirty all dressed in black robes, quite different than the white ones she was used to seeing. Mustafa sat her in the back and went up front to join his colleagues.

Pope Radinsky was on his knees in prayer at the altar. Blaine was thrown off stride when she didn't see the usual symbols. Instead of Jesus hanging on a cross, there was a circle with what appeared to be an upside-down cross with it arms broken downward. To one side of that was the image of a man with a goat's head, black wings spread wide, horns curved upward and outward, holding a quarter-moon in his right hand. To the right was a five-pointed star. On a table in front of the altar was a skull sitting atop what looked like a Bible.

Blaine was scared and thought about slipping out the back door, but hesitated because then Vladimir would be disappointed in her. She assured herself that he'd have some legitimate explanations for the bizarre imagery, although it was quite creepy. Then she remembered that she'd felt the same way the first time her parents hauled her inside the Catholic Church and seeing the dead man nailed to the cross.

Before she could give it further thought, Pope Radinsky rose, faced the congregation, spread his arms and lifted his head toward the heavens. "In nomine Magni Dei Notri Satanus introibo ad altare Domini Inferi," he pronounced in a deep, tremulous voice laden with worshipful fervor.

She remembered what Vladimir had advised and closed her eyes, centered herself, and opened up to receive all that the spiritual world had to offer.

"Ad Eum Qui laetificat juventutem meam," the congregants responded, sending chills throughout Blaine's body.

"Adjutorium nostrum in nomine Domini Inferi," the Pope intoned majestically.

"Qui regit terram," came the response, equally fervent.

The Latin actually helped to calm Blaine's nerves, sounding so familiar to the Masses she'd attended as a young girl before they switched to English.

"Domine Satanus, Tua est terra. Orbem terrarium et plenitudinem ejus Tu fundasti. Justitia et luxuria praeparatia sedis Tuae. Sederunt principes et adversum me loquebantur, et iniqui persecute sunt me. Adjuva me, Domine Satanus meus. Custodi me, Domine Satanus, de manu peccatoris," Pope Radinsky implored, his voice rising in intensity.

Blaine felt warm arms embrace her. She opened her eyes but no one was there. She smiled, closed her eyes and returned to the wonderful sensation of being held and comforted as though she were an infant. As Vladimir had suggested, she gave herself fully to this spiritual being. She didn't care if it was Jesus, Buddha, Muhammed or any of the other names we give to God. Those were merely human constructs. This was the real thing.

"Et ab hominibus iniquis eripe me," the congregants responded in a uniform singsong.

"Domine Satanus. Tu conversus vivificabis nos," the Pope cried out.

"Et plebs Tua laetabitur in te," was the response.

Blaine began to tune out the service itself, concentrating entirely on this new, internal sense of being loved, protected, cherished. She was a little embarrassed to find that she was becoming sexually aroused. But God was a He, after all, so perhaps this was natural when coming into a close encounter with Him.

"Gloria Deo Domino Inferi, et in terra vita hominibus fortibus. Laudamus Te, benedicimus Te, adoramus Te, glorificamus Te, gratia agrimus tibi propter magnam potentiam

Tuam: Domine Satanus, Rex Inferus, Imperator omnipotens," Radinsky howled into the heavens.

Blaine's spirit rose upward with the sound of the Pope's voice, carried into the heavenly places. She was soaring above the earth, flying high with the angels. Voices in the background were lost as she heard another voice within herself.

"You are mine," the deep, soothing voice said. "To have and to hold forever."

"Credo in Satanus... Dominus Inferus... Veni, Magister Templi, Veni, Magister Mundi...," cried the Pope.

"Ave Satanus," came the response.

"We shall be wedded in the spirit," said the warm, loving voice within Blaine. Time and space disappeared, replaced by an overriding sensation of eternal bliss.

"Fratres et sorores, debitores sumus carni et secundum carnem vivamus. Ego vos benedico in Nomine Magni Dei Nostri Satanus," Radinksy's voice soared with Blaine's spirit.

"Ave Satanus, Ave Satanus, Ave Satanus," the congregants cried out in elation.

"Say it," said the voice within Blaine. "The service is ending. Say it so that we can be one."

"Ave Satanus," Blaine cried out along with the congregants and fainted into a delirium of exquisite ecstasy.

Chapter Forty-Three

The scouts returned from their four-day trip to San Gabriel with a favorable report about the old hideaway. The area had been changed drastically by the tsunami that struck before the Global Government was formed last year. Most of the landscape had been flattened and drawn back out toward the shoreline with the vast receding tide. Whereas once the hideaway entrance was concealed by a small forest at the top of a small rise, the trees were gone and some of the hill had washed away, leaving a gaping open wound directly into the once-hidden retreat.

Guards were posted immediately outside and at four corners about one hundred yards away. A small cadre of technicians appeared to be living inside, continuing their attempts to revive flooded equipment and glean data about other hideaways and the organization that had established this one. From conversations recorded on breaks they took outside, it appeared they were making some progress.

This reinforced the need for speed to General Wycliffe, who was able to talk Morrison into advancing the time-table by a few days. Two long weekend days of training and rehearsal found the troops eager to get going. Most were sick and tired of the one-world government that was becoming more and more intrusive. Most, however, had gone along and received their RFID chips.

"You don't expect our families to starve to death, do you?" they responded incredulously to the warnings of the "right-wing whackos" who'd held out because of some Biblical lunacy. However, both groups were united in their desire to strike back at the "liberal nutcases" who had sold freedom and the free-market system down the drain.

Some of the militia were flown overnight to the remote camp in the Angeles National Forest northwest of San Gabriel in their small fleet of helicopters and light planes. The remaining soldiers traveled in a caravan of surplus military troop transport vehicles that travelled under darkness for two nights, skirting around metropolitan areas, bivouacking during the day in a small, deserted canyon outside St. George, Utah that the scouts had found on their trip back.

When all the troops had reconnoitered at the remote camp, they ate heartily, slept soundly and were refreshed and ready to go to war. They set out in the cool, early winter night just after sundown, marching down the mountain toward the hideaway. There was no need to be wary of being seen when they emerged from the forest into once inhabited communities. The tidal wave had so thoroughly destroyed the area, that people were only beginning to resettle Los Angeles, let alone the surrounding suburbs.

It was just before dawn when the militia arrived in the valley near the hideaway, where they broke into separate groups as had been planned and practiced. Unlike the shock-and-awe attack on the detention center in New Mexico, this time General Wycliffe had prepared a surgical strike that would enable them to get inside the hideaway before anyone knew they were coming.

Snipers took up positions that encircled the hideaway. As dawn broke, they targeted the guards and waited for the signal. When everyone was positioned and ready, Wycliffe blew into the whistle that hooted like a Great Horned Owl. Three hoots were quickly followed by the whispers of silenced rifles. All the guards fell as one without a scream or a shout.

One militia team ran forward to ensure that each of the guards was dead, while another team rushed up to and down into the hideaway entrance. They found everything exactly as Morrison had laid out on the floor plan. A few workers were just beginning to resume fiddling with the shorted out electronic gear in the central chamber. Silencers masked the shots from the Glock handguns, but there were a couple of cries of shock and alarm that brought a few people out of the dining room where breakfast was being served.

But that was the next target, as the militia team split up into six teams. The first team took out the people in the dining room, while the other five made their way down each of the five tunnels. Now it was time for brute force. MK-47s filled the air with the racket of bullets followed by screams of terror and death. A few armed workers emerged from their quarters and fired back, wounding several of the militia. But they were quickly cut down and soon there was only quiet as the remaining workers and guards surrendered, hands held high in the air.

General Wycliffe and his two aides strode triumphantly into the hideaway and assessed the situation. "Find out whether anyone was able to signal the outside world."

The captives were split up and interrogated. No one worried about the Geneva Convention restrictions on torture. Two people admitted to calling 911, but in the aftermath of the tsunami, there was no answer. Another captive confessed reluctantly to getting a quick text message off to his superior officer. Not good. But the General had prepared contingency plans for every imaginable situation.

So instead of attempting to occupy and hold the hideaway, the demolition team began to set up explosives at predetermined locations that Morrison's engineers guaranteed would implode the entire structure, burying and forever destroying all the electronic equipment. There was no need for recovering any written or printed materials, since each hideaway was instructed not to keep any sensitive information around at any time.

They herded the captives outside and released them to scurry down to Los Angeles. Then the troops retreated up the hillsides and gathered to watch as the explosives were set off remotely. A series of loud rumbles were followed by an enormous cloud of dust and debris that rose into the air and then fell back on itself. When the dust settled, the demolition team ran forward to check that the hideaway had been completely buried and destroyed.

When they reported back in the affirmative, the militia gathered back together for the return trip. They were surprised when General Wycliffe took out his electronic bullhorn.

"Congratulations on a job well done," Wycliffe began addressing the troops. "However, we are not completely done. There is a new detention center built just outside the area where the city of Glendale used to be. We are going to hike over there and release the thousands of people they've illegally incarcerated."

The sounds of surprise rippled through the militia. Then some began to cheer, flush with the excitement and satisfaction of victory. They wanted to extract more blood from the enemy and were ready to go wherever Wycliffe led.

However, some were quite concerned, knowing that there had been no special training for this new mission. Were there even plans? Even if there were, Hank and Bill knew that at most four people knew of them; the general, his two aides and the militia commander. That was far too few. This sounded risky and dangerous.

When Wycliffe reported back to Morrison about their success in destroying the hideaway, he neglected to tell him of their new plans. He'd grown tired of having to get Morrison's agreement about military matters. With a sign of contentment, Wycliffe gave the signal for the Commander to organize the troops and begin the circuitous march to Glendale.

Chapter Forty-Four

Word of the girl's miraculous healing and the raising of the dead spread like wildfire throughout all of Bali. Soon, Aadi's small home enclave was besieged by thousands of people who wanted healing or restoration from the Sanghyang Widi Wasa. Aadi explained that this was the Balinese phrase for "Supreme Being," which was almost never spoken. But now that they thought the Supreme Being, or at least His representatives, were in Bali, it was alright to say.

Abraham and Gabriel insisted that Aadi talk to every new group of people arriving almost hourly and tell them that they were not gods, but rather disciples of Jesus Christ who alone was God, and that all other presumed gods were not true gods, but rather demonic, born of the devil.

Aadi was greatly alarmed. "I can't go tell them to renounce centuries of belief. They'll get mad and attack me, maybe even kill me."

"We will pray over you and Jesus will protect you," Gabriel quickly asserted, for time was of the essence. General mayhem was spreading and who knew what form of mob hysteria might break out.

Aadi was still very reluctant. "If they don't attack me, they might just turn around and go home."

"That would be all right with me," Abraham stated emphatically. "There's too many people with too little understanding to handle at the moment anyway."

"Wait, let's anoint Aadi to also pray over the people, to heal and save them," Gabriel said. "After all, the Bible says that all believers can be empowered to do so."[91]

Abraham suggested they pray about it first. It took only a few moments to sense the Lord's strong confirmation. So they anointed Aadi with oil, laid hands on him, prayed that the Lord's power would flow through him, and then sent him off.

As Aadi moved out into the surging crowd, Gabriel and Abraham set up prayer stations on either side of the front porch. Several strong local men, two of who had been raised from the dead, formed a barrier to control access to the two ministers.

Neither Abraham nor Gabriel attempted to communicate with the Bali citizens, most of whom knew some English. All they felt led to say as they laid hands on and anointed the people was, "Be healed in the name of Jesus Christ."

Many were indeed healed, some quite dramatically, but many others were not. The Lord's two representatives didn't have time to think about it much as the unending line of people continued to grow despite their efforts to be quick and efficient.

All of a sudden there was a great commotion just down the road. People were screaming, some jumping up and down hysterically. From the porch, it seemed as though their worst fears might be realized, and a riot was starting.

But then they saw people backing away into a circle with Aadi in the center. Several children were hugging his legs and climbing up into his arms. Aadi waved at them excitedly and they waved back, still not quite sure what was transpiring.

But word quickly spread across the crowds up to the porch. "They are saying that Aadi healed those children,"

Uncle Putu explained. "One was blind, another paralyzed and one had been dead for almost thirty-six hours."

Gabriel and Abraham smiled and breathed a sigh of relief. Thankfully, they wouldn't have to carry this burden all by themselves. Perhaps the Lord would raise up dozens of Aadi's to handle the revival that was breaking out in Bali.

*****

Word not only spread across Bali, but also across all of Indonesia, for the Balinese were not a backward people. Cell phones, the Internet, even Twitter had become major avenues of communication.

Muslim leaders in the world's most Islamic nation were incensed to hear that many Balinese were converting to Christianity. In fact, they had been looking for a chance to force conversion to Islam on the last bastion of Hinduism, but were held back by threats of sanctions from the Global Governance Committee who wanted peace at all costs, or at least the appearance thereof.

Soon Mustafa was hearing about it back at the Vatican. Pope Radinsky then called Alexis, all within the first twenty-four hours. "It is fortunate that this so-called Christian revival is taking place on an isolated island," Alexis observed as his agile mind filtered through many different courses of action.

"So, first of all, we need to ensure that no one leaves that island," he quickly decided. "Tell Mustafa to have the Indonesian navy seal off all maritime traffic while the army is airlifted in to shut down the airports. Then we'll send in our global army to establish detention centers where we'll incarcerate anyone who refuses to renounce Jesus Christ."

Within another twenty-four hours the island was sealed off from all incoming or outgoing traffic. Three remote compounds were identified and crudely fenced off. Thousands of well-armed troops streamed into Bali, capturing control of all the major cities with virtually no resistance, for Bali was a peaceful place with no standing army.

Word of these activities came quickly to Gabriel and Abraham. They told Uncle Putu to tell the crowds of people not to panic, for they were protected by Jesus Christ, the Creator of the universe, who was all-powerful. Then they took a timeout from their healing ministry to convene in prayer to determine what they should do next.

What they heard and saw from the Lord shook them to their very core, so they redoubled their prayer efforts and even invited Aadi to join them, for they had to be absolutely certain that what they were hearing was truly the Lord's plan.

Chapter Forty-Five

C IA-East in the Tennessee Valley was almost complete. Word of General Wycliffe's success in San Gabriel inspired Jim and Abby to stop work on the finishing touches and hold a celebratory dinner. They had noticed that the round-the-clock work had dampened morale, due mostly to tiredness. People were getting snappy with one another. "All work and no play...." Abby said and Jim was quick to agree.

The underground chamber was three times as large as Havenwood1. Instead of rock-hewn floors and walls, it was built with reinforced concrete that could withstand bunker-busting bombs. The amount of electronic gear was ten times as much and a thousand times more sophisticated. Finding someone to operate the equipment had been the most diffi-cult task of all.

Where do you find another Fran? The answer was, you don't. When they got that notion out of their heads, they realized that perhaps a small team with diverse skills could also do the job. Of course, they'd also have to be born-again believers who had not received the "mark of the beast." Then, they would be trained and supervised from afar by Fran.

They sent word out to all the hideaways and remote camps. Fran came over for the interviews and just last week they "hired" one from the upstate New York camp, another from the Texas hideaway and a third from one of Morrison's companies.

Jim had to laugh at the thought that they were "hiring" people. "Great job. No salary, just room and board and lots of danger," he said to Abby afterwards.

Now they were initiating the even more daunting task of forming a militia. They were rather disturbed at the men General Wycliffe had recommended for leading the Eastern militia. They were each ungodly, overbearing men, much too full of themselves.

"Something like Wycliffe himself," Abby observed, and wondered once again about the expediency of using people who were not Christians devoted to their cause.

Nonetheless, they both felt the need to stop all the work, take a deep breath and celebrate what they'd already accomplished in a remarkably short time. Since it was a Friday, they decided to halt all work for the entire weekend. Immediately the cheers went up and spirits were uplifted.

Brandon and Juanita drove down for the weekend as well. They were almost ready to embark on their journey to all the hideaways and remote camps, so this would be one last vacation before they plunged into their new roles. Juanita would train more prayer warriors while Brandon would raise up small militia groups at each location for both offense and defense.

When word got back to CIA-West about the eastern celebration, they too thought it was the right time to have a joyful weekend. With Wycliffe's successful mission and Fran's ability to circumvent the Universal ID System, there was much to be thankful for.

Jerome and Sue decided to hold their wedding that weekend as well. When Sue approached Fran about being her maid-of-honor, she could tell that Fran was depressed. Most people wouldn't have noticed, because a subdued Francine was still more animated than most people.

Sue insisted Fran take a break from monitoring all the global databases. She had trained enough assistants who could manage the basic functions. When they were alone in Sue's room, she got immediately to the point. "What's the matter, Fran? Does it have to do with you and Jesse?"

Fran sighed and began to pace. "I hate to say this, but I think the problem isn't me and Jesse, but rather Rev. Braintree and his wife. They are so negative and so depressing, I just can't stand it any more."

Sue was somewhat taken aback. "Does Jesse feel the same way?"

Fran paced to the far wall, turned around and threw her hands up in the air. "There's the real problem. He thinks just because Braintree is a 'man of God' that everything he tells us is the God's honest truth."

"And you don't?" Sue asked cautiously, wondering where this would lead.

Fran paused, feeling hesitant herself to be critical of a minister. "No, I guess I don't," she admitted, and promptly felt relieved to have finally given voice to the dark shadows that had clouded her heart these past weeks.

"What specifically is he telling you that's not right?" Sue asked reluctantly, not wanting to get into some theological dispute for which she felt woefully inadequate.

Fran paced, stopped, thought a moment, paced some more and then, to Sue's surprise, actually sat down. "It's not any one thing, it's the overall attitude. If there's anything negative to find, he'll find it. Even if the glass is 99% full, he'd still focus on the 1%. Instead of feeling the joy that the Bible talks about so often, it's like we're supposed to be solemn all the time. Like all the "shalt nots" of the Old Testament are still hanging over our heads all the time. Like Jesus is still carrying His cross and we're not yet victorious."

Sue thought about that awhile. She remembered back to the first church she'd attended after Jesse had led her to the

Lord back at the FBI, of all places. It was full of pomp and circumstance, but formal and austere. When she told Jesse about it, he'd immediately understood and recommended a few other churches he knew about that were much different. He didn't want Sue coming to his church because it might raise questions with both their increasingly anti-Christian bosses as well as Jesse's wife.

After sampling a few, Sue finally settled into a Calvary Chapel that was kind of a midpoint between the liturgical mainline denominations and the charismatic congregations that scared her with all their carryings-on. There she'd found the "joy of the Lord" that fit her laid-back personality. It was more of a calm assurance of her eternal salvation and the loving camaraderie that gave her the foundation she needed.

When she thought about Fran's journey in the Lord, she realized how the perpetual motion machine had never really settled into any one camp, but flittered from church to church, unwilling to commit to any of them. Sue had shrugged it off as being Fran's way of doing things, but now she could see that it had come back to haunt her. Without that solid foundation, she had no fallback position when someone like Rev. Braintree threw her off stride.

She could also understand how Jesse had fallen victim to the joyless, non-victorious attitude of some churches which seemed to feel that if you weren't suffering, there was something wrong with you. After his wife left him, Jesse had become morose and prone to self-loathing, so if that was Rev. Braintree's message, Jesse was probably eating it up like a dog wolfs down chocolate, not realizing it could kill him.

Without Pastor Gabriel or Pastor Wally around, Rev. Braintree had assumed the mantle of spiritual leadership by default. No one really knew him or understood what he stood for, or against.

"What about Mrs. Braintree?" Sue finally asked, breaking the long silence. She looked over at Fran, astonished to see her still immobile. *She must really be depressed!*

"What? Oh, her? She's even worse. It's like she's afraid a smile might crack open her face. A laugh would probably do her in. The only change in her expression is from a scoff to a scorn."

Sue was never one to allow a problem to fester. "We've got to go talk to Mr. Morrison," she pronounced. "He's like our overseer, except we hardly ever see him. But he's our only hope in changing this situation."

Fran looked up, her normally bright eyes dark and heavy-laden. "I don't see what he can do about it, but I guess it can't hurt to try."

Chapter Forty-Six

General Wycliffe perused the area from atop a hill high enough to have escaped the tsunami's fury. Down below were mostly carcasses of once sturdy homes and buildings. The only undamaged aspect of what was once Glendale was the pavement. Just roads and parking lots, covered in debris. He was trying to remember the lyrics to that song, something about paving Paradise and putting up parking lots.

Well it sure didn't look like Paradise, despite all the pavement. However, it meant that he could still use the street map he'd acquired back in Denver before they'd set out for San Gabriel. It had always been his plan to move on to the Glendale detention center. The hideaway was mere child's play, a ruse to get Morrison to release the funds that would get his army on the move.

Now that they were out and about, he wasn't going to return to confinement on Morrison's ranch until he'd proven that he knew better than all of them how to bring it to the enemy. No fiddling around while Rome burned for him. He didn't need to make elaborate plans to attack a detention center. He'd already done it successfully back in New Mexico. They'd all be about the same, because the government always sacrificed creativity for the cookie-cutter approach. Supposedly more efficient, but somehow the bureaucracy still found a way to run up the costs.

Wycliffe shook himself out of his internal anti-government rant in time to find his two aides staring at him. "What are you two fools doing just standing there like lamp posts. Can't you see that I was formulating our plan of attack? You should have been off making sure the troops weren't getting disorderly."

The aides turned to go. "Now where do you think you're going? That's what you should have been doing before, but now that I have developed our plans, I need you to go and scout out the detention center."

Lt. Evan Holliday and Lt. Mary McBride stopped in their tracks and obediently turned back around, standing at attention. That's what General Wycliffe liked the most about them, their unfettered obedience. He gave them some sage guidance about how to carry out their mission and then sent them on their way. The fact that they had never done anything like that before troubled him not in the least. It was a simple task.

Down below, in a small valley that hid the militia from sight, Hank and Bill had watched Wycliffe and his two aides through their binoculars. When they saw the aides scamper off down toward Glendale, they just shook their heads.

"We're the ones with all the training and expertise," Hank complained. "We're the ones who mapped out the strategy for attacking the New Mexico detention center, but do you think he'd ask us to do it? Of course not. He'd rather have Tweedledee and Tweedledum do it. Well, the hell with him. I'm not going to get myself killed on account of his arrogance and stupidity."

Some of the other soldiers glanced over, having caught a few of Hank's words. The troops had split off emotionally into two camps. The majority were still ecstatic over their first victory and thirsted for more, seeing General Wycliffe as a hero. A minority, led by Hank and Bill, were quite uncomfortable with this sudden change in plans, believing that Wycliffe was turning into an egomaniac.

However, mutiny was not in their character, so they bitched and moaned among themselves instead of doing anything. Dusk came and went with no further instructions from above other than to eat their MREs and not light any fires. Just when they were about to turn in for the night, Lt. General Bernard went around to his unit leaders alerting them to the new battle plan.

Hank and Bill swallowed their rebellious spirits, reluctantly saluted, and then set out to gather their units together, albeit with a deep sense of apprehension. No matter what, though, they were good soldiers who followed orders. The plan was quite similar to the one they'd enacted in New Mexico. Presumably, the detention center was set up and manned in a similar manner. Leave it to the government to repeat their mistakes.

They moved out just after midnight, skirting the hills, slinking down whatever ravines and gullies the scouts had found, and took up their positions around four a.m. As they quietly reassembled their weapons for another shock-and-awe attack, Hank scurried up from behind the small hill to take a first peek at the compound. It was larger than the one in New Mexico, but appeared to have the same kind of fencing, trailers and tents, with guard towers at the front gate and the two front corners.

When he slid down the hill, Wycliffe was waiting for him. "What do you think you're doing?" the general asked in a loud, scolding whisper. "If I catch you disobeying orders or questioning my authority again, I'll reduce you to private or worse. Now get back to your duties."

As Wycliffe strode off, Hank realized that someone had overheard him earlier and reported his complaints to the general. Maybe he'd quit when they got back to the ranch. But for now, he tried to refocus on the task at hand.

Just like in New Mexico, the guards changed shifts at six a.m. Three hoots of the owl brought forth a sudden barrage of shoulder-fired missiles and grenades, bringing down the towers. As the lead team rushed to cut through the front gate, the entire area was unexpectedly lit up like it was the middle of the afternoon. Blinding lights on tall towers revealed the militia groups scattered around the perimeter.

Before they had time to adjust their eyes and their thinking to the sudden exposure, loud booms resounded from the small hills on the far side of the detention center, followed by enormous explosions that tore up the ground in and around the militia. As they attempted to regroup, a squadron of helicopters came sweeping in from the rear, strafing them with machinegun fire.

The militia scattered in every direction, only to be met by several battalions of soldiers all equipped with night-vision goggles. In no time at all, every single militia member was either dead, wounded or captured. Hank huddled on the ground, trying to stem the red tide that gushed from his belly. He realized they'd walked right into a trap.

Of course, what idiots they'd been. The attack on the hideaway hadn't gone unnoticed. Satellites with infrared filters had probably tracked their movement through the mountains toward Glendale. The scouts had missed it all and Wycliffe's arrogance had undone all the careful work of the past year.

Chapter Forty-Seven

Blaine Whitney sat in her small, temporary office in the Vatican Palace, feeling quite strange. Her mind kept wandering off in directions she'd never experienced before. She could force it back on track, but as soon as she relaxed she began thinking weird and horrible things.

This should be a time of great joy. She'd become part of the Pope's inner circle and now called several Cardinals and Bishops friend. She was even allowed to participate in the Pope's private masses. While there were certainly many joyful moments, she didn't like her mind and emotions being so out of control.

Control had always been her main goal in life. It was a major factor in her successful career, but it was also the reason her relationships were so shallow and fleeting, as Rev. Wainwright had pointed out. Now her job itself was utterly dependent on the whims of the Global Governance Counsel, more specifically Alexis and Vladimir. Worse, in her private time, all these unbidden thoughts dominated her mind.

Why was she so stirred up sexually? A part of her now longed for intimacy with her bosses, Mustafa, some of the unavailable Cardinals, Bishops and priests, even René. But when her mind wandered over to Patrick, she envisioned strangling him to death with her bare hands. The worst of all the foreign, unbidden thoughts was the absolute hatred she felt for Rev. Wainwright, although she knew he'd only tried to be helpful.

The net result of all this mental chaos was extreme emotional peaks and valleys. Maybe her emotions were triggering her thoughts? She tried to watch herself from a distance, but it was impossible to tell which came first. She tried to nap, but was awakened repeatedly after a short time by vivid dreams that weren't quite nightmares, but disturbing nonetheless. Altogether, she felt as though an outside force was attempting to take her over.

The soft knock on the office door jolted her out of the pensive ruminations. "Come in," she called out in a quivering voice. She took a deep breath, sat up straight and attempted to look composed.

Mustafa poked his head inside, began to speak and then stopped. "You all right?"

"Yes, of course. What do you want?" Blaine answered sharply.

Mustafa eyed her a moment longer. "It's time for your meeting with Pope Radinsky."

What? She glanced at her desk clock. How had it gotten so late? Perhaps her brief naps hadn't been so brief. She wasn't ready for the meeting, so what should she do? Stall for more time? Go and admit she hadn't completed her summary of the holographic image tests?

She sighed. "Okay, I'll be right down."

After Mustafa left, she gathered up her papers and tried to organize the information from the four cities mentally, but her brain was foggy. Normally, this is what she excelled at, but now there was only a mental haze. Mustafa was holding the Pope's office door open when she arrived. He gave her a smile of encouragement, as though he knew how woefully underprepared she was.

Pope Radinsky was on the telephone, but he pointed over to the couch, so she sat down and began going through her sparse notes again, unable to retain them for longer than a minute or two. She looked up when Vladimir came over and was quite shocked when he sat on the couch and placed his hand on her shoulder.

"Mustafa was right. You look like you haven't slept. Are you feeling all right?" His fingers squeezed her shoulder. It was only a gesture of fatherly concern, she told herself, but the unbidden thoughts and images suggested otherwise.

She debated within herself for a few moments, and then decided to confide in her new spiritual mentor. After she haltingly described what seemed to be going on inside her, Pope Radinsky inched closer and moved his arm across her back and squeezed the other shoulder.

"Your muscles are so tense, but I understand why," he said as he smiled kindly at her.

Blaine waited for the explanation but finally had to ask, "Why?"

"It's your spirit guide trying to establish communication with you," Radinsky said softly. "If you'll stop resisting, you'll feel a lot better."

"Spirit guide? I thought such things were fiction," she asserted, hoping to be correct.

The Pope chuckled and squeezed tighter. "No, indeed not. They are simply angels who want to help us be all we can be. They only come to the special ones, the awakened ones. This is a wonderful sign that you are one of the chosen few."

Blaine's mind and emotions were in turmoil. She wanted to ask more questions, but couldn't regain mental control. So instead, she did as the Pope suggested, surrendered to the intrusive force that was attempting to take her over.

Her body shuddered uncontrollably for a few moments, then she collapsed against the back of the couch. Radinsky removed his arm and watched carefully. Suddenly, Blaine's eyes shot open, though they were quite blank. In fact, they were completely black. That was just what Radinsky was looking for. Blaine was now inhabited by her spirit guide.

He shook her gently and her eyes returned to their normal bright blue. "Blaine, you nodded off. You really need to get more sleep."

She looked over at him, surprised to see him there. Then she looked around the room and vaguely recalled coming to the meeting. Oh no, she wasn't prepared! That must have been why she'd been so anxious. And Vladimir was right, she hadn't slept well.

"I'm sorry, Vladimir, but you're right. I haven't been sleeping well. I'm afraid that I didn't finish preparing for our meeting today."

"Oh, my child, there's no need to worry. Go get some rest and let me know when you are ready." Radinsky leaned over, hugged her, kissed her on the forehead and stood up.

Blaine was warmed and comforted by his concern. She stood up and pecked the Pope on the cheek. She was feeling so much better now.

As she left to walk down to her office, she tried to remember why she'd been so troubled. Something about not having mental control. She supposed she must have been overtired, because after dozing on the Pope's sofa she felt entirely in control of herself now.

After returning to her hotel room, she laid right down on the bed. When she thought about Vladimir, she felt so loved and cherished. When she thought about Alexis and René, she felt guilty over how she'd been judging them so harshly, for now she felt only love and admiration for them.

Sleep came quickly and deeply. As her body and conscious mind rested well, her subconscious was slowly but carefully being reprogrammed. When she awoke sixteen hours later, she felt better than she had in a very long time.

Then she heard the voice inside her, as clear as could be. "Hello, Blaine. My name is Mephistopheles. I am your very own spirit guide, your guardian angel. Together, we will accomplish great and wonderful things."

Blaine didn't feel the least bit afraid or resistant. In fact, she welcomed her new guide with an open heart. That hole in her spiritual center was filled. At last she felt whole and complete.

Chapter Forty-Eight

The entire nature of the Bali Revival, as the local news media was calling it, changed as Abraham and Gabriel complied with the guidance they'd received from the Holy Spirit. Indeed, they saw that it would have happened anyway, even if they hadn't gone ahead with the plan, because the revival was spreading of its own accord.

Instead of healing and baptizing, they spent their time teaching and commissioning. Aadi would go forth into new pockets of revival, wait for the dove of the Holy Spirit to land on someone, and then take that person back to the two witnesses for training in the basics of the faith. Abraham and Gabriel took over the schoolhouse because they needed the space and classes were cancelled because everyone was too busy celebrating and witnessing. Across the entire island, people were holding spontaneous church services wherever they could find space, indoors and out.

Gabriel and Abraham had to split up and conduct separate classes because the number of people the Holy Spirit was designating for training was growing exponentially. The anointing was so great in the classes, that revelatory understanding enabled the newly converted students to grasp the essentials of the faith right away. Then they were sent forth to heal and save, which resulted in even more students.

Finally, the numbers dwindled and the two exhausted teachers collapsed into bed after forty-eight straight hours without sleep. However, the numbers being saved, healed and taught in Bali continued to grow exponentially without the two fire-starters. They had the deepest most blissful sleep they'd ever experienced. When they awoke in unison, the sounds of celebration were everywhere. The heavy demonic blanket that they had felt covering the island when they first arrived was totally gone, replaced by a sense of freedom and love that had everyone smiling.

Well, almost everyone. The troops sent in by Alexis had finished building and staffing three detention centers. In addition, they had established two military bases where their planes and helicopters could come and go at will, and from which they launched a campaign to take over all the major cities. This is what Gabriel and Abraham had seen. They sighed deeply, and went out to face the day.

Word of widespread assaults spread rapidly at first throughout the island, but as the troops made their way into the major cities, their first order of business was to destroy all communication capabilities. Soon, Bali was completely isolated from the world. Alexis needed to be sure that no one outside Bali would be privy to the havoc he planned to wreak on this lone bastion of Christian awakening. Once he was sure all communication was frozen, he planned to blast the whole island to kingdom come, wherever that was.

After a quick lunch, Gabriel and Abraham asked Aadi to drive them to Denpasar, the capital. When they got to the outskirts of the island's largest city, they immediately encountered a checkpoint. The highway was blocked with several army vehicles. A phalanx of soldiers surrounded the cars and pickup trucks that had stopped in a long line on the two-lane road. The soldiers peered into each vehicle, checking the faces of the occupants against the photos on sheets of copy paper.

When two young soldiers examined Abraham and Gabriel, their eyes opened wide before they regained their composure and pointed their rifles at the occupants. "We've found them," they excitedly called out toward the officers back at the checkpoint. Soon a virtual army surrounded the two witnesses and their protégé.

"Get out," barked the officer in charge. They did so.

"Hold your arms out wide where we can see your hands at all times," he commanded. They did so.

"Search them," he ordered the two young soldiers who'd spotted them. They did so, and found nothing.

"Handcuff them," the officer snapped officiously, already thinking about how this was going to enhance his career.

"No," said Abraham and Gabriel together.

The officer was taken aback. "If you resist arrest," he shot back, "then I'll have no alternative but to use force, violent force, because you two are wanted dead or alive."

"It is you who need to be careful, sir," Abraham responded. "We do not wish to hurt you but will do so if forced."

This was too much. Laughable, really, the officer thought while he smiled at them. The warning from command central about being wary of these two sad sacks was ridiculous. A frail, harmless old man and a pudgy, soft Hispanic were not going to get in the way of his promotion.

"Cuff them now," he commanded the two young soldiers once again. "If they resist, beat them into unconsciousness with the butt of your rifle."

The two young men stepped forward hesitantly, not because they feared these two unarmed ministers, but rather because they didn't want to wantonly beat them. They hoped the two would just submit to the inevitable.

Abraham swept his arm toward the two young soldiers who went flying backward nearly ten feet before they landed with a thud, just as he had seen in his dream-vision.

First, shock immobilized the troops, then they quickly raised their rifles and pointed them at Abraham.

The commanding officer attempted to regain control, both of himself and the situation. "I don't know what kind of tricks you have up your sleeve, but you won't be able to dodge bullets."

"We won't have to," Gabriel quickly responded, gesturing to Abraham that they should get moving. "None of your guns will work."

As the two casually walked toward the checkpoint, the officer slowly, angrily, began the countdown. "Ready.... Aim...."

He paused to give these two idiots one last chance, but they never even looked back.

"Fire!" Click, click, click went all the guns and rifles. Not one bullet fired.

The commanding officer was stunned. All the soldiers were looking at him, waiting, wondering what to do next. He gathered himself up and looked each one of them in the eye. "These are just tricks, illusions. They're playing with your minds. Now go and grab them and throw them into the Hummer." The Hummer in question had a six-foot high cage in the rear.

The soldiers turned as one and stepped toward where the two witnesses had just been a few seconds ago, but now they had vanished. They quickly looked back at their commanding officer who could no longer get himself back under control. He just stood and gaped, his jaw slack and open, eyes wide with wonder.

Chapter Forty-Nine

Sue and Francine were not able to meet with Alan Morrison immediately because he was tied up on an important call, the housekeeper told them. Would they want to wait or schedule a meeting for the next morning? They waited awhile, but then felt awkward having just marched on over without any advance warning, so they made an appointment for the following morning.

This proved to be a worthwhile delay, because they took the intervening time to talk with a few other people about the Braintrees. They thought that maybe it was just themselves who thought there was a problem, but that was far from the case. No one wanted to speak out too forcefully or harshly, but everyone seemed to be quite turned off by the Braintree's negativity.

"They're like a dark cloud hanging over us," one said. "They suck the joy right out of you," said another. "No one wants to attend their Sunday morning or Wednesday evening services anymore because they are so, well, boring and depressing."

When Sue and Fran arrived a few minutes early the next morning, the housekeeper told them Morrison was on the phone. "No, not the same call from last night," she chuckled. "But he does spend most of his time on the phone, running his businesses from the ranch and keeping on top of all our Christian doings as well."

The two women were led into the library where Morrison often held meetings so people could sit at the large, central oak table to take notes. Sue sat, but Fran darted around the room reading off book titles. Both women were surprised at the extensive collection of both Christian and secular volumes.

Neither noticed at first that Morrison was standing in the doorway watching them with a slight smile curling his lips. He cleared his throat and they both jumped.

"What can I do for you ladies this fine morning?" he asked as he came in and settled into the chair at the head of the table.

Sue began a somewhat circuitous monologue that, to Fran's estimation, was taking way too long and was avoiding the central issue. She waited for Sue to pause slightly and then leapt in quickly.

"Look, Mr. Morrison, we don't want to slander anyone, but the fact of the matter is that Rev. Braintree and his wife Bonnie are raining on everybody's parade back in the underground shelter," Fran said rapidly.

She took a quick breath and continued on before Morrison could respond. "We've talked with a number of people over there, and we all like them okay as people, but they make everyone so uncomfortable with their negative attitudes about pretty much everything while they act as our designated ministers. But who made them the pastors over us? Did you? Can we do something about it? What do you think?"

Morrison had to suppress the grin that threatened to explode all over his face. The motor-mouth was quite a gal, he realized. Jesse was a lucky guy.

"Whoa, hold up," Morrison said as he saw Fran's mouth open for another barrage. "Let me answer the first set of questions before you add any more to the list."

The twinkle in his eye caused both Sue and Fran to laugh, perhaps a bit too heartily, but they were each, in their own way, quite nervous about bringing up such a spiritually charged topic to the man in charge whom they barely knew.

"First of all, I didn't appoint Rev. Braintree to any position of authority. He stepped in to fulfill a need, and everyone seemed to accept them, or so I thought. I saw no reason to interfere, until perhaps now."

"So, can you do something about it? My potential marriage hangs in the balance," Fran blurted as her face became consumed with pain and sadness.

So that's what's going on with Jesse and Fran, Morrison realized. Well, he couldn't have his technical expert and the operations director in a funk because of some unenlightened, old-school preacher.

Morrison's hackles were easily raised when it came to the "church" at large. He'd been burned too many times by denominations and ministers who weren't grounded in the Word. He'd sensed that Rev. Braintree fell into that camp and so had steered away from all the religious activity at CIA-West.

Well, now he'd have to deal with it, but he'd better get his anger in check and his facts straight before venturing onto holy turf.

"Excuse me, Mr. Morrison," the housekeeper said through the open doorway, "but you have an urgent call from a Mr. Hank Bradkowski. He says he's with the militia and there's a major problem."

Morrison excused himself from the meeting with Sue and Fran, but asked them to wait. He really wanted to help them with this situation. Fran once again began roaming around, spouting off book titles, occasionally opening one up and reading some interesting passages.

This time, they both kept their eye on the door, not wanting to be startled again. But they were anyway, by the shocked, ashen face that transformed the ever-confident, composed leader into a wasted shell that stumbled back into the library.

"What's the matter?" Fran asked urgently, rushing forward to help the staggering man into the chair.

His empty eyes remained unfocused for a few moments, and then began to harden. "Damn that Wycliffe. That arrogant so-and-so went off on a second mission without telling anyone and the whole militia was decimated"

"Decimated?" Fran repeated, not quite understanding what that might mean.

"Yes, all but Hank, who's nearly dead himself. They thought he was, and left him out in the field with all the other bodies. Then they took the wounded and captured into the detention center. While they were doing so, Hank crawled away and is hiding in a culvert under one of the nearby streets. He's badly wounded, but was able to call me on his cell phone."

A great many questions rushed through Fran's mind, but for once she thought she ought to keep them to herself for now. She ran outside the library calling for the housekeeper.

Sue slid over in her rolling chair and took Morrison's limp hand. "If General Wycliffe did this on his own, then it's not your fault," she said softly.

Morrison raised his head and looked over at Sue. Tears began to wind down his cheeks. "I should have seen it coming. I'd expected that his pride would become a problem at some point, but I never anticipated anything like this."

Fran returned with the housekeeper who brought a glass of ice water. The three women fussed over Morrison who politely refused to be comforted and left for his office. They heard the door close and the lock click. Sue shrugged her shoulders and the housekeeper shook her head. Yet another man who would rather lick his wounds alone.

Chapter Fifty

The festivities at CIA-East had begun with a sumptuous brunch that left everyone stuffed and well satisfied. The new chefs had outdone themselves with Eggs Benedict, Belgian waffles, deviled eggs, spinach-feta quiche, salmon crepes, country-fried steak, blueberry pancakes, chocolate French toast, rice frittata and fried bananas. Contentment reigned supreme as the new band began to play and everyone stood or sat around getting to know each other.

With the heavy work schedule they'd endured to complete the facility in record-time, there had been little time to socialize. Jim and Abby stood off to the side, taking it all in. Jim had his arm around her and squeezed hard as he saw her eyes glisten. In the midst of all the world's travail, what a joy to partner with such beautiful people on such a worthy project.

A tap on the shoulder shook Jim out of his reverie. It was the switchboard operator. Jim thought her name was Kate, but decided not to take a chance. "Yes, what is it?"

"An urgent call for you from Mr. Morrison at CIA-West," Kay answered. Though Morrison hadn't disclosed anything, she had been able to read his tone of voice. Something was wrong.

Jim kissed Abby and followed Kay back to the communications center. After listening for a few moments, Kay saw his face drain of all its color. Something was really wrong.

"Uh, Kate, I'll take this call in my office," Jim stammered and handed the receiver back to her. Normally she hated it when people got her name wrong, but this wasn't the time or place.

Jim closed the office door and listened quietly to Morrison's tale of woe. "That's just what Abby and I were talking about yesterday. All of Wycliffe's picks for our militia leaders were arrogant, pompous jerks too, even the Christian ones."

"Yeah, I guess I should have known better," Morrison sighed. "I thought I could keep him under control. Boy was I ever wrong."

"Hey, don't take it all on your shoulders," Jim said sternly. "Did anyone object to Wycliffe? Did anyone come and warn you? This is on all our shoulders."

"I suppose," Morrison answered, not at all convinced.

"So, what do we do now?" Jim asked, never one for lingering in a cesspool. He'd had to deal with too many screw-ups at the Agency, so he was quite accustomed to simply moving on in the face of adversity.

Morrison was silent awhile and Jim allowed him time to compose himself. "Well," Morrison finally answered, "I've sent out a team in a chopper to see if they can rescue Hank and then assess if there's any way of getting our people out of the detention center. I don't see how, but maybe they'll see an opening or something."

Jim knew Morrison was grasping at straws, so he let it pass. "I've been so anxious to get on the offensive," Jim admitted, "that maybe we've both overestimated our ability to strike back at this monolithic one-world government. Maybe we're better off staying with our guerilla-warfare tactics instead."

Morrison didn't respond. "I'll convene a meeting here and see if we have any advice or wisdom to give you," Jim said, not knowing how to lift Morrison's spirits.

"Okay," came the weak reply and the line went dead.

Jim sat still a moment. What lousy timing. Just when they were celebrating. He decided not to bring the good cheer crashing down, and limit the information to just Abby, Brandon and Juanita until tomorrow.

He put on his happy face as he left his office, slapped a few backs, shook a few hands, and was eventually able to get the other three down to his office without creating a stir.

"So what's the good news?" Brandon asked as they assembled inside. Then he saw Jim's plastic smile dissolve into a severe frown. "Or should I say bad news?"

"Yeah, it's bad news all right," Jim admitted as they gathered around the conference table. He explained what had happened and watched each of them sink into the same gloomy muck he was mired in.

Finally Juanita got up and began to pace, muttering to herself. They knew she was praying, so they each closed their eyes and sought wisdom and comfort from the Holy Spirit.

"Yes, that's the real problem," Juanita exclaimed.

"What is?" Abby asked.

"We covered the militia in prayer for their successful San Gabriel mission, but since we didn't know about Wycliffe's plans to attack the detention center in Glendale, they were bound to fail. Or, perhaps we would have heard from the Holy Spirit that they'd be walking into a trap and could have warned them not to proceed. In either event, it was the lack of a prayer cover that did them in."

Abby nodded. "And that's the problem with not having a strong Christian leading the militia. They don't know that the battle is the Lord's[(97)], not theirs. The militia should only undertake a mission if it's sanctioned by the Lord and confirmed by our prayer team."

"It's not by might nor by power, but by my Spirit saith the Lord,"[61] Juanita quoted one of her favorite verses.

"So, does that mean we shouldn't even have a militia at all but simply rely on the Lord?" Abby asked, now genuinely perplexed.

"I believe we are still called to have some militia groups," Juanita answered, "because we prayed about it way back when Pastor Gabriel was still here. Mr. Morrison, Jermaine and I all felt certain that there would be times when we would have to use physical force backed by spiritual power."

"Well, maybe that was then and this is now," Brandon suggested carefully, not wanting to ruffle any feathers, least of all those of the wife he adored and respected so much.

Juanita's eyes flashed anger momentarily, and then faded into blankness. They all waited quietly a few moments while their prayer leader communed with God.

"You're right, Brandon, we do need to pray about this again." She reached over and squeezed his arm to show there were no hard feelings. "But not for the reasons we think. Beyond that, I don't have a clue what the answer is."

Chapter Fifty-One

Aadi had remained frozen inside the Mercedes as Abraham and Gabriel faced off against the army troops. When they disappeared from sight, he watched the soldiers scurry around this way and that, desperately seeking to find the two ministers. With all that distraction, Aadi decided to take a chance. He gunned the engine and roared down and around the blockade at the checkpoint and heard only a few bullets bounce off the speeding vehicle as it plowed on toward Denpasar.

He didn't know where to go, or where his mentors had gone, so he stopped on a side street and prayed. "Lord Jesus, I'm still just a beginner and don't really know how to pray. I don't know what to do or where to go. Please help me."

He was distracted by an image of his cousin Komang's house just off downtown. He pushed the image aside and asked again for the Lord to help him, but the image kept recurring. Finally, he remembered how Gabriel talked of the Lord speaking to him in images, so he asked Jesus if that's where he should go. He felt an odd sensation, a sense of knowing the answer was yes without really having heard a voice or anything. Most peculiar.

Nevertheless, he quickly pulled off the side street and crossed to the other side of Denpasar. As he drove, he saw soldiers setting up more barricades on the main streets, so he veered off and took a roundabout route. When he pulled up in front of the small but tasteful home he saw Gabriel and Abraham sitting on the porch as though they didn't have a care in the world.

"Very good, Aadi," Abraham called out as the young man climbed out of the Mercedes. "Pastor Gabriel and I had a little bet on how long it would take you to hear the Lord and come to your cousin's house."

Aadi stopped and thought about that for a moment. "So neither of you doubted that I would come?"

"No we didn't," Gabriel answered, smiling broadly. "Apparently we have more faith in you than you do."

"Furthermore," Abraham added, "the Lord showed us you would come."

Aadi shook his head in wonder. "This will still take some getting used to," he admitted. "But I can see that it's quite handy to be guided by an omniscient, omnipresent, omnipotent God instead of a lowly spirit guide."

Abraham turned to Gabriel and winked. "Well, well, our student actually has learned his lessons quite well."

Just then a shout came from the front door. "Putu, it is you after all. Who is this Aadi they were talking about?"

Aadi waved at his cousin but seemed embarrassed. Gabriel and Abraham raised their eyebrows questioningly. Aadi sighed and shrugged.

"I changed my name when I became an Indonesian translator," he reluctantly explained. "I didn't want people to think I was just Balinese. Besides, there are thousands and thousands of Putu's here. I think it's ludicrous that traditionally we have only a few names for so many people."

"Ahh, yes, Putu the non-traditionalist who did everything in his power to leave Bali and now here you are back again," his jovial, rotund cousin Komang scolded gently.

It appeared to Abraham and Gabriel that this was a long-running family feud, friendly but irksome. That explained some of the initial aloofness of Aadi's family. They didn't like hearing him called by another name, and resented those who had stolen him away from Bali. Only when it became clear that the two ministers were not at fault and had actually brought him back did they loosen up.

By now the two cousins were hugging and Aadi was answering rapid-fire questions in Balinese. The name Jesus came up several times, so Gabriel and Abraham knew they were talking about Aadi's conversion and the revival in Bali. Apparently it hadn't touched this area of town yet.

As Aadi witnessed to Komang and told him of the miraculous healings, the raising of the dead, and how the two ministers had escaped from the Army checkpoint, the cousin fell to his knees in tears. The anointing of the Holy Spirit was so strong that Aadi had to grab the banister to keep from falling over.

Abraham and Gabriel went and laid their hands on Komang as Aadi prayed in Balinese and then prompted Komang to confess his sins and accept Jesus as his Lord and Savior. When he had done so, there was a crack of thunder and a bolt of lightning that struck a tree outside just down the street, setting it on fire.

Neighbors came running outside and stared in wonder at the burning tree. Though flames sprouted upward throughout all the branches, the leaves weren't consumed by the fire. Aadi glanced over at his mentors, eyes wide with wonder.

"Go speak to them, Putu, for these are your people," Gabriel prompted. "Tell them about Moses and the burning bush,[103] and about Jesus."

Aadi felt the unction and anointing of the Holy Spirit strongly, so he rushed over to the crowd gathering around the burning tree and excitedly spoke to them in their own language. Komang followed and added his testimony. Abraham and Gabriel watched like proud papas as one by one people fell to their knees, tears streaming down their

faces. Soon all had been saved and several healed of debili-
tating illnesses.

"Now that's what I call revival," Gabriel said haltingly,
choking back his own tears.

Apparently the lightning strike and burning tree had
attracted the attention of the authorities. Sirens announced
the arrival of a fire truck, two police cars and an ambulance.
The crowd backed away from the tree and laughed delight-
edly as the firemen weren't able to quench the fire.

Aadi and Komang led the entire group over to witness
to the fire, police and ambulance personnel. As they
approached, two policemen brandished their handguns while
another reached inside the vehicle to grab the microphone
and request backup.

Gabriel got up to run over and help Aadi, but Abraham
grabbed him. "I think our boy will do just fine," Abraham
said reassuringly.

Aadi recalled the earlier incident at the checkpoint. "Lord
Jesus, show me what to do," he quickly prayed.

The two policemen saw that Aadi was the chief instigator
and ordered two others to grab hold of him. Aadi waved his
arm as Abraham had done, and the two officers were flung
backwards onto the street. As the two officers went to pull
their triggers, Aadi waved his other arm and the guns went
flying onto the sidewalk.

The power of the Holy Spirit then fell upon the new
arrivals and they too were swept away into the arms of Jesus
as the tree continued to burn brightly.

Soon the sound of sirens and helicopters filled the air.
Massive local and Global Governance troops surrounded
the area, only holding back because of the wild reports from
the checkpoint and the recent transmission from the newly-
converted cop.

Bullhorns were raised and orders to disperse were barked
from several directions in both Balinese and English. The

crowd all looked to Aadi for direction even as he looked over at his two mentors. Abraham and Gabriel were still sitting on the porch steps, but now with clasped hands and closed eyes as they prayed for guidance.

More orders were shouted and warning rounds were fired into the air over the heads of the crowd. The two witnesses rose as one and spread out their arms, leaned back and cried out into the heavenly places, "Lord Jesus, cover us now completely with Your Holy Spirit. Place your armor of light[60] over us so that the darkness cannot penetrate."

A flash of light temporarily blinded everyone. When everyone's eyes refocused, everything seemed almost the same, except brighter. The captain ordered his troops to move in and forcibly break up the unauthorized assembly. When the closest soldiers got within ten feet of the cringing crowd, it was as if they had bumped into an invisible force field, like in Star Trek.

Other soldiers walked up and pressed their hands against the transparent barrier, feeling all around to see if there were any holes or weaknesses. The captain grew agitated and fired his handgun at the force field only to have the bullet ricochet upward and then bounce harmlessly to the ground.

The captain then ordered one of his men to arm a shoulder-fired grenade launcher and shoot it at the invisible bubble after the captain cleared everyone from the vicinity of the target. The grenade too bounced upward, exploded in the sky and rained down hot particles over the astonished troops.

The captain was bewildered. This was beyond anything he'd ever seen or heard. It was also beyond his rank to figure out, so he radioed over to General Asimoto who was over-seeing the global forces in Bali.

Chapter Fifty-Two

Blaine was ordered back to Jerusalem immediately. She wanted to see Vladimir, Pope Radinsky, again before she left, but he was tied up in important meetings. That didn't sit well with Blaine, despite Mustafa's excuses and explanations. She then tried to seduce Mustafa, and was especially miffed to be rebuffed yet again.

But her tirade was stopped in its tracks when she finally heard what Mustafa was saying. "I'm gay," he kept repeating until finally he saw it sink in. "Don't take it personal."

Her eyelids fluttered nervously. She used to think of gays as perverts. That's why she had been so repulsed by René's advances. But now she was confused. The thought of René sent chills of desire up her spine. Surely, then, it couldn't be wrong.

Mustafa was a good person, so how could she condemn him for his sexual preferences? Besides, hadn't she read that it was genetic? So how could he help himself? For that matter, how could she help herself next time she saw René?

But what would God say? a small voice inside her said. God? Why would He care? Only those Neanderthal's with all their "shalt nots" would care, but surely not God. Weren't we supposed to love everyone? She'd have to ask Rev. Wainwright about that when she got back. Just the thought of the self-righteous old fool brought her blood to a hard boil.

Mustafa watched the flood of emotions swirl in and around Blaine. When things appeared to have settled down, he coaxed her into leaving without further ado. Blaine arrived back at her hotel room in Jerusalem in the early morning hours. She was exhausted but restless. She realized it was right around the time Patrick would be available following his nightly newscast.

Perhaps it was time to have it out with him. She'd never felt stronger, more herself than ever before, and that was saying something. She dialed his cell phone.

"Well, if it isn't my long lost love from the past. How nice of you to return my dozen calls," he said mockingly.

Now Blaine's dander was really up. "You're the one who disappeared when I needed you. I thought I could count on you for support. Instead, you're busy cozying up to your new ingénue."

"My, my, jealous are we?" Patrick said, somewhat disdainfully.

"Not in the least," Blaine answered quickly. "In fact, the reason I'm calling is to tell you that we're through."

Patrick laughed. "That's old news. I've known it was over ever since you started working for that bunch. Then, when you started imagining demons and such, it was goodbye tutti-frutti."

Now Blaine was absolutely incensed. Memories of the demons conflicted with the recent acceptance of her spirit guide. Were they the same entities? No, couldn't be. Good angels and bad angels, she remembered. But had she heard that from Boris or Vladimir? Why was she getting so confused? Here she thought she was back on top of her game.

"Blaine, you still with us dear?" Patrick chortled, enjoying Blaine's discomfort more than he expected.

Blaine threw the cell phone across the room where it crashed against the far wall and broke apart into three pieces. That actually made her feel better.

Maybe it was time to have it out with Boris, the would-be father figure, the counselor extraordinaire. She dialed him on the hotel phone next to the couch. It rang quite some time before his sleepy voice answered. She'd forgotten it was the middle of the night.

"Oh, sorry Boris, I didn't mean to wake you. I lost track of the time," she apologized, sort of. She'd thrown it out there, but she wasn't really sorry at all. The old goat needed a comeuppance.

"Blaine? Is that you? Is everything all right?" Rev. Wainwright coughed and tried to clear the sleep out of his throat and his mind.

"Yes, it's me and things couldn't be better. I was just calling to say I won't be needing any more sessions with you." *Let him twist in the wind for awhile.*

Rev. Wainwright paused to try and figure out what was going on. This didn't even sound like the same person he'd met with last week. "Well, if you don't mind, I'd like to meet with you one more time. It's customary to have closure at the end of a counseling relationship, and I'd rather not do it over the phone in the wee hours of the morning."

Hmmph. He just wants to get into my pants. Or try to talk me out of quitting. Maybe both. But I'll show him a thing or two. "Okay, Boris, have it your way. How about tomorrow night, seven o'clock?"

He agreed and she hung up quickly. Somehow she wasn't getting the satisfaction she wanted out of these phone calls. Must be the late hour. And the travel. She quickly unpacked, got ready for bed, and slept soundly.

She felt bright-eyed and bushy-tailed, whatever that meant, when she arrived a few minutes early at Alexis' office. He was on the phone and was not at all pleased about something. *Oh well, that's his problem.*

She looked around for René and was disappointed not to see her. It was good not to feel so scared of these people.

Vladimir had taught her so much, and she felt much more confident having her spirit guide with her.

Alexis slammed the phone down and waved her into the office. "Those two goddamn witnesses are causing more problems than I thought they would," he muttered.

"Who?" Blaine asked casually, not really caring much about whatever was vexing the Global Czar. "Where's René?"

Alexis looked directly at Blaine for the first time that morning. Radinsky was right. She was a new creation. She was one of them now. He could trust her with more information. He gave her a quick summary of who the two witnesses were and the trouble they were causing in Bali, of all places.

"And why should I care about all this?" Blaine remarked casually as she studied her nails.

Alexis marveled at the changes in her, not sure whether he liked the new Blaine or not. In some ways, Lucifer's children were more difficult to deal with because they were more rambunctious, rebellious, independent. But they were also more powerful and useful, so the good outweighed the bad.

"Because, my dear, this afternoon you're going to explain to the media why no one can get through to Bali, and how we've crushed a rebel uprising," Alexis said, all the while carefully watching and analyzing Blaine's reactions.

"Oh, is that all? Piece of cake. What do you want me to tell them?" Blaine looked up and smiled sweetly. *I wonder how the Global Czar is in bed?*

Chapter Fifty-Three

True to his word, and despite the great letdown, Morrison scheduled a meeting with Rev. Michael and Bonnie Raintree the day after hearing about the militia's demise. They arrived promptly, dressed prim and proper, expressing their condolences.

"But we believe violence is a work of the devil, Mr. Morrison, so perhaps this is a lesson for us," Rev. Braintree stated smugly.

Morrison wanted to strangle him, but kept his peace. "Be that as it may, that's not why I asked to meet with you today. I've had a number of complaints about your ministry."

The Braintrees looked as though someone had hit them over the head with a frying pan. "What? Who? Of all the nerve!"

"I don't want to say who at this time," Morrison said, glad to have shifted the blame game to them. "But I would like to hear your side of the story."

"What story?" Mrs. Braintree snorted. "We present the Word of God as it was meant to be understood. Anyone who has a problem with that is obviously not in the right relationship with the Lord Jesus Christ."

"And what is the right relationship?" Morrison asked, a question he had posed to many a minister.

"Why to do His commandments," Rev. Braintree responded quickly, somewhat miffed that he had to explain himself to this pagan. "That's what He said. If you love me, then keep My commandments."[104]

"Yes, He did say that," Morrison agreed. "But what happens to those who aren't perfect, who slip up and don't always do what the commandments say?"

The Braintrees looked at Morrison as though he were an imbecile. "Punishment, of course. As a man sows, so shall he reap,"[105] Mrs. Braintree finally responded as though it were beneath her to engage in this conversation.

"And who or what does the punishing?" Morrison continued his line of questioning.

"Jesus, of course. After all, He is the Judge!"[106] Rev. Braintree sniffed, his nose pointed upward.

Morrison held back the laugh that was trying to force its way out. These were caricatures he was talking to, not real flesh and blood people. Products of cookie-cutter seminaries that churned out robots, not shepherds.

"Don't the sowing and reaping passages suggest that it is our own actions that cause repercussions in the world rather than Jesus punishing us each time we fail?" Morrison asked pointedly.

Rev. Braintree harrumphed again while the Missus snorted. "That's the problem with you liberals, always trying to water down the gospel."

"What about forgiveness?" Morrison asked and watched the facial expressions and body language carefully. Spouting scripture was one thing. What people really felt lay below the surface.

"The Lord will not always strive with the spirit of man,"[107] Rev. Braintree intoned seriously. "The reality of hell is real. People don't like to hear about the fire and brimstone anymore, but it's still true."

"Are you happy?" Morrison asked, purposely switching gears.

The Braintrees were quite taken aback. "Happiness is overrated," Mrs. Braintree finally responded. "It is better to be content, as the Apostle Paul so eloquently stated."[108]

"Doesn't the Word also say that the joy of the Lord is our strength?[109] And didn't the Apostle John write several times that our joy should be full?[110] And didn't the Apostle Peter write that we should be glad with exceeding joy,[111] and that we should rejoice with joy inexpressible?[112] The Apostle Paul wrote frequently about joy. Where's your joy?"

The Braintrees were at first shocked and then sputtered, unable to get their thoughts together. Their minds had suddenly been thrown into disarray. They felt under attack, and yet also guilty of something they couldn't quite put their finger on. A great sadness fell upon them.

Morrison pounced gently when he saw he'd broken through their hardened veneer. "When you first arrived here, I saw two older people who were happy and in love. That gave me hope. Now I see two hard, bitter people who've lost touch with one another and with all of those around them. You've become joyless. Doesn't that go against Jesus' commandments? After all, He said we should enter in to the joy of the Lord,[113] and that His joy would remain in us.[114] I think you're missing out on the greatest gift of all, and I feel sorry for you."

Shock gave way to sorrow and then to tears. Mrs. Braintree looked over at her husband who looked away, embarrassed. She took his hand. "Remember how we felt lying together in the sleeping bag under the stars? We felt free and in love again. We were looking forward to a fresh start despite all the terrible things that were happening. But all we did was recreate our old, stale lives in this new place. Mr. Morrison is right. I want to taste that joy again I felt so briefly."

Rev. Braintree's shoulders started shaking as he tried to suppress a lifetime of remorse and resentment. When Bonnie stroked his head for the first time in a very long time, he finally gave in and sobbed uncontrollably. Morrison excused himself and quietly slipped out of the room so they could mourn in private. Then he got on his knees outside the closed door and prayed that they would come to know the richness of mercy and grace that the Lord has for all His children.

When the door opened some time later, the Braintrees saw Morrison bowed over the bench seat outside his office. Bonnie leaned over and kissed him on the cheek Then she took her husband's hand, kissed it gently, and led him out the door determined that this time they would get it right.

Chapter Fifty-Four

Pastor Wally sat and scratched his head for the third time. Not that it itched. It's what he did when he was mystified. Two phone calls in the space of fifteen minutes threatened to shake up his entire world. He'd become quite satisfied with his life as it was. Pastoring a group of dedicated, sold-out Christians was a whole lot easier and more fun than being the famous pastor over one of the largest churches in the Washington, D.C. area, where even Presidents and Congressional leaders often came to worship. More likely for photo-ops, he thought.

Even the challenge of integrating the gang members into their close-knit family had worked itself out after a few bumps along the way. Bumps? In hindsight it seemed that way, but at the time everyone wondered if they'd made a big mistake taking in Reaper, Shauna, Yolanda, Izzy, Rowanda and her daughter Missy. They had come of their own free will, as much to get away from their increasingly unstable gang leader, Big Dog, as to have shelter and food.

Even more problematic had been the capture and incarceration of Dukester and Tat. Those two were quite the experiment, one that almost backfired. Wally had been convinced that, with Jermaine's assistance, he could reason with them from both a practical and spiritual direction. Too many times he'd had to wipe the spit off his face. The fact that he was white and a pastor was too big a barrier to broach.

So he'd left it up to Jermaine to deal with them, while he worked more closely with those who'd joined them voluntarily. Building trust was the key, and the entire Havenwood team helped by always being kind, correcting them gently, and giving them total freedom. At first there were thefts of food and supplies, arguments, contentions, attempts at seductions, manipulations, and a host of other problems he couldn't quite recall at the moment.

As trust grew, Pastor Wally was able to start teaching them about Jesus and the Bible. However, he found that he couldn't counsel the women individually. Too many female issues exacerbated by their previous wanton lifestyles as well as their distorted view of men. Raised in the ghetto and forced into gang slavery was not a good foundation. These weren't black issues, but rather circumstantial and environmental concerns.

So he'd trained Tara to counsel the women. With her prayer background and natural empathy, she proved to be an apt pupil and a first-rate counselor. It was Tara who led each one to the Lord. Wally would then meet with the group of four women from time to time to shore up certain areas and, eventually, for deliverance from demonic forces. Once their spiritual house was cleansed and filled with the Holy Spirit, they became one with the other Havenwood residents and never had to be treated separately again. This would make a great chapter in the book on counseling he was writing.

Meanwhile, Jermaine had taken a tough-love approach with the two hoodlums. It was the only way to break through their defenses, he said. It was difficult for Wally to watch, or even hear about, Jermaine's extreme measures. When Dukester and Tat behaved, they were granted all the privileges of residency except the right to leave. The potential of their disclosing the location of the hideaway to their former gangbangers, or even to the authorities, was too great a risk.

Everyone treated them with love and respect. But when the two hoods were uncooperative, rebellious, or hostile, they were locked away in isolation and forced to do hard labor. Jermaine used food as an inducement or reward, much like training dogs. If Dukester and Tat behaved they were allowed to enjoy the regular meals plus ample goodies. When they misbehaved, they were only given basic, unflavored nutrition.

"These young men have had a lifetime of learning the wrong lessons," Jermaine explained. "Or, as you've taught us before, their minds were programmed to the point of being hard-wired. Such mindsets, or strongholds, need to be shattered before reprogramming can begin." Jermaine's methods and the love and support of all the residents eventually prevailed, although they were still not allowed outside without an escort. Trust still needed to be earned.

Of course, Juanita and her prayer team also had a tremendous effect on the outcome, which brought him back full circle to the two phone calls. The first had been from Juanita inviting him down to CIA-East to pray and plan for the militia issues. The second had been from Morrison at CIA-West, asking him to come out and work with the Braintrees so that they could fulfill their calling to be the pastors there.

The first request was more of a one-shot deal at a relatively nearby location. The second, however, would require him to stay out west for awhile. If he did so, should he take Michelle? What about their two children, Jennifer and David? While he was noodling about these things in the lounge, Tara wandered in and asked if he was all right. Apparently, he looked troubled when he noodled.

But that's the way his mind felt, like wet, squishy noodles. So he unloaded on his protégé and was pleased with the way she led him through a logical, spiritual and emotional review of all the questions and concerns. Yes, he was getting a little too set in his ways, maybe getting a little stale. Afraid of a new challenge? He didn't think so, but he supposed that could be part of it.

What would Michelle think? She rather liked it at Havenwood now. It had taken a long time for her to fully settle in. Sure she missed Abby and Juanita, but she had lots of other friends now. Of course he would ask her. The children? They had taken the longest to acclimate to the new and different living conditions, but they seemed solidly grounded now. Hate to mess that up.

"Have you thought about the longer-term implications?" she asked after he thought they'd hashed through everything.

"What long-term implications?" Wally asked back.

"You mean it hasn't even occurred to you? Even with Juanita's example?"

Then Wally got it. The roving pastor for all the hideaways, remote camps and CIA compounds. Not just the occasional visit to the remote camp and CIA-East, both in relatively nearby in Virginia and Tennessee. Whew, this was a whole different ballgame. Too big a change to contemplate now, he told Tara.

"Don't you think you should ask Jesus what He would like you to do?" Tara nudged gently.

Pastor Wally laughed out loud. How dumb he felt. The mighty counselor had neglected rule number one, two and three. Now he knew how his counselees felt when he caught them short on that very point. How easy it is to get embroiled in your own mental and emotional machinations and forget who the real Counselor is.

"Point taken. And I must say, you have turned into a fine counselor!" Wally came over and gave Tara a grateful hug.

"Now I'll go talk to Michelle and then the two of us will seek the Lord together. I hope your prayer team will do so as well, just in case we can't see the forest for the trees."

Chapter Fifty-Five

It was quite odd inside the force field or bubble as Abraham called it. After everyone calmed down and gratefully realized they were safe from the army and their weapons, other questions began to form. What if they used up all the air inside? Could they get out if they wanted to? How and where would they go to the bathroom? What about food?

While most people fussed and fidgeted, Gabriel sprang into action. Assuming this protective force field was of the Lord, then He must have anticipated all their needs. He looked around to try and ascertain the boundaries of the bubble, but that was hard because it was transparent except when the light reflected off it just right. However, it appeared to cover just the area of the street where the small crowd had congregated.

Gabriel trotted over to Komang's house. He slowed and walked up the front steps and into the house. The captain sent some soldiers down the sidewalk, but when they approached the porch they bounced off the invisible shield. A few of the people had been watching Gabriel. They began to shout and draw the attention of everyone to Gabriel as he disappeared inside the house, leaving the exasperated soldiers behind.

However, when the others inside the bubble attempted to return to their homes, they were able to do so but were outside the force field. When soldiers ran to capture them, they scurried back inside the protective bubble while the soldiers appeared to run into an invisible brick wall.

The awesome display of God's supernatural power was not lost on many of the soldiers. One of them approached the bubble and called out to an aunt inside. Although the soldier and aunt talked in Balinese, Abraham could hear the name of Jesus Christ come up often. He motioned for Aadi to go over and soon the soldier was crying and nodding, calling loudly on the name of Jesus. Aadi waved to the man to come and he walked through the bubble as though it didn't exist. Others ran up to the very same spot and bounced right off.

Abraham, Gabriel and Aadi huddled together. "It would seem that this bubble of God's protection is only for believers," Abraham noted.

"Yes, and it expands where we go, but not for the others," Gabriel added.

"So, what do we do now?" Aadi asked, breathless with excitement.

"We pray," answered Abraham and Gabriel simultaneously. As they did, each received a glorious vision from the Lord, individually different but built upon the same premise.

Their eyes opened wide with anticipation and amazement. They quickly compared notes, hatched a plan, and then Abraham and Gabriel moved out in two different directions. Abraham walked down the street toward the captain and his troops, while Gabriel went down the street in the other direction toward the soldiers gathered there. When they approached the opposite ends of the force field, it expanded to accommodate their movements. There was a great, holy anointing on God's two witnesses.

The captain ordered his troops to stand their ground, but they were pushed back as the field expanded. The empty police cars and military vehicles became encompassed by the bubble. When Abraham reached the end of the street he stopped to survey the situation. The soldiers scrambled to their feet and ran away in terror.

The captain called in the helicopters which strafed the bubble with bullets that bounced right off. Then they dropped some type of explosive ordnance which made a spectacular sound and light show, but didn't make a dent in the force field.

Abraham, Gabriel and Aadi reconvened once again. "What we saw in our visions is coming to pass. I think this test showed that, not only are we safe, but we can use the bubble offensively to sweep the enemy off the island," Abraham pronounced.

"Hold on," Gabriel cautioned. "Let's approach this one step at a time. What the Lord showed me was that this protective shield would keep us safe wherever we go. However, it wasn't clear whether it would remain behind in places we left. I wouldn't want all these new believers to suddenly be vulnerable."

"What did you see?" Abraham asked Aadi, deciding to hold off on describing his own vision until he could incorporate what the others saw.

"I saw a great revival spreading from here down every street, with this fantastic bubble spreading over every area where the revival took hold," Aadi answered, almost delirious with anticipation.

Abraham nodded seriously. "How we get from here to there is the issue. So I agree with Pastor Gabriel, one step at a time."

Aadi was a little deflated. He was so excited about the awesome display of the Lord's power that he wanted to push it to the max as quickly as possible. But he also respected his mentors, so he took a deep breath, sighed and asked, "So, what's the next step then?"

Gabriel suppressed amusement at their precocious star pupil. "Do you have a map of the island?"

Aadi shook his head. Then he remembered where they were. "Wait a minute. Komang is a taxi driver. He must have some maps. Hey Komang, over here!" he yelled.

Soon they were huddled over a large map unfolded across Komang's kitchen table. They asked Aadi and Komang all sorts of questions about the various facilities and terrain of the island. Gabriel took copious notes while Abraham tried to focus on the big picture.

When the steady stream of questions finally died out, Aadi and Komang sat back exhausted. Abraham and Gabriel also collapsed into their chairs.

"Gabriel sighed with satisfaction. "Well, you know what Jesus said, '*For which of you, intending to build a tower, does not sit down first and count the cost, whether he has enough to finish it?*' [115] That's what we're doing and why it's so important to scope a big project out before setting off willy-nilly."

"Willy-nilly?" Aadi asked seriously. "Is that a Biblical term?"

Abraham's and Gabriel's uproarious laughter gave him the answer, and was a fitting way to end an exhilarating if exhausting day.

Chapter Fifty-Six

B laine's new attitude was immediately apparent to the media gathered on the portico of the Global Palace, as they were calling the monstrous conglomeration of spiritual building styles. The press corps was beginning to get a little snippy following the initial, worshipful euphoria over the Global Czar, the one-world government, and, most of all, global peace.

Blaine stumbled through her notes about the situation in Bali while inserting a few crude jokes. It seemed as though she didn't really care. She didn't. Her mind appeared to be elsewhere. It was. She ridiculed the first few questions and mockingly imitated some of the reporters' voices and pronunciations. That she enjoyed.

Then a question caught her off guard. "We've heard rumors to the effect that the so-called 'rebel uprising' in Bali is actually a revival sparked by the two men you call the 'world's most dangerous charlatans and fugitives.' If so, why are you covering up this information?"

Blaine was shocked speechless. *Why hadn't Alexis said anything about a revival? What is a revival? Who is this twerp? Oh yes, he's the one from that Christian magazine. We need to ban him from future press conferences.*

"That's the most ludicrous question we've heard today," Blaine finally answered. "I'm not going to dignify it with a response. This press conference is over."

With that, Blaine held her head up high feigning both confidence and disdain. But the reporters weren't fooled. They had seen the shock register on her face, lending credence to the question that surprised them all.

Normally, the *Christianity Today* reporter was shunned by all the other media types. Now, he became the center of a circle of questions about his sources, which he refused to reveal. When they saw that they weren't getting anywhere, they heaped some choice invectives upon the despised reporter and rushed off to see if they could find any confirmations of this rumor. Most likely, though, it was just the hopeful imaginings of yet another Christian whose mind was blinded by his absurd faith.

Blaine was angry and gave serious thought to storming into the Global Czar's office and giving Alexis a piece of her mind. Then she remembered that he said he was hosting delegates from all the world's financial sectors to shore up a few loopholes in the Universal ID/Banking System.

So instead she went looking for René, not entirely sure why, but feeling an intense need to see her. René, however, was "out of the country," according to her young, handsome but dumb male secretary, who refused to tell Blaine where exactly.

Blaine stormed out of the building, hailed her driver and went back to the hotel. Although the work day wasn't yet half over, she felt some satisfaction in quitting early. It was the only way she could think of to get even with Alexis for the time being. Back in her room, she changed out of her work clothes and ordered the most expensive items on the room service menu. The Global Governance Committee paid for her hotel, meals and sundries, so this also felt a little like retribution.

After a delicious lunch, she napped for awhile, took a luxurious bath and then slipped into a comfortable but revealing negligee. It was only after she'd lounged back on the sofa with a new romance novel, a genre she'd never been interested in before, that she realized Boris, Rev. Wainwright would soon be coming by. A wicked little smile played across her face as she decided to remain just as she was.

She was surprised that the banalities of the romance novel were definitely turning her on. Sex had never been of much importance in her life. Boris said it was because of her father's abuse. Sex had always seemed dirty, which turned her off. Now, it seemed the opposite was happening. The dirtier the better. She'd been freed!

She threw on the heavy, white hotel bathrobe and scurried down the hall to the room she'd leased so that her counseling sessions would be free from the prying eyes of the Global Governance Committee. Now she secretly hoped that there would be eyes to see what she had planned. Once inside, she hung the robe in the closet and paced nervously until the knock on the door finally came.

She cracked the door and peeked out, a coquettish smile on her face. "Blaine, is that you? You look different. You even sounded different on the phone last night. What's going on?"

She threw the door wide open and struck a vampish pose in her semi-transparent negligee. She licked her lips as she took in the reverend's surprised countenance. She saw the desire flash into his eyes, so she grabbed his hand and pulled him inside, slamming the door behind them.

Before he could say anything, she stepped back, released the shoulder straps and let the negligee fall to the floor. This was so much fun, so intoxicating, she thought. A whole new world was opening up to her and she lusted after it with every fiber of her being.

"Blaine, stop, this isn't right," Rev. Wainwright protested and averted his eyes.

"C'mon, Boris, you want me. I saw in it in your eyes. Your wife left you, you're lonely, and I want you, so it's okay."

"No, Blaine, it's not okay. Sex outside of marriage is not right." Wainwright turned to leave.

Blaine's lust turned instantly into blind fury. "You self-righteous, arrogant, holier-than-thou s.o.b. You make everything that's enjoyable in life a sin. Shalt not this, shalt not that. I hate you and all your Christian garbage!" she screamed and threw herself at him, pummeling his back with her fists.

Wainwright sensed there was more going on than just seduction as her fury morphed into gasping, choking sobs. "Devil, demons of lust, in Jesus' name I bind you up[116] right now and command you to cease and desist your attacks on this vulnerable young woman," Boris said authoritatively and waited while Blaine's sobs dwindled into soft whimpers.

"Go put some clothes on," he ordered. "Then we need to talk."

Blaine felt like the dirty little girl her father left behind after he'd had his way with her. She slunk off to retrieve the thick robe, since she kept no other clothes in this room.

When she turned around, she saw that Boris still had his back turned to her. "It's safe now," she said softly, and sat demurely on the couch. She could hardly believe the love she saw in his eyes rather than the disgust she expected and felt for herself.

Rev. Wainwright pulled one of the chairs over to the opposite side of the coffee table and sat down. "What happened to you, Blaine? We'd made such progress!"

Blaine's mind was mush, her emotions all mixed up. She didn't know how to even begin answering the question. What, indeed, had happened? Now it all seemed like a blur of images and feelings. She felt anger welling up again inside, but somehow it felt disconnected from her core being, and yet it was taking her over.

Wainwright watched carefully and saw the demonic anger transforming Blaine's face into a hateful glare. Before she totally lost control again, he commanded, "Demons of anger and hate and all your cohorts, I also bind you up according to the Word of God who is Jesus Christ, and I demand that you leave Blaine now!"

A snarling howl wrenched Blaine's body into a twisted, contorted convulsion that threw her violently against the back of the couch. Wainwright waited as he saw Blaine's body relax and then collapse into a heap, no longer rigid but soft and pliable.

He waited until she came to, sat up and looked at him with questioning eyes. "What happened to me?"

"Jesus just delivered you from several demonic entities that had taken up residence within you," Rev. Wainwright explained.

Blaine blinked nervously. "You mean I was demon-possessed?"

"No, that's very rare. In fact, that phrase is a mistranslation. What it really means is that *you* possess 'little devils.'[117] They are around because you allowed them to be. Your thoughts and emotions were strongly influenced by these demons, but you retained overall control. We always have a choice as to whether we reject or follow what the demons are encouraging us to think and do. However, the more you yield to them, the more control they get."

Blaine looked away. "I feel so empty now. Some of it felt very good, very right. They were helping me. How could it all be bad?" she asked plaintively.

"Because they first come bringing tempting presents, making you feel good, awakening your carnal desires. But eventually, they want control and tend to afflict their host, much like a virus will infect but not kill its victim. Now that you're rid of them, you need to fill up that void with Jesus so that they can't come back again," Wainwright pushed ever so gently. "Because each time they come back, it gets worse and worse."[118]

Blaine didn't respond at first. He thought perhaps she hadn't heard him. Then she looked at him with sad, tired eyes. "I appreciate what you've done, but I still don't think I'm ready to take that step yet."

The reverend tried to hide the disappointment from his eyes. He wanted to push her harder, yet couldn't. "Well, then, you must be very careful that you don't allow them to gain a foothold again," he warned instead.

Blaine laughed, a little too forced. "Don't worry, Boris, I know what to watch out for now."

He hoped so, but she didn't know how persistent and clever these demons were, and how they used other people to reopen closed doors. He sensed, though, that he shouldn't pursue it any further, so he tried a different tack.

"If you're up to it," Wainwright suggested gently, "I'd like you to tell me what you've done recently. I'd like to find out how you got so quickly and deeply infected."

Blaine sighed deeply. She couldn't yet betray Vladimir. The Pope had been so kind to her. She needed to talk this over with him before she continued any further with Boris. Always best to get a second opinion, she convinced herself.

"I'm not up to it now," she finally said truthfully, leaving out the greater truth. "I'll call you again in a day or so, and I promise I won't try to seduce you again," she said sincerely, even as the embers of desire started to stir again. *I'm still here, baby doll,* Mephistopheles said within her. She shivered and pretended to be cold as she closed the door behind Rev. Wainwright.

Chapter Fifty-Seven

Michelle's world was rocked by Wally's suggestion that she consider whether he should become a roving pastoral overseer for the hideaways, remote camps and the two Counter Insurgency Agency campuses. She had grown so used to this new life, that to undertake a whole new paradigm so soon was quite unnerving. So she only agreed for now to go down with Wally to CIA-East for the important prayer meeting about the militia.

The news of the militia's massacre was disturbing enough. As they drove southwest from the hideaway to the CIA campus in the Tennessee Valley, she thought that maybe she could also accompany Wally to the western campus to work with Morrison and the Braintrees, assuming that they were only talking about a couple of weeks, maybe a month.

Of course, if they were to go out west, she'd have to ask someone to watch over the children. Not that they needed much attention now that they were so well integrated into the underground community. Their days were pretty well scheduled and supervised, with school five days a week, music lessons, Bible studies, outdoor exercise, arts and crafts, etc. And they had lots of friends who they bunked with overnight.

But still, she'd feel better if there was a designated someone who accepted overall responsibility for their well-being. God forbid they were hurt or got sick while she was gone. She pushed that thought aside. It was her greatest fear in this increasingly troubled world. She didn't understand why Jesus had to take so long to come back. Weren't things bad enough as they were?

So, who to ask? Since Abby left with Jim to build CIA-East, Michelle had become closest with Carmelita, Pastor Gabriel's wife. She marveled at how well Carmelita managed to cope with her husband's continued absence, Even more so, Michelle was in awe of how Carmelita was able to ignore the terrible things the world said about Gabriel and Abraham, turning them into the most reviled persons on the face of the earth.

She thought Pastor Gabriel was quite remiss in not even contacting his wife. Surely there was some way to do so without compromising their secret location. She'd only brought it up once, because she saw the hurt in Carmelita's eyes. But still Carmelita carried on as the overseer of the women, the kitchen, the school and many other programs. She was an endless fount of enthusiasm and encouragement.

Yes, she would ask Carmelita to watch over the children while she was gone. With that decided, she napped until they were sneaking into the Tennessee valley through some unpaved back roads, which made her a little nervous. In the dusk of early winter, the shadows turned the densely wooded hills into brooding mounds of hidden danger. She shivered in spite of herself.

"Are you all right?" Wally asked, not taking his eyes off the rough dirt road.

"Yes, just caught a little chill. Would you please turn the heat up a bit?" Michelle wrapped her sweater tighter around her body, but the chills were coming from within. Even with all the counseling, fear was still the door she had trouble keeping closed.

Finally, they turned into a wider expanse. She breathed a sigh of relief, not feeling so closed in. She was amused that there was no evidence of an underground shelter that she could see with the naked eye. No vehicles, no signs of human life. Wally stopped briefly, looking for the opening on the far side of the valley into a stand of trees that concealed the opening to the underground garage.

After he drove into the narrow gap between two trees that were ever so slightly marked with a dash of green paint, he stopped in front of a thick barrier of evergreen bushes. He then placed a 5x8" laminated barcode on the dash of the automobile for a hidden camera to send to the computer for verification.

"It's still amazing to me that every worldly barcode has had three sixes built into it since they were first widely employed. That's the devil's number," Wally remarked to Michelle for perhaps the third time in the last twenty-four hours. What *she* found amazing was how men were driven to repeat themselves so often. It used to bother her on behalf of womanhood, but they even did it to one another, endlessly.

"*Our* bar codes do *not* have three sixes," Wally continued proudly but unnecessarily.

Fortunately, the bushes began to rise up in the air before Michelle was forced to come up with a reply. Instead, they both watched in awe as the ground opened wide like a giant mouth, revealing a steel ramp that led through a dimly lit tunnel into the bowels of the earth. As they drove down the ramp, the ground automatically closed up behind them, while ahead a steel wall lifted up to welcome them into a brightly lit parking garage where there were many other vehicles.

Signs led the way to an elevator whose options were to go down one, two or three levels. Wally pressed the number one as instructed, and they rode down silently, in awe of the massive, modern structure that made their hideaway seem like a prehistoric cave. When the doors opened, a welcoming committee rushed forward to greet them with hugs and kisses.

Both Wally and Michelle were overcome with emotion, an awkward surprise. They hadn't realized how much they had missed Jim, Abby, Brandon, and Juanita. It gave both of them pause, midst the animated greetings. Perhaps their time at Havenwood1 had indeed come to an end.

Chapter Fifty-Eight

Out at CIA-West, the entire emotional and spiritual climate had been indelibly altered by two vastly different events. The wipeout of their entire militia was almost overwhelming. The news that Hank had bled to death before the two new scouts could reach him, plunged the whole group of eighty people into a severe funk. However, the transformation of the Braintrees provided a light of hope at the end of the tunnel

Sue and Fran were the first to notice the difference in their de facto pastor and wife. Since they were the ones who had instigated the meeting between Morrison and the Braintrees, they had kept watch for any signs of changed behavior after the Braintrees returned.

They knew something drastic had occurred when they saw the couple go straight to their room with reddened eyes and slumping postures. But it wasn't until dinner time that they could tell something truly extraordinary had happened. Meals were served buffet style for one-hour periods for breakfast, lunch and supper. Most people came early and lingered, needing greater human contact to mitigate the isolation they all felt living underground away from their friends and family, as well as from the world in general.

They rotated the responsibility for going out into the world to buy supplies and necessities, spreading that taste of freedom across the whole group. Although there were still some jitters when they were scanned, Fran's programs continued to successfully run interference, tricking the Universal ID System into approving all their purchases.

When Rev. Braintree and his wife Bonnie made a late appearance for dinner, just as the buffet table was being cleared, both were clearly downcast and avoided all eye contact. Fran and Sue were the only ones left in the dining hall when the apparently distraught couple finished eating, having not spoken a word to each other.

Just as the Braintrees were getting up to take their trays over to the cleanup crew, Sue and Fran took a deep breath and went over to say hello and ask them if they were okay. Bonnie began to cry while the reverend slipped away with the two trays.

Sue went around the table and put her arm across the sobbing woman's shoulders. Not knowing what had happened over at the ranch house, she simply said, "Mrs. Braintree, no matter what, we want you to know that we love you."

That broke the dam wide open. Bonnie collapsed into the chair, wailing loudly. Sue and Fran were at a loss, so they began to pray over her, asking the Holy Spirit to bring comfort and guidance. They waited patiently as the wailing subsided and finally wound down to choking sobs.

In between gasps, Bonnie began to explain. "We're so..... embarrassed.... Joyful.... but very... embarrassed."

That was quite confusing to Fran and Sue, but Fran was never one to shrink away from things she didn't understand. "What's so embarrassing?"

Bonnie choked a couple of times attempting to hold back more sobs. "Because we.... were... so... pigheaded... so... foolish."

"About what?" Sue asked gently.

Bonnie took a deep breath and finally got her voice under control. "About our being so legalistic. About not knowing the joy of the Lord. About being so blind."

That confession took Sue's breath away, leaving it up to Fran to keep the conversation alive. "I'm sure you did the best you knew how." Fran chastised herself for uttering such a banality, but couldn't think of anything else to say.

Bonnie, however, was touched by the love and support being offered by the two women who had borne the brunt of the Braintree wrath. "Well, we did as we were raised and then taught by our bishop. We thought we were doing the right thing, and stuck to our guns no matter what. Even in our misery, we consoled ourselves by believing we were suffering for Christ, carrying our cross. But then....."

Sue and Fran kept quiet as Bonnie choked back another few sobs, not wanting to disrupt the flow of words now that they'd finally started. "But then over at the ranch house we were touched mightily by the Lord. It was as if a veil was lifted off our eyes. Actually, more like we were given new eyes to see and feel things from the Lord's vantage point."

Bonnie sighed deeply and looked up at the two women. "On the one hand, we felt such love and so much joy it was overwhelming. But then we also felt deep shame over how poorly we have represented Him. Misrepresented Him, actually."

Fran hesitated, and then plunged ahead. "I'm sure the Lord doesn't want you to remain stuck in shame. Once we see the error of our ways, we need to repent, accept Christ's forgiveness and let it go."

Sue was appalled, but not surprised, at Fran's boldness. She couldn't imagine giving advice like that to a minister's wife. She took a quick glance at Bonnie to see if she was offended. Instead, Bonnie smiled. Sue couldn't recall ever having seen her smile before. It changed her whole countenance.

"Fran, dear, that's our biggest problem. We've never been able to let go of things. So now we're stuck between joy and shame. It's like being on an emotional roller coaster," Bonnie admitted ruefully.

"But not for long," Morrison said from behind them. "Help is on the way."

The three women turned around as one, doubly surprised because Morrison seldom ventured underground. No one was sure whether he was just an aloof leader or perhaps had claustrophobia.

When none of the women responded, Morrison continued. "Pastor Wally Alfredson and his wife Michelle, from Havenwood1, have agreed to come out here to do several weeks of counseling. From what I've heard, Pastor Wally has been able to work wonders with all kinds of people, from gang members to drug addicts to virtually everyone he's counseled. And, he understands the special strain on those of us in the resistance movement who are forced into isolation and living underground."

"How soon can they be here, because Jesse and I could really use some help?" Fran jumped right in.

Sue saw the pained expression on Bonnie's face, heaping more guilt and shame on herself. "Yes, they can help us undo the harm we've caused," Bonnie said remorsefully.

"Don't look at this negatively," Morrison advised. "Pastor Wally and Michelle both have gone through some of the same things you and Rev. Braintree have. This is an opportunity for all of us to learn and grow in the future."

"Yes, I suppose so," Mrs. Braintree admitted, but didn't seem too convinced.

Sue finally summoned up the courage to say what was burning in her heart. "In the face of all the adversity we're dealing with, we need to do what the Lord Himself did when he had to face up to what the future held for Him."

Then she quoted the one Bible verse that had sustained her through so many difficult times. *"Let us lay aside every weight, and the sin which so easily ensnares us, and let us run with endurance the race that is set before us, looking unto Jesus, the author and finisher of our faith, who for the joy that was set before Him endured the cross, despising the shame, and has sat down at the right hand of the throne of God."*[119]

Chapter Fifty-Nine

Abraham and Gabriel were awakened just after dawn by a loud banging noise. At first they thought someone was knocking on their bedroom door in Komang's home, but when Gabriel opened the door there was no one there. Instead, the banging continued, sounding like it was coming from outside.

Komang sleepily emerged from his bedroom, while Aadi peered out cautiously from the living room. They advanced on the front door together, but stood back to allow the actual homeowner to open it. There was a whole crowd of people on the porch, some of whom were still banging their fists against the door and walls while others were stomping their feet on the wooden planks that vibrated precariously beneath them.

At first, the shouting voices made a cacophony of unintelligible noise. Komang motioned for them to calm down, holding his hands over his ears and shaking his head. "Can't understand you," he shouted back at them.

Finally the volume declined to a level where the spokesperson at the front of the pack could make himself clear. He spoke in rapid, frantic Balinese to Komang who leaned forward to catch all his words midst the continued racket.

"What did he say?" Gabriel asked when the man finished talking.

"General Asimoto of the Global Army says he is going to blow up our entire neighborhood to smithereens, as you Yanks say," Komang reported. "Our neighbors are understandably a bit agitated."

Gabriel looked back at Abraham. "About what we expected," he said, and Abraham nodded with a look of grim resignation. Being one of the Lord's two end-time witnesses was no picnic. *In fact*, Abraham thought grumpily, *it's getting to be a royal pain.*

But then he immediately apologized to the Lord. *It's also a great honor,* he admitted, *but it would be nice to get some vacation time too.* Then he laughed out loud, causing everyone to look at him strangely.

"Tell them," Abraham said to Komang, "that we'll take care of the situation after we've had a chance to get dressed and have some breakfast. Tell the general to keep his pants on."

Somehow, that didn't translate well and the people on the porch looked at Abraham as if he was a madman. Abraham simply shrugged and walked back into the bedroom. He hadn't slept well, thinking over and over about how they should employ this new, God-given power of theirs. He knew that he should simply wait for the Lord to lead him step-by-step along the way, but it was hard not to speculate about how it all might turn out.

Gabriel wandered in after him, giving him a quizzical look. "I suppose it's a sign of progress," Gabriel noted, "that we've gone from doubting to believing to nonchalance."

Abraham laughed. "I suppose so. But I also think it makes a good statement to those people out there, and in particular to the army, that we're not here to be pushed around, that the Lord God Almighty is not to be told what to do and when to do it."

"Sounds good to me," Gabriel agreed with a wink. "So let's get dressed and see what's for breakfast."

Komang and Aadi were still standing nervously by the open front door, trying to calm and appease the crowd.

"Close that door," Abraham ordered, and they did so, somewhat reluctantly.

"Komang, we appreciate your hospitality, but we also know it's been a great imposition on you," Abraham continued in a quieter tone of voice, now that the mob noise was muffled.

"We'd like to have some breakfast and are willing to pay for it," Abraham offered.

Komang was horrified at the thought. "No, no, no," he protested, forgetting all about the crowd outside. "It is an honor and a pleasure to have you here, although a little unnerving to be sure. But please, let me make some coffee and cook something for you."

He rushed into the kitchen to get things started. Aadi sidled over and whispered, "He's been very lonely since his wife passed away last year. The family was getting worried about him. Now he looks alive again, so don't worry about being an imposition."

Whatever it was that Komang prepared tasted good, so Gabriel and Abraham decided not to ask what it was. The fact that Aadi knew and didn't tell them only bolstered their resolve not to know.

The crowd outside was growing quite restive. Apparently the general had made some more imminent threats, so Abraham and Gabriel finally finished off the last of the coffee, took a deep breath and stepped outside to see what was what.

The mob parted like the Red Sea, which caused Abraham to chuckle out loud. They continued to look at him as though he were crazy, which in worldly terms he supposed he was. Crazy for Jesus.

Gabriel whistled in awe as he looked around. The two ends of the street were now thick with military personnel, vehicles and weaponry as far as the eye could see. He could understand why the neighbors were so agitated. Even he began to feel a bit nervous, wondering whether the force field or whatever it was would hold up against such massive power.

Then he remembered that the Bible said the two witnesses would prophecy and do miraculous things for three-and-a-half years before being temporarily killed, so clearly this was not their time to die.[120] They had only barely begun.

Some impressive looking officer wearing a spiffy uniform covered with all sorts of sparkling medallions was shouting at them. Just for fun, Gabriel waved at him to come on over. The general must have thought they were allowing him passage through the force field, so he strode forward and banged face first right into it. The people laughed and Gabriel was glad to see that their protection from the Lord was still in place.

But enough of the fun and games. Now it was time for he and Abraham to go on the offensive, to carry out the plan they'd hatched the prior evening. They strode forward to meet with the General Asimoto face to face. The general, however, was quite angry at having been embarrassed in front of his troops, so the smallish Asian man launched into an angry tirade in flawless English.

The two witnesses simply waited for the harangue to end. Then Abraham told him what was going to happen. "Listen to me, General Asimoto. You either pull your troops back, or we will have to destroy all your vehicles and weaponry. We'll try not to harm you or your soldiers, but there might be what you military types call 'collateral damage.'"

The General was about to have a full-scale conniption. "How dare you speak to me like that! And how dare you throw empty threats around that you can't back up! Now you have one minute to surrender, or I am prepared to have those airplanes circling above drop heavy-duty bombs that will destroy this entire neighborhood for blocks around."

Abraham sighed. He wished he could convince the military to pull back, but the Lord had already shown him that wasn't going to happen. So he simply spread his arms, turned his face to the heavens and spoke directly to the Lord of Hosts, his Commander-in-Chief.

"Lord Sabaoth,[121] I ask that you to send Your fire down from heaven and consume as many of these military vehicles as necessary to make these fools turn back. Please don't hurt any of them, but use this demonstration of Your power to cause them to fall on their knees in repentance and turn to You for their salvation."

Immediately, a rumble began to sound and the ground began to shake. It grew into something like rolling thunder that grew louder and louder, the earth now shaking as though a great earthquake was about to swallow up the entire area. Suddenly, there was an enormous flash of light and bolts of yellow fire flew down from the sky in many directions, instantly incinerating dozens of tanks, and other military vehicles.

When the noise stopped and the ground ceased shaking, it was the general and his troops who were quaking. Many of the soldiers turned and ran, which infuriated General Asimoto even more. He ordered his men into a tactical retreat, and then spoke into a handheld receiver and looked up at his B-52 bombers circling like hawks high in the sky, giving them the orders to blow these insurgents to kingdom-come.

Gabriel shook his head. How much did they need to see before they realized they can't war against God. The two witnesses and the nervous neighbors watched as the B-52s began to spiral downward. Some of the people cowered in place, while others ran back into their homes. Abraham wondered what they were thinking, but didn't have time to deviate from the plan.

Not wanting to destroy the aircraft with the personnel inside, the two witnesses waited patiently until the bombs were released and sufficiently removed from the bombers. Then Gabriel cried out, "Lord God Almighty, I pray that You disarm those bombs and turn them into ashes to rain down harmlessly upon us and the army." And so it was.

Everyone stared in disbelief as each mighty bomb went poof, with a slight whisper of sound and a tiny flash of light, as though they had been mere toys. Then all the neighbors gathered around the still burning tree and shouted and sang their praises to the Lord of Lords, the King of Kings. Midst the great celebration, no one noticed Abraham and Gabriel slip out of the protective zone, walking directly toward the general and his army, who had retreated about three blocks away.

Chapter Sixty

Alexis was absolutely beside himself about the events in Bali. Fortunately, the clamps on the media were still holding except for some sheer speculation in the now largely discredited Christian publications. He had expected that the two witnesses would be difficult to contain, but he hadn't expected such an across-the-board revival to break out over an entire population. Nor had he expected Abraham and Gabriel to create such strong protection over an area.

What if they were able to expand their little protective bubble to unlimited dimensions? That posed severe potential problems for his plans to place further controls over the general masses. If he couldn't depend on traditional military might, then what could he do? Go nuclear? Blow Bali off the face of the earth?

This required an emergency meeting with Pope Radinsky and René. And, he supposed, Blaine should also be there too, now that she was one of them, Lucifer's children. He continued to stare out the window of his private study high atop the Global Palace in the peak of the obelisk. Here he looked down upon the Dome of the Rock, and further off in the distance, the recently reconstructed third temple of the Jews.

Both of those would be destroyed in due course, but it was still much too soon to be thinking about that. Instead, he must focus on the problem at hand. Soon, they would gather and commune with Master Lucifer. He breathed a sigh of relief. This was Lucifer's problem, not his.

It was Lucifer who'd decided to allow the witnesses to fulfill their Biblical destiny so as not to disrupt the prophetic time line. Then, he planned to manipulate the dimensions of this four-dimensional world of space and time by employing the techniques that Sir Isaac Newton discovered but couldn't bring to fruition due to a lack of computing power. So, Alexis decided with a shrug, let Lucifer decide how to deal with the events in Bali that seemed to be spiraling out of control.

Blaine was the first to arrive. Alexis immediately noticed yet another change in her. He wondered whether the Pope had erred by moving too fast with her demonization. Now she sat quietly and demurely, not making eye contact, responding to his inquiries with terse, monotone replies.

Before he could think of how to probe further, René arrived in her usual brisk fashion, sweeping into the room, immediately becoming the center of attention wherever she went. This time, she went straight for Blaine. She'd been looking forward to her alleged transformation, so she sat down right beside her, placed her hand on Blaine's thigh and gazed alluringly into her eyes.

However, she did not receive back what she expected. Blaine avoided René's eyes and leaned away from her touch. René snapped around on the couch and focused her dark, angry eyes on Alexis. "We've been deceived. She isn't one of ours yet."

Blaine was wondering what that comment meant when Pope Vladimir Radinsky glided through the doorway, also vexed. "Why must we meet up here? You know I don't like heights. And that fool elevator stops two floors short. I hate stairs." Fortunately, he was wearing casual attire, not all that dreadful Papal regalia.

Alexis glanced from one to the other. Good, they were stirred up too. Why should he be the only one feeling out of sorts? "You know it's too narrow here for the elevator shaft," Alexis responded in kind, always enjoying edgy repartee.

Radinsky saw the furious look on René's face. "What's eating you?" he sniffed in disdain. He still resented her presence, although she filled out their unholy trinity.

"You are, because you're an abject failure," René snapped back. "Look at her. She's regressed, if she ever really was converted."

Radinsky slid onto the couch on the other side of Blaine, who glanced back and forth between them. "Converted to what? I don't understand what's going on here, even though it seems like it has something to do with me."

"Avé Satanus," Radinsky said reverently and probed Blaine's eyes.

"Huh?" Blaine was totally perplexed.

"You're right," Radinsky reluctantly admitted to René. He turned back to Blaine. "Have you been with Wainwright again?"

The fear that flashed across Blaine's entire countenance was all the answer he needed. "I told you to stop seeing him," he roared at Blaine, as she shrank away from him, only to wind up in René's welcoming arms.

Blaine jumped to her feet with a shriek. "You people are all crazy!" she declared and tried to get past Radinsky to escape out the door. But the Pope grabbed her and threw her back down on the couch.

"You know far too much to walk out on us now," Radinsky snarled.

Alexis had watched the episode play out as though it was a theater performance staged for his benefit. He quite enjoyed it, but now it was time to take over.

"All right, the three of you, put a lid on it," he ordered and walked away from the window, stopping in front of the couch.

Blaine's hopeful eyes brought a smirk to the Global Czar's lips. Despite his two partners' vain attempts to claim their prize, he always knew that Blaine belonged to him. Now it was time to take possession.

"Hold her down," Alexis commanded. Radinsky and René knew that tone of voice. He wasn't to be trifled with when he sounded like that. They immediately complied.

Alexis spread his arms and faced the image of Lucifer with the goat's head and unicorn's body on the wall behind his desk, right next to the blazing star. "Oh mighty Lucifer, we ask you to join us now. One of your children has gone astray. In your great mercy, we ask that you reclaim what was yours."

Alexis opened the narrow cabinet that ran along the backside of the desk and pulled out a vial of blood and the human skull. "As we rededicate ourselves to you, we also offer Blaine to you as our holy sacrifice."

He poured the blood into a compartment inside the skull. "Let this blood wash away all the contamination of the enemy from our bodies, minds and souls."

Alexis drank from the skull and handed it to Radinsky who tipped it forward and sipped from its mouth. Then he passed the skull on to René who eagerly slurped from it and then licked up the drops that were about to drip off the jaw bone.

Blaine's eyes were wide with fright. This seemed somewhat familiar. Like that mass she had attended but about which she recalled very little. A black mass, Rev. Wainwright said.

As the Pope and the Mother of Harlots held her arms, Alexis squeezed Blaine's nose to force her mouth open and then poured the rest of the blood down her throat. "Let the blood pour through the doorway to her soul that she willingly gave to you, O Lucifer. She has been unfaithful, but she didn't know any better. Take her back into your arms once again, make her yours, let your holy spirit, Mephistopheles, merge with hers and take up residence once again."

Blaine was choking on the blood, red spit flying every which way. Then suddenly her body went rigid and her eyes blank. She moaned, quivered and fainted into oblivion.

Chapter Sixty-One

B ack at CIA-East, Pastor Wally and Michelle awoke somewhat disoriented. Then they remembered where they were, and why they had such a large bedroom all to themselves. Not that they minded having Jermaine and Tara as roommates back in the hideaway, but a touch of privacy was a nice way to start the day.

Michelle was feeling a lot better about things and was glad she had told Wally to go ahead and make plans for them to spend some time at CIA-West. They slept in awhile and then enjoyed a late breakfast in the spacious dining room, all sparkling clean with gleaming stainless steel everywhere. What a change from their earthy domain.

But now it was time to get to work. Jermaine had just arrived, having eaten along the way down from Havenwood1. So all the players were there, ready to chase after God and a solution to the militia conundrum. They convened in a brightly lit, spacious conference room that made Jermaine a little jealous. However, he quickly reminded himself how much he had grown to love the Virginia hideaway and the people there, especially his new wife Tara. He was a lucky man and he knew it.

After Juanita led them in an opening prayer, Jim asked to speak. "In a sense, I feel somewhat responsible for the militia's demise," he admitted to the surprise of everyone else, except for Abby, his wife and confidant.

"I was the one who clamored for us to go on the offensive, to take it to the enemy. And though I know we're doing so through our spiritual warfare groups, I was the one who really pushed for there to be a physical army as well." Jim paused, trying to contain his emotions and gather his thoughts.

"None of this is your fault alone," Juanita quickly responded. "We all prayed together and felt like the Lord approved of those plans."

"Well, then, why did it go so horribly wrong?" Jim asked mournfully.

"Because I made a terrible misjudgment," Alan Morrison interjected through the partially open door. He had flown in on his private jet after Wally informed him of the meeting.

When the excitement of his surprise visit had calmed down, Morrison went on to explain. "I thought we could make use of an ungodly man like General Wycliffe to perform the dirty work for us. I mistakenly believed that I could manage him. That proved to be a fatal error."

Morrison allowed those words to sink in before continuing. "Not only that, but the militia was rife with people who were part of it for all sorts of reasons, but only a small contingent for the Lord's true cause. I believe we need to go forward with a militia, but smaller in scope and comprised only of dedicated believers who understand what we're trying to accomplish."

"What are we trying to accomplish?" the always direct Abby asked.

That brought the conversation to a dead stop. Jim felt obliged to try and summarize what he thought it meant for them to go on the offensive. "It was my belief and understanding when we made the decision to go ahead and form the militia, that it would serve three purposes. First, to protect our hideaways and remote camps from attack; second, to rescue believers who were being unlawfully detained; and third, to strike at strategic points of vulnerability in the one-world government in order to prevent major attacks against Christians."

Everyone was impressed with Jim's ability to wrap it all up in such a concise manner. But they had never seen him in operation back when he was the Deputy Director of the actual CIA. They'd only known him as a baby Christian who'd grown up among them. They still tended to think of him as Abby's husband. Now, though, with the completion of the eastern campus of the Counter-Insurgency Agency East, they were beginning to see him in a different light.

"Yes, I think that about sums it up," Morrison agreed. "Our success in retaking the San Gabriel hideaway and destroying it to prevent the authorities from tracking down our other hideaways and remote camps, was a prime example of fulfilling that mission."

"But then Wycliffe went haywire," Brandon noted. "Which goes back to your earlier point. We need to have godly, Holy Spirit-led officers and soldiers who understand the cause."

"Let's not forget that the militia's demise happened not only because they went off on their own, but they did so without any prayer covering," Juanita added.

"Yes, that's true," Abby agreed. "So, if we decide to reform a militia, it needs to be comprised of only strong Christians who believe in what we're doing, and they should only undertake a mission when it has been approved by the Lord and covered with prayer."

Wally laughed. "You two are certainly of like minds and abilities," he said, looking admiringly at the happy couple.

"It was your spiritual warfare course that enabled us to understand how much we need to depend on the Lord in choosing our battles and devising a plan of attack," Jim returned the compliment.

"Oh, all right, let's stop patting each other on the back and get back on point," Juanita said, although her bright smile and wink showed she too felt the love and camaraderie in the tight-knit group. "Does anyone have any other thoughts or questions before we take it to the Lord?"

After a brief silence, Michelle spoke up softly and shyly. "I've never been part of these meetings before, and I appreciate your allowing me to attend. I don't want to be disruptive, but there is a question I'd like to ask."

"By all means," Jim quickly assented. "We're quite pleased that you're fully one of the team now."

Wally looked on proudly as Michelle continued. "Wally explained to me the Biblical case against the pre-Trib rapture that Pastor Gabriel presented before he…. before he became one of the two witnesses."[122]

Michelle paused, not wanting to appear foolish, but really wanting to get an answer to the question that had been plaguing her for some time. "However, I don't understand why we think there won't be a mid-Trib rapture, instead of the so-called pre-wrath rapture you all talk about?"

That brought the proceedings to a grinding halt. "Where's Pastor Gabriel when we need him?" Abby finally asked. "Probably out gallivanting around the world," she answered herself and they all laughed.

Juanita's eyes lit up. "Maybe he's off in Bali where that supposed revival is taking place, according to some of the Christian media? Of course, the mainstream media is calling it a revolt."

That caused everyone to sit back and ponder what the two witnesses might be doing. Their spirits and imaginations soared as they thought about revival breaking out in Bali, of all places.

"Ahem," Jermaine cleared his throat to recapture everyone's attention. "I think Michelle has asked a good question, one we should all be prepared to answer, because that's what we're basing much of our plans on."

"You're absolutely right," Juanita quickly jumped in, "and you're just the man for the job. You've worked most closely with Pastor Gabriel on those plans and I think you're pretty adept with Scripture, so maybe you could sort it all out for us."

Jermaine shook his head. "I knew it was a mistake to open my mouth, but if that's what you want me to do, we need to take a recess so I can get my thoughts and Scriptures in order."

That made sense to everyone, so they decided to adjourn for an hour and then reconvene to address this specific issue before they made any decisions about the militia.

Chapter Sixty-Two

As Abraham and Gabriel advanced on General Asimoto's global army, they paused and glanced back toward Komang's block, straining to see whether the bubble of protection had remained in place. Everything seemed normal, but no troops had attempted to reenter the zone, so it was hard to tell. The force field, or whatever it was the Lord had done, was invisible so there was no way for them to see if it still stood firm.

Meanwhile, General Asimoto had just gotten off the satellite phone with the Global Czar himself. Normally he was unshakable, but he was shaking now. He was stuck between an enormous rock and an extremely hard place. While he thought of the two witnesses as the rock side of the equation, he didn't realize that it was *the* Rock[123] that was his problem.

On the other side was the hard, unrelenting savagery of Alexis D'Antoni, a man like no other. What the general didn't know was that there was indeed no other man in all the world like the Global Czar, because he was almost completely possessed by the devil himself. Had Asimoto understood the spiritual nature of his dilemma, he might have made better choices.

As it was, he had a premonition that things were going to work out badly, but he had a job to do, as D'Antoni had made abundantly clear. "Throw everything you've got at them, and if that doesn't work, destroy the entire island and everyone on it. Use any means necessary, and I mean *any* means." He presumed that meant the nuclear option, left unstated to give the Global Czar plausible deniability.

He held his ground and stood rigidly at attention as the two witnesses approached. When they finally were standing right in front of him, he formally pronounced, "At the direction of the Global Czar, I am commanded to tell you that this island and everyone on it will be thoroughly destroyed if you do not leave Bali immediately. We may or may not be able to counter your powers, but do you wish to see millions of innocent people die because of your stubbornness?"

The two witnesses were clearly surprised at the rapid escalation to the maximum level. They looked at one another for a moment, and then Abraham spoke passionately. "It is not we whose power you are opposing, but rather the Creator of the universe. And it is not we who are being stubborn, but rather the King of Kings. This earth is His footstool[70] and He will not allow you to destroy this island or His people on it."

Now it was the general who looked a little taken aback. But both had said what needed to be said. Now it boiled down to a test of wills and might. "You have twenty-four hours to comply. If you do not leave, the consequences are on your consciences," Asimoto concluded.

Gabriel and Abraham nodded at the general, turned around and headed back to Komang's place. They would have to move more quickly than they'd expected. In fairness, though, they realized that they had merely interpreted the timeframe of their visions. Neither had heard the Lord say how long it would all take to unfold. It was human nature to stamp their own expectations on it.

Back at the house, they gathered up the maps and notes and got in the taxi. Komang was at the wheel and Aadi rode shotgun. Gabriel chuckled to himself. An apt phrase, except their weapons weren't shotguns but the spiritual might of the Lord.

Komang drove through downtown Denpasar and headed south to the Renon area where the government had its official offices. They were surprised to see so many people out and about. The revival had taken on a life of its own. Many people knew nothing of the two witnesses, but had encountered others who had been healed and/or saved by Jesus Christ.

The anointing on the island was so great that anyone who opened up just a crack of their soul to the Lord received a blinding light of truth and revelation almost like Paul received on the road to Damascus. Fortunately, no one was blinded for any length of time. Instead, spontaneous celebrations were breaking out all over Bali. Komang had to weave his way through and around enormous block parties.

When they reached the government offices, Komang and Aadi waited in the taxi while Abraham and Gabriel went forth to do what the Lord had shown them. While they had marched down to confront General Asimoto, Komang had prepared anointing oil according to the specifications they gave him directly from the Lord. It was an unusual mixture of olive oil and several of the island's essential oils.

Komang had been surprised to find just what he needed in the kitchen cabinets. His wife had been quite the cook, but he never did more than the very basics. It dawned on him that this Jesus Christ to whom he had just yesterday committed his life, knew those oils were there all along, giving him a big faith boost.

Now each of the two witnesses carried small vials of the special anointing oil prepared for just this purpose, this very day. Nothing came as a surprise to the Lord of Lords. Because of the revival and the military action around Komang's house, which most of the revelers knew nothing about, the government offices were closed. Very convenient.

Gabriel and Abraham anointed the doors of the main government building with the special oil and prayed out loud as instructed. "In the mighty name of Jesus Christ, who is coming back soon in Person to retake possession of His Kingdom, we proclaim here in the capital of Bali that the entire island and all of its people are now and forever more part of that Kingdom. We separate it out from the ways of the world and ask Father, in Jesus' name, that you forgive this government and the population of their pagan ways.

"We further ask, Father, that you break off all the curses that they brought upon themselves through their sinfulness, and wash them clean with the water of Your Word[124] and the shed blood of Your precious Son, Jesus Christ.[125] And finally, we ask now that you keep this island and all its people under the shadow and protection of Your wings. We declare that under your wings, Bali shall seek and find refuge from the perilous pestilence that walks in darkness and the destruction that lays waste at noonday.[126] Thank you Father, in Jesus' name we pray. Amen."

Komang then drove north out of Denpasar, which was near the southern coast of Bali, toward the ancient colonial capital, Singaraja, about fifty miles away, across the breadth of the entire island. Komang had explained earlier that Singaraja was the Dutch colonial administrative center for Bali and the Lesser Sunda Islands until 1953. It was the port of arrival for most visitors until the development of the Bukit Peninsula area in the south where the two witnesses had flown in last week.

Singaraja was also the regency seat of Buleleng, Indonesia. A regency, Komang explained, is a bigger area than a city, and has a regent appointed by Indonesia over it. Most people forget that Bali is not an independent nation, but rather part of Indonesia. It was for this reason that the two witnesses knew they must also pray similarly over this previous capital of Bali, because that's where its ancient spiritual roots had first grown.

They were pleased to see that the revival had spread all the way north as well, and that those government offices were also shut down. They anointed the doors and prayed the same prayers as in Denpasar, but added, "We take the axe of the Holy Spirit to the roots of the bad spiritual trees that grew here and spread across all of Bali, and in Jesus' name, we cut down those trees and cast them into the fire according to Your holy Word.[127] We ask now, Father, that you cleanse Bali from all the sins and curses of the past, from the indigenous tribes to the Dutch influences to past and current Indonesian authority.

"We further declare, in Jesus' mighty name, that Bali is a new creation in You, a new people, a new nation, no longer rooted in the past, forgetting those things which are behind and reaching forward to those things which lie ahead, pressing on toward the goal and the prize of the upward call of God in Christ Jesus."[128]

When they had finished their mission in Singaraja, Komang drove them west into Lovina Beach, where they relaxed and ate a large meal in a small, family-run restaurant overlooking the ocean. From this vantage point, everything did indeed look new and fresh, as the tides swept away the debris.

However, they knew they had one more journey and one more task to complete before General Asimoto unleashed whatever military response was up his sleeve. They piled back into the taxi and headed east.

Chapter Sixty-Three

When the CIA-East group reconvened, including Alan Morrison from the western CIA campus, Jermaine had several pages of hand-scribbled notes drooping out of his well-worn Bible. Michelle still felt a little awkward at having caused the meeting to go off agenda to satisfy her own curiosity, despite everyone telling her it was actually a good thing it came up now.

Understanding the Biblical rationale for a pre-Wrath rapture wasn't so important earlier on when they were positioning themselves against the pre-Tribulation viewpoint. But now that the seven-year Tribulation had begun, they needed to better understand the arguments against a mid-Tribulation rapture and what exactly a pre-Wrath rapture meant.

When they had all been seated and quieted down, Jermaine stood up at the head of the table. He had set up a portable flip chart off to his left. Speaking like this in front of groups was not Jermaine's thing, no matter how small nor how well he knew the participants. He was quite nervous, but well prepared.

"Okay, I guess we should get started." Jermaine took a deep breath and plunged right in. "Before talking about the pre-Wrath rapture, we need to understand the core reason why a mid-Trib rapture is not feasible. The Lord said that we would not know in advance the day when we would be taken up into heaven. We now know the day the Tribulation started, that is when the "peace pact with many" was signed as prophesied in Daniel 9:27.

"We also know from Daniel 9:24-27 that the Tribulation is to last seven years. Therefore, we can say with certainty when the midpoint of the Tribulation will occur. This violates Jesus' admonition that we won't be able to predict the day of the rapture, and since He is not a liar,[41] there can't be a mid-Trib rapture." Jermaine paused and glanced anxiously at the seven people gathered around the conference table. The nodding heads seemed to indicate that everyone understood and was satisfied with this key point, so he pushed forward.

"Now the case for the pre-Wrath rapture requires some more background that is not familiar to most Christians. It begins with understanding what the Bible means in its many references to the 'Day of the Lord', also called 'that Day' or 'this Day' or '*the* Day.' Malachi 4:5 calls it 'the great and dreadful day of the Lord.' So, what exactly is this Day?"

Jermaine saw that he had the rapt attention of everyone, so he continued. "Here are some additional verses that describe that day." He then began writing them out on the flip chart, wanting everyone to see them all together. "Now, remember, these are just a few of many verses that refer to this day:"

> ➢ Psalm 110:5 *The Lord is at your right hand; He shall execute kings in the <u>day</u> of His <u>wrath</u>. He shall <u>judge</u> among the nations.*
> ➢ Revelation 11:18 *The nations were angry, and Your <u>wrath</u> has come, and <u>the time</u> of the dead, that they should be <u>judged</u> and that You should <u>reward</u> Your servants the prophets and the <u>saints</u>, and those who fear your name, small and great, and should destroy those who destroy the earth.*

> ➤ 1Thessalonians 5:4 *But you, brethren, are not in darkness, so that this <u>Day</u> should overtake you as a thief.*
> ➤ Ezekiel 30:3 *For the day is near, even the <u>day of the Lord</u> is near; it will be a day of <u>clouds</u>, the time of the Gentiles*
> ➤ Joel 3:14 *Multitudes, multitudes in the valley of decision! For the <u>day of the Lord</u> is near.*

"Whew. That's going to be some day!" Abby exclaimed. "I didn't realize the Bible said so much about that particular day. Is so much really going to happen in just one day?"

"Good question, one I spent some time just now verifying," Jermaine responded enthusiastically. He was pleased that he'd thought ahead about the questions that might come up.

"Both the Hebrew and Greek words used in this context can mean a twenty-four hour day or some indeterminate amount of time, usually of short duration," Jermaine explained. "So it's not entirely clear, but that goes along with the overall premise that we won't know exact dates and times in advance."

Everyone appeared to accept that point, so he moved on. "We can see from these verses I wrote out on the chart that the 'day of the Lord' involves Jesus coming to execute judgment on the earth with great wrath, but the saints will be rewarded. In several other Scriptures, we're told that we don't receive our rewards until we are in heaven,[129] immediately after the rapture. That's why it's a 'great' day for Christians."

"Even the reference to clouds evokes imagery similar to Revelation 1:7 which tells us, *'Behold, He is coming with clouds, and every eye will see Him.'*" Also, 1Thessalonians 4:17 says, *'Then we who are alive and remain shall be caught up together with them in the clouds to meet the Lord in the air.'* This verse refers to the rapture, which comes from Latin word *rapieumur,* for the English phrase "caught up."

Wally laughed out loud and wound up with everyone looking at him, waiting for an explanation. "Sorry, but I was remembering back to my Lutheran pastorship days when so many people would state that the King James Version was the only one to use, all others being faulty. So I would ask them what language the Bible was originally written in, which tended to give them pause or make them angry. Others would tell me the word 'rapture' wasn't in the Bible, as if English was the only language God uses."

Several of the others nodded their heads knowingly, having run into the same hardheadedness themselves. Jermaine waited till he was sure there were no other comments, then picked up his presentation. "So let's look a little more closely into why Malachi calls it a 'great' day as well as a 'dreadful' day, even though he originally wrote that verse in Hebrew." He waited to see if anyone caught his little joke. They did and rewarded him with a few smiles. He was actually beginning to enjoy this.

"Let's look at a few verses that show us how truly dreadful this day will be for unbelievers," Jermaine said as he turned to a blank flip chart page:

> ➢ Isaiah 13:6,9 *Wail, for the day of the Lord is at hand! It will come as <u>destruction</u> from the Almighty... <u>Cruel</u>, with both <u>wrath</u> and <u>fierce anger</u>, to lay the land <u>desolate</u>; and He will <u>destroy</u> its sinners from it.*
> ➢ Jeremiah 46:10 *A day of <u>vengeance</u>... the sword shall <u>devour</u>.*
> ➢ Joel 2:11 *The day of the Lord is great and very <u>terrible</u>; who can endure it?*
> ➢ Joel 2:31, Acts 2:20 *The <u>sun</u> shall be turned into <u>darkness</u>, and the <u>moon</u> into <u>blood</u>, before the coming of the great and awesome day of the Lord.*

➢ Matthew 24:21-22 *For then there will be <u>great tribulation</u>, such as has not been since the beginning of the world until this time, no, nor ever shall be. And unless those days were shortened, no flesh would be saved; but <u>for the elect's sake those days will be shortened</u>.*

➢ 2Peter 3:10 *The <u>heavens will pass away</u> with a great noise, and the <u>elements will melt</u> with fervent heat; both the earth and the works that are in it will be <u>burned up</u>*

"You're right, Abby," Brandon remarked, "it hits home much harder when you see all these verses together. I'm glad we get to escape the brunt of it all."

"That's right, and there are even more verses that speak about how awful it will be," Jermaine agreed. "But let's look at a couple of important points contained in these Scriptures, beyond how awful it will be. First of all, notice what it says in Acts 2:20 that repeats Joel 2:31. A major, cataclysmic event will blot out the sun and cause the moon to appear red. There's been lots of speculation about how this will occur, from volcanic eruptions to nuclear war.

"But that's just speculation. We're more concerned about *when* this will occur. Turn in your Bibles to Revelation, chapter five, beginning at verse twelve and read along with me. *'I looked when He opened the <u>sixth seal</u>, and behold, there was a great earthquake; and the <u>sun</u> became <u>black</u> as sackcloth of hair and the <u>moon</u> became like <u>blood</u>. And the stars of heaven fell to the earth... Then the sky receded as a scroll... and every mountain and island was moved out of its place.'* Then in verse seventeen, *'For the great <u>day</u> of His <u>wrath</u> has come, and who is able to stand?'*

"We can see that this event, which is triggered when Jesus opens the sixth seal, fulfills Joel's prophecy, with verse seventeen tying it to the 'day of wrath.' Jesus also refers to these signs in Matthew 24:29-31: Jermaine turned there in his Bible and read, *'Immediately after the tribulation of those days, the sun will be darkened, and the moon will not give its light; the stars will fall from heaven, and the powers of the heavens will be shaken. Then the sign of the Son of Man will appear in heaven, and then all the tribes of the earth will mourn, and they will see the Son of Man coming on the clouds of heaven with power and great glory. And He will send His angels with a great sound of trumpets, and they will gather together His elect from the four winds, from one end of the heaven to the other."*

Of course, we don't know the exact day when this will occur, but for the *'elect's sake,'* that is for believers, those days will be *'shortened'* by the rapture, the catching away of the saints. *'For the Lord Himself will descend from heaven with a shout, with the voice of an archangel, and with the trumpet of God. And the dead in Christ will rise first. Then we who are alive and remain shall be caught up together with them,"* Jermaine quoted from 1Thessalonians 4:16.

After Jermaine finished reading those verses, a holy hush fell over them all. It was as if the presence of the Lord had come to give further witness to the truths of the Scriptures just read. Everyone forgot the original purpose of the meeting, and began to spontaneously pray and worship the Lord. It was an awesome experience, one they would never forget.

Many tears flowed, much joy was received. But more importantly, everyone was also given a heavier burden for all those unbelievers out there who would remain on the earth as all hell literally broke loose upon them. They shuddered as they recalled the awfulness of the trumpet and bowl plagues that were to occur after the rapture when Jesus opened the seventh seal.[146] And each realized in their own way that whatever missions the militia eventually executed, the primary goal was to save souls.

Chapter Sixty-Four

Since Bali did not have any major roads that crossed the island from east to west, Komang drove them along Jalan Serrit – Singaraja, the beginning of a coastal route that first wound eastward and then to the south, changing names several times along the way. Komang soon turned off that route and headed south on Jalan Gunung Batur.

Abraham and Gabriel were asleep in the back, the large lunch and the day's excitement and awesome responsibilities catching up to them. Aadi used the time to catch up on family matters with his cousin, and then answered many of Komang's questions about Jesus, the Bible and Christianity in general.

When Komang turned off the main road an hour or so later, Aadi reached back and shook Gabriel and Abraham by their knees. It took a little while for them to reorient themselves. The sun was still shining brightly in the middle of the afternoon. "Where are we?" Gabriel asked.

"We've just made the turn toward Besakih, which will take us to the Mother Temple," Komang answered. "I thought, perhaps, that I should tell you a little about the temple before we get there."

"Yes, that would be very useful," Abraham agreed.

"Well, it is the most important of all our temples," the longtime taxi driver and tour guide began. "It is also the largest of our holy sites. But, of course, they are no longer holy to us now that we have been set free by Jesus," Komang quickly amended.

Gabriel chuckled. It was always difficult for new converts to shed the language of the past. "No worries. We know your new faith is real."

Relieved, Komang continued his spiel. "The temple is located on the slopes of Mount Agung, an active volcano and the highest point in Bali at 3,142 meters high, that's over 10,000 of your feet. The temple is comprised of three main complexes dedicated to the Hindu Trinity, Brahma, Vishnu and Shiva." Komang was pleased with himself for leaving off the 'lord' before each name of the false gods.

"The Pura Besakih temple was built during the late 8th century AD. A series of eruptions of Mount Agung in 1963 killed approximately 1,700 people and also threatened the temple, but the lava flows missed the compound by mere meters. The saving of the temple has been regarded as miraculous, and a sign from the gods that they wished to demonstrate their power but not destroy the monument the Balinese faithful had erected."

Komang reprimanded himself now for implying continuing belief in the Hindu gods. But wasn't it possible they were just lesser gods? Before he could begin to sort that out, Abraham spoke up. It was as though he had read Komang's mind, but it was merely heightened discernment through the Holy Spirit.

"There are only three possibilities behind the temple avoiding destruction. It could have just been an accident of nature, but I don't think so. Otherwise, it is either of the Lord Jesus or the devil," Abraham stated firmly.

"But why would the devil wish to do us good?" Komang asked, genuinely confused.

"Oh, the devil is always offering something that feels good, or what *seems* good. Otherwise, how could he trick people into going along with him? In this case, it reinforced your belief in the false gods that Satan himself raised up, so it was most likely his doing," Abraham explained.

Komang was soaking that in as they broached the entrance to the temple grounds. It was all quite beautiful and impressive. It was easy to see how people could be duped into translating natural beauty into holiness, connected to the gods to whom the splendor was dedicated. Satan was very adept at taking what God created and twisting it to his own purposes.

Gabriel checked his watch. It was after four p.m. General Asimoto's 24-hour deadline was going to make things difficult. They'd have to finish the climb up Mount Agung in the dark, but there was no way around it.

After parking the car, Komang and Aadi both began pleading with the two witnesses to postpone their arduous hike up the mountain to the following day. "It is a difficult hike that takes at least four hours," Komang pointed out again. "And that's for those who are in excellent shape."

Abraham and Gabriel laughed. The elderly rabbi and the paunchy pastor were obviously not in the best of shape. But they knew without a doubt that the Lord was calling on them to finish their mission before Asimoto's deadline expired.

"Komang, Aadi, we truly appreciate your concern. If the Lord hadn't called upon us to do this, you'd be right. It makes no sense and we probably wouldn't even make it to the top. But if this is indeed His will, then He will assist us along the way, you'll see," Gabriel asserted, pushing his own doubts aside.

There was no time to waste sightseeing, so Komang reluctantly led the foursome through the temple complex and onto a path that traveled continuously upward on a steep narrow spur through open jungle. They paused many times, since they would have to climb nearly 2,000 meters, or around 6,600 feet to reach the top.

Each time they stopped, Gabriel and Abraham prayed for supernatural strength. Although strained and tired, they were able to keep going. Four hours came and went. Still they plugged along, following Komang who had his industrial-strength spotlight illuminating the path. The wild sounds of the jungle gave way to odd chirping and rustling noises as they reached higher, more barren elevations.

Komang stopped when he came to a fork in the path. "Here is where many tourists get lost," Komang said as he pointed ahead to the fork that looked the most promising. "That will take you into a small valley, a dead end. We need to go the other way, even though it looks like we're doubling back."

Abraham and Gabriel were exhausted. Komang and Aadi weren't much better off. They swigged some more of the water in the canteens Komang had supplied for the hike. Then they prayed yet again, and set off at a markedly slower pace. As they approached the peak of the volcano several hours later, the only sound they heard was their labored breathing.

Finally, Komang stopped, searched the area with the spotlight, and pronounced they had arrived. They collapsed into four heaps on the ground. No one said anything for quite some time. When at last they seemed to have caught their breath in the thin mountain air, Abraham said, "Okay, before we fall asleep on the job, let's do it. Komang, can you take us to the rim of the volcanic crater?"

"Sure, but you'll have to watch your step. Take it real slow. Stay within the circle of the spotlight." Komang led the way and the group stayed tightly packed together, moving very cautiously. Although it wasn't a large distance to cover, it still took quite some time over the rocky ground. When they finally got there, Aadi held on to Abraham, and Komang grabbed hold of Gabriel as the two witnesses leaned over the edge. Each of them held a vial of the special anointing oil.

Abraham began the prayer that the Lord had spoken to him in his vision the previous day. "Father in heaven, Creator of the universe, God over all gods, we come to You tonight on the highest point in all Bali. But You are the Highest of the high. We ask tonight that You forgive the people of Bali for worshiping false gods on all the high places of Bali, for worshiping the creation instead of the Creator."

Gabriel picked up where Abraham left off. "Jesus Christ, Son of God and Son of Man, Savior and Judge. We thank You for this revival that Your Holy Spirit has sparked across the entire island. Yet the Global Czar and his General Asimoto are threatening to destroy Bali and its people tomorrow morning. We implore You to save this island, save these people who are now calling on Your holy name. Make an example of Bali for all the world to see how Your power is so much greater than anything the devil and his one-world government have at their disposal. We ask this Father in the name of Your precious Son, Jesus Christ. Amen."

Abraham and Gabriel then poured the remainder of the anointing oil into the crater, and then threw the bottles far out over the edge, hoping they would reach the bottom. They did so with such gusto that it was all Aadi and Komang could do to keep them all from toppling over. Instead, they all tumbled backward and rolled away from the edge.

"What happens now?" Aadi asked.

"We don't actually know," Gabriel admitted. "The Lord didn't see fit to show us. But we've done our job, thanks to you two. Now it's up to the Lord."

At that very moment, the ground began to shake under them, and a low rumble resounded from out of the crater. "I think we ought to get going," Abraham said. "It appears that the Lord is up to something."

They stumbled to their feet and began to jog behind Komang who led the way with his spotlight. It was certainly easier going down than up, but still they needed to exercise caution on the sloping, slippery trail. Each of them stumbled several times, enduring cuts and scrapes, but not breaking any bones.

The shaking and rumbling grew more pronounced as they continued onward. They were about halfway down when an enormous explosion behind them caused the ground to heave upward and then collapse inward. Small rocks and debris cascaded down on them causing more bruises, but nothing serious.

Suddenly there was some light. They thought dawn was breaking, but it was just the volcano spewing molten lava up and over the rim. A plume of thick ash roared up into the sky. "Run, run," Komang called out urgently. "The lava will be rushing down toward us. We must get out of here."

The four struggled to their feet and were propelled forward by adrenalin and the Holy Spirit. Soon they were flying down the mountainside as though they had wings. Abraham recalled how Elijah was empowered by the Lord to outrun the chariots to Jezreel after his triumph against the prophets of Baal.[147]

Behind them they could hear the thunderous roar of explosion after explosion. Though the ground shook furiously, they were able to keep their feet and keep going. Reddish light cast eerie shadows, providing just enough illumination to see their way.

As they neared the bottom of the trail, they could hear the growl of the lava following them down the mountain, along with the snap, crackle and pop of trees and bushes being ripped apart and burned instantly. The dawn's light fell on the temple complex. The few remaining priests and workers ran frantically toward their vehicles.

Komang led the way to his taxi where they each fell inside gasping for breath. They were relieved to hear the engine fire up. Komang wasted no time putting it into gear, because they could already see and smell the lava flow just a few hundred yards above them. As they drove away, Abraham and Gabriel looked back out the rear window and watched as the lava began to consume the outer areas of the compound, and then ravage the main temple buildings.

Komang fell in behind a line of vehicles headed back out to the main road, but were now far enough along that they felt safe. However, instead of the breaking day bringing more light, it was getting darker and darker as the voluminous ash cloud began to drift over the island. Occasionally the ground shook, even miles away from the volcano. Finally, they reached the small town of Redang to the south and stopped to rest.

"Is this what your God wants to do to save us? Destroy our homeland?" Komang cried out, angry and frightened.

"What time is it?" Abraham asked.

It seemed like a foolish question at such a time as this, but Aadi looked at his watch and answered, "Almost seven a.m."

"Well, we have another hour till General Asimoto's deadline. Then we shall see whether the Lord is destroying us or saving us," Abraham said emphatically. "As for me, let's go find something to eat. I'm famished."

Chapter Sixty-Five

"What do you mean you can't reach General Asimoto?" Alexis screamed into his office phone and slammed it down. "Damn incompetents."

He quickly dialed General Warren Falstaff whom he had appointed Chairman of the Joint Chiefs of Staff of the Global Military Command. "I don't care whether it's the middle of the night. Get him on the phone now!"

Alexis paced nervously around the perimeter of his office. Finally, the sleepy general was on the line. "How can you go to sleep at a time like this? You're supposed to be in charge of this Bali operation, aren't you?"

"Sir, as Commander-in-Chief, you said you were overseeing that operation, or did I misunderstand you yesterday?"

Alexis thought he could detect a little sarcasm but let it go because the matter at hand was too important. He'd deal with this insubordination later.

"Listen, general, get up to speed fast. I lost all contact with General Asimoto. I need to know what's happening over there, immediately."

"Yes, sir," General Falstaff said snappily and hung up.

Alexis began pacing again as he waited and waited. He hated waiting for anything. His blood was boiling by the time the phone rang.

"Sir, it appears that at least three volcanoes have erupted on Bali," the Falstaff reported tersely. "The entire island is covered with a volcanic ash cloud. No communication channels are operational. We cannot reach General Asimoto right now."

"That's not good enough, General Falstaff," Alexis snarled. "I've had it with all this waiting around and giving them twenty-four hours. Send in the nuclear bombers now."

There was a lengthy pause on the other end of the telephone line. "Sir, that simply is not possible. That black cloud has risen to over 60,000 feet. There's no way any aircraft can fly in there."

Alexis was about to explode. "Then I order you to destroy Bali with your nuclear missiles. I don't care if General Asimoto and his troops are still there, do it anyway."

Another pause raised the Global Czar's blood pressure even further. "Sir, the guidance systems will fail inside the ash cloud. Furthermore, the missiles would be destroyed by all the debris circulating at very high speed. We simply must wait until things settle down a bit."

Alexis flung the phone across the room where it struck the blazing star and brought it crashing down on the carpet. The Global Czar screamed at the top of his lungs and collapsed onto the couch.

Epilogue

The island of Bali, its people, and the revival are safe for now. *The End of Peace*, the fourth book in this series, continues the journey of all our characters and story lines through the end-times toward the Day of the Lord, the pre-Wrath rapture, and the Millennial arrival of Jesus Christ upon the earth to claim His Kingdom.

Appendix – Scriptural References (NKJ)

1. Revelation 11:3-13
2. Matthew 17:1-3; Zechariah 4:3-14
3. Acts 4:13
4. 1Corinthians 1:27
5. Mark 9:35
6. 1Corinthians 11:3; Ephesians 5:24-28; Colossians 3:18-19; 1Peter 3:1-7
7. Proverbs 31:10-31
8. Genesis 3:16-19
9. Genesis 2:18
10. Revelation 9:20-21; 16:9-11
11. Psalm 95:8; Daniel 5:20; 1Timothy 4:2
12. Genesis 12:1-3
13. Genesis 17:4
14. Judges 6:11-40
15. 1Corinthians 12:10,28-30; 13:1; 14:5,18,39
16. Joel 2:28-29; Acts 2:17-18; Isaiah 10:27; 1John 2:27
17. Joshua 6:1-21; Hebrews 11:30
18. 1Chronicles 14:14-15
19. Revelation 13:8
20. 1Corinthians 12:11
21. Proverbs 16:18; 1Timothy 3:6

22. Exodus 7:22; 8:7
23. Exodus 14:21-22
24. Exodus 17:6
25. Numbers 20:8-12
26. Joshua 7:1-8:29
27. Psalm 19:12; 139:23-24
28. Psalm 19:13
29. Revelation 13:16-18
30. 1Samuel 23:1-5
31. 2Samuel 5:22-24
32. 2Kings 7:3-16
33. 1Samuel 17:4-52
34. 2Kings 19:14-20; 35-36
35. 1Samuel 14:1-15
36. 1Samuel 13:6-14
37. 1Samuel 15:9-26
38. 1Kings 22:31-34
39. 2Samuel 11:1-12:14
40. Judges 13:5; 16:17-21
41. Titus 1:2; Hebrews 6:18
42. 2Timothy 1:7
43. Psalm 56:11; 118:6; Hebrews 13:6
44. Revelation 13:7
45. Revelation 2:7,11,17,26; 3:5,12,21
46. Romans 8:37
47. Isaiah 60:1-5
48. Daniel 8:23; 9:24
49. Revelation 21:1-2
50. 2Timothy 2:15 (KJV)
51. John 15:4-8
52. Exodus 34:29-35
53. Matthew 28:20; Hebrews 13:5b
54. Revelation 17:5-16
55. John 8:44
56. 2Corinthians 11:14

57. James 4:7
58. Isaiah 54:17
59. Matthew 18:19-20
60. Romans 13:12
61. Zechariah 4:6
62. 1John 3:8
63. John 10:10
64. John 16:33
65. Revelation 19:20-21
66. Psalm 23:5
67. Revelation 12:11
68. Psalm 139:13-14; Job 31:5, Isaiah 44:24; Jeremiah 1:5
69. Psalm 50:10
70. Isaiah 66:1
71. Jeremiah 32:17
72. Exodus 16:13,31
73. Hebrews 13:2
74. Luke 4:41; Luke 8:30; Matthew 25:41; Mark 16:17; 1Corinthians 10:21; Jude 1:6, 2Peter 2:4; Revelation 12:7
75. Matthew 28:18; Mark 1:27
76. Exodus 12:7-23
77. Proverbs 13:22
78. 2Corinthians 10:4-5
79. Hebrews 12:15
80. Proverbs 21:1
81. Genesis 1:26-28
82. Genesis 3:1-6
83. Matthew 4:8-9
84. 2Corinthians 4:4
85. Ephesians 2:2
86. Matthew 28:18
87. John 5:27
88. Mark 9:12
89. Revelation 21:5
90. Luke 10:19

91. Mark 16:17-18
92. 1John 5:14
93. Acts 17:10-13
94. Psalm 91:7
95. Psalm 91:11-13
96. Ephesians 6:13-17
97. 1Samuel 17:47
98. Psalm 33:10
99. Psalm 91:4
100. Isaiah 53:5
101. Romans 6:4; Colossians 2:11-12
102. Revelation 13:14-15
103. Exodus 3:2-3
104. John 14:15
105. Galatians 6:7-8
106. Acts 10:42
107. Genesis 6:3
108. Philippians 4:11
109. Nehemiah 8:10
110. John 15:11; 16:24; 1John 1:4,12
111. 1Peter 4:13
112. 1Peter 1:8
113. Matthew 25:21,23
114. John 15:11
115. Luke 14:28
116. Matthew 16:19; 18:18
117. Matthew 4:24; 8:16,28,33; 9:32, etc.
118. Matthew 12:45
119. Hebrews 12:1-2
120. Revelation 11:3
121. Romans 9:29; James 5:4
122. Chapters 22 & 24 of *"The Beginning of the End"*
123. 1Corinthians 10:4 Psalm 18:46
124. Ephesians 5:26
125. Matthew 26:28

126. Psalm 91:4-6
127. Matthew 3:10
128. Philippians 3:13-14
129. Matthew 5:12; 19:21